ALSO BY TURK PIPKIN

Fast Greens

Barton Springs Eternal

Born of the River

When Angels Sing

The Old Man & The Tee

The Tao of Willie

The Moleskin Mystery

Requiem for a Screenplay

ALL FOR LOVE

ALL FOR LOVE

A NOVEL BY
TURK PIPKIN

Softshoe Publishing

To my family,
and the memories of our years
on the South Llano River,
and to good times on the Cortez
with Gilberto, Tony, Bradley,
Marko, Jay & Steve

For everything that's lovely is
But a brief, dreamy, kind delight.
O never give the heart outright,
For they, for all smooth lips can say,
Have given their hearts up to the play.
And who could play it well enough
If deaf and dumb and blind with love?
He that made this knows all the cost,
For he gave all his heart and lost.

– William Butler Yeats

THE PLACE WHERE
THE RIVER BEGINS

From deep within him, Michael Parker could hear the whispering of the water, echoing in the murmur of his heart as it had for thirty years. Then once again he was ten years old, full of wonder as he watched the cold, clear stream rush out of the old rock and fall into the limestone channels at the place where the river begins.

Kneeling closer, he tried to decipher the sound, hoping to learn the language of the water so he could know what it wished to say to him. For one moment, he thought that he had it, but then the word was washed away, swept down the river where it joined countless other freshets that stream from the rock, each with their own word, the waters and the words chattering noisily as they pass over ancient granite outcroppings, then quieting for the long, slow journey to the sea, where all words— like the men and women who believe in them—are forgotten.

TURK PIPKIN

ONE

June 14, 1991. Baja, Mexico

Dear Jamie,
School is out and summer is finally here. Mom drove me to the airport this morning, but she wouldn't go in and Dad wouldn't come out.
I'm never going to fall in love. It makes you do stupid things.

Stopping for a moment, Hope wanted to cross out the last part, but her rule was no erasing. Once a thing was written, it could not be unwritten.

From the bar across the pool from their room, Hope heard her father laugh. "Like a person who's trying to sound happy," she was about to write. But then Michael and his pal Cooper both laughed harder, like people who really were happy.

"That's not a good sign," she wrote in the diary. "We're supposed to go fishing."

There's an old saying in Mexico. *One tequila, two tequila, three tequila...floor.*

Michael wished it had only been three.

He knew the sound of the waves lapping at the shore, but not much else. Flopped across the bed, but still wearing his cowboy

3

boots, he needed a moment to remember where he was.

Oh yeah, Mexico. Then it came back to him. They'd toasted the memory of Cooper's father, then Coop had turned to his bartender.

"Elvis, *dos mas!*" he ordered.

Every time they drank, Cooper said it again.

"Elvis, *dos mas!*"

Shading his eyes in the bright sunlight, Michael found Hope sitting on the front step of the *casita*. Even from behind she didn't look happy.

"Why didn't you wake me?" he asked.

"Don't blame me," she said. "We were supposed to go fishing and you got drunk."

Michael looked out at the sun well above the horizon, then sat down beside her.

"Sorry, Kiddo. I guess I blew it."

Hope fixed her eyes on a column of sugar ants. She was twelve years old and their annual adventure was off to a bad start.

Every summer since she could remember, Hope had come with her parents to Campo Buenavista on the shores of the Sea of Cortez. The past two years, her mother had bowed out, but Michael and Hope had carried on, snorkeling at Cabo Pulmo, hiking to mountain waterfalls, and catching all kinds of fish. Despite the situation at home, Michael was determined that this year would be equally great.

"You seen Gilberto?" he asked.

"He's on the phone. Something's up."

"Something better not be up. We're still going fishing."

At that moment, he saw Gilberto Martinez walking across the lawn toward them, his hat in hand.

"*Miguel, lo siento,*" Gilberto apologized.

"What's the problem?"

"The two professors," Gilberto explained, "the ones from San Diego."

"Yeah, the dolphin doctors. What about 'em?"

"They called to say they arrive this morning." Gilberto's eyes were now averted to the ground. "Two weeks; good money."

"Then you gotta do it."

"But I am supposed to take you fishing. Three mornings we hunt big tuna for your girl."

"He'd just throw up," Hope said as she tried to divert the ant column with a twig. When a couple of ants grabbed the stick, she flung them onto her father's boots.

Seeing none of this, Michael put his arm around Gilberto's shoulder.

"Hey, it won't be the same without you, but we'll get somebody else. What did Cooper say?"

"He is still asleep."

"I'm not surprised. What about Martín?"

"He has a charter."

"Anselmo?"

"His wife is having a baby."

"Don't tell me we have to go with Nacho."

The year before, Michael and Hope had fished one day with Hector "Nacho" Sanchez, a sloppy fisherman with a bad habit of grabbing the rods whenever there was a strike. Yanking to set the hook, he'd play the fish a while to make sure it was on, then hand the rod to his customers to reel it in. To Michael, it was as much fun as fishing in a fountain at the mall.

Over the gentle lapping of the waves on the beach, they heard the distinct zipping sound of something ripping across the surface of the water.

"Roosterfish," Michael said wistfully, thinking he and Hope might find some decent shore fishing.

"Just a little one," said Gilberto. "Listen—today you take a boat yourself—then go tomorrow with Martín."

"Whose boat today?"

"Nacho's."

Michael tried to remember the condition of Nacho's boat, but his mind was still thick from the tequila. Cooper didn't like screwing with outboard motors, and like his father before him, he only operated diesel cabin cruisers. But sometimes Nacho or another captain used their own outboards to take up the slack. Thinking back, Michael concluded that his problems with Nacho had been more about the boatman than the boat.

"Okay," he said. "It's a plan."

"*Bueno,*" said Gilberto. "*Gracias.*"

By the time they cleaned the spark plugs on the outboard and loaded the cooler and tackle, the morning was half gone. Rising from the shade where she'd sat without helping, Hope gave the boat a suspicious once-over.

"How long do you think it'll float?" she asked.

"You want to go or not?" her father asked as Gilberto helped him push the boat into the water.

Realizing he wasn't bluffing, she scrambled aboard as the two men waded the boat through the gentle waves.

"*Dondé vá?*" Gilberto asked.

Michael scrambled aboard. "South. Coop said the dorado and tuna are good near Pulmo."

Though he said nothing, Gilberto looked dubious.

"Okay, what do you suggest?" Michael asked as he pulled on the starter rope, then pulled again.

"This afternoon we have too much wind for Pulmo," Gilberto advised. "Maybe it's better in the north. You find wahoo, tuna, many dolphin for Hope to see. Maybe even a marlin; big excitement in a little boat."

On Michael's third pull, the motor sparked and roared to life, emitting a small cloud of black smoke as it found its stroke.

"Okay! North it is!" Michael shouted over the motor.

"*Vaya con Dios,*" Gilberto called.

With the motor running smoothly, Michael slipped it into gear and the boat jerked forward. As he steered north past the rockslide that marks the end of the road, all signs of civilization fell away.

The wind was fresh in their faces, and Michael's hangover and Hope's attitude both gave way to growing enthusiasm. Kneeling in the bow, Hope thrust her arms forward to embrace the spray, screaming with delight as they bounced into each little swell.

"That's my girl," Michael thought. "I knew I could count on her."

The boat was a 23-foot panga—the same fiberglass skiff found in every coast town of Mexico, this one built around 1980, Michael guessed. Despite its age and shoddy maintenance, the broad beam, high stern, and three molded seats for added flotation gave it a solid feel on open water. The cooler had been stocked by Cooper's cook, Juana, with sandwiches, apples, oranges, sodas, and three liters of water. Michael also had a full day's supply of the diabetes pills he took to control his insulin level, so his chief concern was the sun. Gilberto's panga had a big canvas sunscreen, an expense for which Nacho had never managed to save. Six or eight hours on the Sea of Cortez can cook you, but Hope and Michael had wide-brim hats and plenty of sunscreen, something Kate had stressed repeatedly over the phone.

"If she comes back burned like a beet, I'll never forgive you," Kate had warned.

"For that or a hundred other things," Michael nearly said out loud. As their problems had mounted, he sometimes had to catch himself from speaking what came to mind. Eventually he just quit talking. One day he found himself in a bookstore thumbing through a self-help book that listed the warning signs of a marriage on the rocks.

"Do you imagine responses to your spouse after he or she has left the room?"

Thinking back on the two years that he'd been saying to himself a thousand things he should have said to his wife, Michael decided a short break was in order. In truth, he thought she'd tell him not to go. When Kate said, "maybe it's a good idea," he realized how far they had fallen. Not once in the two months he'd been flying charters in Mexico had Kate asked when he might be coming home to stay. Deep down inside, Michael was waiting for an invitation. What he wanted, he kept telling himself, was to be wanted.

Half an hour north of the hotel, he angled back toward the coastline and throttled down to enter a small cove on the north side of Pescadero. Many times he'd come here with Gilberto. They'd switch places in the boat, with Michael moving back to steer them through the shallows. Standing in the bow, Gilberto watched for submerged rocks, which he pointed out with a single word, *"Cuidado."* Peering through the glare of the sun, Gilberto would spot a school of baitfish hiding from the predators of the open sea.

Unfurling his casting net, Gilberto held the free line in his teeth till he saw the fish racing by, their sides flashing silver beneath the ocean's mirror of blue. In an instant, his net was airborne, opening wide in mid-flight and landing level on the water in a ten-foot circle. A pause, then he'd stamp his feet on the bottom of the boat, scaring the sardines up into the closing net like a tap-dancing wizard casting his spell on all who dwelled below.

Only once had they failed to come away with live bait, and that because Gilberto failed to notice a rocky point that would have been harmless at a higher tide. Even with the low tide, the hull of the boat cleared the rocks, but the propeller struck the rocks, snapped its cotter pin and plunged straight to the bottom. Though they'd been moving slowly, the shock of the impact had almost knocked Gilberto overboard, an eerie reminder of a similar accident just two years before when Gilberto's father, despite decades of experience on the water, tumbled out of his boat in a similar fashion. Landing headfirst in the shallows, the old man climbed back aboard with nothing more than a sore neck. The pain was worse the next day, so Gilberto drove his papa fifty miles to the hospital in La Paz for an x-ray. After the pictures came back clean, Señor Martinez was sent home with a handful of aspirin. For the next three months, though, the old fisherman was rarely able to even get out of bed. Finally, he returned to the hospital where they x-rayed him again and discovered major fractures of the fourth and fifth vertebrae.

Looking back to the first pictures in the file, the doctor discovered that the lab had switched the old man's x-rays with those of another patient, a young man who had been subjected to dangerous and unnecessary surgery. Before the year was out, both patients were dead.

"Mistakes," Michael remembered his grandfather telling him back home in Texas when the boy forgot to unbridle and water a horse after a long ride. "One must always be on guard against mistakes."

"Yes sir, I know," the boy answered automatically.

"And do you know why?" his grandfather asked.

"Because they're... mistakes?" Michael answered, knowing instantly that his reply was both stupid and sarcastic, and if there was ever a time when he deserved a thump on the ear, this was probably it.

Josh Parker let out a long sigh. "Yes," he said, "and because later on, providing they're the type of mistakes we survive—we're forever faced with the knowledge that what happened was preventable. If that horse had stood in the barn all night and died of sweats or thirst, you'd have to live with having killed her. Pay attention, son. The things you bring about in the world are both your blessings and your burdens. Knowing that is a big part of what makes you a good person. This isn't about me being proud of you; it's about you being proud of yourself."

With that the old man hugged the boy closer and longer than Michael had ever known.

"I love you, son. Don't ever forget it. And all I really want is for you to find some happiness in this world."

Holding tightly to his grandfather's neck, the boy noticed that the old man didn't seem so powerful and solid as he once had.

Almost thirty years later, in a boat on a bay in Mexico, Michael realized that Hope was the same age he'd been that long ago day when his grandfather suddenly began to treat him like a man.

"Sit back here and keep us balanced," Michael said to Hope. "I'll move forward with the net."

"Leave the motor running," she told her father. "I can steer us close."

"I know you can, Kiddo, but I might not see the rocks. We'll just have to let the fish come to us."

Switching off the motor, he picked up a scoop cut out of a bleach bottle and began to bail seawater from the ocean into the live bait well in the floor area between the front seat and the bow.

"Dad!" she pleaded. "We're way late and it'll be lots faster."

"Sorry, Sweetie. We gotta do it my way, okay?"

"Yeah, *fine.*" Her tone was anything but fine.

He'd known this trip was going to be hard. He'd always been Hope's knight in shining armor, a fearless and faultless father who could do no wrong. Now everything seemed different, and the question was, had he changed, had she, or had they both?

Standing on the bow, he scanned the surface without the slightest glimpse of any baitfish and began to wonder if Hope was right. Maybe they should start the motor and cruise through the shallows. When Gilberto fell in the boat, the only damage was to his pride and to the easily retrieved propeller, which was bent and would not fit back onto the motor. Michael was already considering the long hike from the beach to the highway and hitchhiking for a spare when Gilberto opened the flotation compartment under the center seat and pulled out an emergency kit that even included a spare prop.

With a real fisherman there was rarely a problem that had not been anticipated. Before leaving Buenavista with Hope as his charge, Michael had checked to make certain the same bag of emergency gear was on this panga.

"Forewarned is forearmed," Coop's father, Colonel Cooper, had said a thousand times, though he was usually talking about weather reports, landing conditions, or anything related to safety when flying.

Nearly twenty years a pilot himself, Michael knew more about ailerons and elevators than he did about cast nets. He'd practiced gathering the folds of the net and holding the lines in his teeth while gathering the various sections in one hand. But accomplishing it while bouncing up and down on choppy waters was entirely different. To complicate matters, the drifting boat began to blow away from the shallows where the fish were likely to be. And when he cast, either the net opened too soon and popped back at him or it opened too late and splashed noisily into the water like a rock.

"Lemme try!" Hope pleaded when he'd failed half a dozen times.

"After I catch some," he answered.

Then he noticed the look on her face—the "bad-dad, you-never-think-I-can-do-anything" look.

Stepping down from the bow, he offered the net to her as if it were some talisman of her coming-of-age. Then he started the motor and steered for the shallows.

With her father looking on, Hope stepped to the bow and spread her feet the way Gilberto had taught her the summer before. Coiling the lines in one hand with the net gathered in the other, she flexed her knees slightly and rode the gently rocking boat like it was an extension of her own body.

"To the left," she told her father as she surveyed the water around them.

As Michael brought the boat about, a silver glimmer on the port side flashed once, then twice, then the net was sailing through the air, hitting the water in a wide, flat circle.

"Stamp your feet," Michael prompted, but not before she'd already done it.

Just seconds after seeing the fish darting through the open water, Hope was dragging the net hand over hand to the boat and dropping fifty beautiful sardines swimming in their bait well.

"Should I try again, or do you want to?" she asked.

"Not me," Michael said in awe. "No way I'm gonna follow that. Let's go fishing!"

"All right!" said Hope. "And let's find the dolphins. I want to race 'em across the ocean!"

"Dolphin-ho!" Michael shouted, opening the throttle.

"Dolphin-ho!" repeated Hope, as the bow rose up and crashed down on a small wave, splashing the spray into the air around her. "Faster!" she shouted with joy. "Faster!"

TWO

A little before noon when most fishermen were already heading home to beat the heat, Michael and Hope finally had two lines trailing behind the boat. One was rigged with a sardine on a small tuna hook, the other with a heavy circle hook and a bigger bait that Hope had netted, a skipjack that raised a little plume of water as it bounced along the surface behind them. Between the two, Michael felt they had a shot at tuna, dorado, or anything else the ocean had to offer.

Twenty miles north of Buenavista and ten miles out to sea, they were trolling steadily north. With both rods in their holders and one hand on the tiller, Michael pulled out a golden apple, took a juicy bite, and handed it to Hope. Taking a smaller bite, she compared the size of their teeth marks.

"You never got to fish with your dad, did you?" she asked.

"I was just a baby when my father died. But you know how much Grandpa liked to fish, right?"

"Yeah. At the River Ranch. You already told me"

The year Hope turned seven, Michael took her to see the ranch where he'd been raised. Driving west from Austin into the Texas Hill Country, they'd watched for deer and hawks as they sped down the winding highways that led back into his youth. After two hours, he eased onto Main Street in the town of Junction. Surprised at how little things had changed, he showed her the elementary school, where he'd flushed red when Geena Harris kissed him on the playground, and Junction High, where his basketball jersey, tattered and faded, still hung from the rafters.

Turning onto Highway 377, they headed up the valley of the South Llano River, drawing closer to the land of never-forgotten dreams.

"When will we get there?" seven-year-old Hope asked yet again.

"Soon," he told her. "Soon."

Years had passed since Michael had last seen his old home, and it had taken plenty of nerve just to call the present owners and ask for permission to visit. As he drew nearer, Michael wondered if perhaps this part of his life wasn't better left in memory. Stopping for milk and sandwich-makings at the Telegraph store, they looked at the faded photos of trophy deer and giant catfish that adorned the wall above the iron-grated post office window.

Ten miles further on, he stopped again at a roadside park atop a steep bluff that offered a view of the entire river valley below. Standing on the low wall that separated him from his past, Michael pointed down at the stone house and metal barns on the banks of the river.

"Is that it?" Hope asked, trying to match this vista with the one her father's bedtime stories had painted in her mind.

He nodded, but said nothing.

"Wow! Look at all the water!"

He tried to see it all through her eyes, but found it hard to consider even through his own. The rock house looked smaller, but the water was even more magnificent than he remembered.

"What's this?" Hope asked.

She was standing by a small limestone cross at the edge of the bluff, the letters worn nearly smooth by thirty years of weather.

Michael walked to the little monument that had been placed in memory of his father, who had not come back from Korea.

"Oh, that's been there a long time," he told her. "I'll tell you about it someday."

Looking at her in the boat, Michael realized that he still hadn't explained that cross. Their future had always seemed so infinite, but lately he was beginning to realize just how short life really is. Taking the rest of the apple back from her, Michael began to work on it himself, knowing he'd get jittery if he didn't eat. It was a near-perfect day on the Sea of Cortez, and in the midday calm, the water around them had turned smooth as glass.

"I was only three years old when Josh first took me fishing," he told his daughter. "And we kept at it for years. It was our favorite thing to do."

"That's what you said about finding arrowheads and Indian junk," Hope corrected her father.

"Junk?" he asked.

For a long moment the two just stared at each other, their stubborn Parker sides making both of them think they cared about something this minor.

"Okay, junk," he finally said. "Have it your way."

"You like to talk about the River Ranch, don't you?" she asked.

"Yeah, when I'm talking to you. Remember the Blue Hole?"

Taking one last bite of the apple, Michael tossed the core into the low wake behind the boat and watched as a large fish rose up and sucked it down.

"It was blue, right?" He couldn't tell if she was being sarcastic or not.

"Bluer than the sky. And the water was so clear, you could see all the way to the bottom, twenty feet in places. When I was your age, I'd float on an inner tube and look down at the big catfish in the deep."

"That sounds cool."

"From the Blue Hole downstream, the South Llano is one continuous river, running all the way to the Llano, the Colorado, and the Gulf of Mexico. And we were the headwaters of it all."

"I used to wish we lived there, you and me and Mom."

Michael looked off to some birds circling the water on the far horizon. "Me too, sweetheart. Me, too."

While they talked, he steered according to the color of the ocean, looking for the deepest blues with water so clear that even from two hundred feet down, the tuna could see the baits trolling behind the boat. Deciding they were still too close to the shore, he angled the boat further out.

"Josh and I used to take his big seine down to the Blue Hole, and we'd stretch it across the flats in the shallow water where the minnows were as thick as flies on cow flop."

"That's gross."

"Then we'd bait the cane poles with minnows and stack rocks on the base of the poles. After lunch, we'd walk back to the water and usually the poles would be gone."

"Gone where? Did somebody take them?" He could see she was starting to get interested.

"No, the fish would pull them in, so we had to go out in Grandpa's old canoe and paddle for all we were worth until we chased 'em down. Then I'd lean over the side and grab the pole. Usually there was a big bass or maybe a catfish on the hook."

"That's cool, but when are *we* gonna catch something?"

"Soon," he told her. Michael had been fishing these waters for fifteen years and he'd never gone this long without hooking something. The birds he'd seen were moving north now in great swooping circles, chasing baitfish that were also being worked by tuna from below. But even when Michael trolled faster, he didn't seem to get any closer to the action. And before long the fish must have sounded, for the birds began to scatter in all directions.

As they trolled on, Hope opened a bottle of water and drank thirstily.

"You too, Dad." She held the bottle out to her father. "You never drink enough water unless I make you."

Grinning at his take-charge daughter, Michael accepted the bottle. Taking out one of his diabetes pills, he washed it down.

"So was Grandpa the best fisherman you ever knew?"

"Well, I thought so at the time, but now I think maybe Gilberto is the best. The son of a son of a son of a fisherman, and he's never tried to hide what he knows like a lot of guys. If he thinks someone is proud to learn something, then he's proud to teach it."

"Like throwing the net?" She asked, happy to rub it in a little.

"Okay. Some things I never got the hang of. But I do all right with the basics: knots and baits and trolling speeds. And somewhere along the way, he started telling me about this ocean and what happens in it and on it. You could spend your whole life out here and not learn half of what Gilberto knows."

"I like Gilberto," she told her father. "He reminds me of you."

"Thank you, Kiddo," Michael said, surprised at the compliment. There was a light in her eyes now that hadn't been there earlier. This was what they'd come for—to remember how much they loved each other.

As they trolled further north, Cerralvo Island came into view. Without a radio, Michael didn't want to venture too far from home, but in a pinch Cerralvo would do as an emergency landing area. Besides, Gilberto and his scientists would be camped there for the next two weeks, hiding from civilization with radios off, communicating only with the dolphins.

On the other hand, Michael knew Cerralvo was a prime destination for adventurous divers who go to see the giant sharks that lurk there in the deep. With that knowledge leaning upon his hand at the tiller, he steered them away from the island and further out to sea. A big shark was one thrill of the natural world he'd just as soon skip. In any event, they were running out of fishing time. They'd started with two seventy-liter gas cans, and the first tank was now half empty.

"A mile or two more and we start back," he told her. "We've got other days to fish. Other days with better captains."

"Dad, look!" Hope shouted. "On the right!"

Michael turned his gaze east, where a big flock of seagulls and frigate birds had regrouped over a school of fish. Steering in that direction, he and Hope trolled closer as a huge school of tuna boiled to the surface.

"Wow!" Hope yelled. "Look at that!"

Just ahead of the boat, big yellowfin tuna were driving schools of baitfish completely out of the water, where they were snatched up by seagulls. Climbing higher with their catches, the gulls were attacked by pterodactyl-like frigate birds, which knocked the small fish free or stole them directly from the mouths of the gulls.

Hoping for a strike on one of their lines, Michael circled the tuna, but the fish sounded and the ocean grew calm. Surveying the surface around them, father and daughter waited in anticipation.

"There!" Hope shouted. "Dead ahead!"

Racing toward the action, Michael and Hope were soon surrounded by one of the sea's most astonishing sights. On all sides, stretching halfway to the blue horizon, thousands of dolphins arced in and out of the water as they moved across the ocean in a giant seething mass, surfacing for the air that gives them life before diving back into the water that gives them speed.

Lying on the panga's prow, Hope thrust her hands down toward the splashing foam while several dolphins took turns surfing the bow wake. Then one big dolphin, old and weathered to a splotchy gray, moved directly beneath her. Still racing along, the dolphin rolled onto its side so that one eye looked straight up at this radiant creature of the land.

"He's beautiful!" Hope yelled to her father. "I can almost touch him!"

And though the dolphins were beautiful to Michael, it was the picture of his daughter, her hair flying about her like some goddess of the foam that made his heart race.

"More beautiful," he thought, "than all the paintings in all the museums in the world."

For five minutes they matched the dolphins' pace. Then as suddenly as they'd begun, the school halted their race and began to mill about. Cutting back on the throttle, Michael coasted into the school, wondering what would happen next and trying to imagine where this amazing day would take them.

In the tourist towns along Mexico's Pacific coast, young men spread their blankets on the sidewalks near the fishing docks and display their carved wooden figures of whales and sharks, pelicans and dolphins. Michael had taken several of these figures to Hope, but he'd never known who had the patience or the skill to carve them. Then one day in San Jose del Cabo, he happened by an old man sitting on the front step of a one-room house. In the man's left hand was a half-formed block of ironwood, in his right, a homemade knife.

"What are you making?" Michael asked, unable to think of the Spanish verb for carving.

"Quien sabé?" the man answered. Who knows.

"Cuando sabrá usted?" Michael asked him. When will you know?

"No sé," the old man replied, peeling off a long shaving between his knife and thumb.

Michael was reminded of his Grandfather Josh, who after the passing of Gramma Parker, spent most of his time sitting on the front porch of the old rock house looking out at the squirrels and birds, and the orphaned deer that he'd adopted. With a gnarled piece of oak or pecan in his hands, he would work the magic of his keen eye and his Old-Timer pocketknife to reveal the spirit and form hidden in the scarred heart of the wood.

"I'm not making anything," Josh Parker once told his grandson. "All these rings of thick and thin have accumulated over good years and bad. I'm just looking for what's already there."

All around Hope and Michael, the dolphins milled about on the surface, awaiting some mysterious sign to renew their circuitous journey of the Sea of Cortez. In the meantime, the collective mind of the giant school had given way to the independent play of the ocean's most spirited mammals. Dozens of six-foot-long adults were jumping eight or ten feet out of the water, spinning like corkscrews to survey the horizon, then falling back into the expanding circles of water from which they had come. Not to be shown up, two babies, not much larger than footballs, displayed their own aerial acrobatics, leaping over each other again and again. But all were outdone by a big gray male who came racing from the deep and blasted into the air, showing the old scar of a shark attack on his mottled skin as he arced fifteen feet above the surface.

"That's my friend!" Hope yelled as the falling dolphin took in her gaze.

Both father and daughter had forgotten their lines and baits still trailing behind the boat when a sudden screaming of the drag on Hope's reel sent Michael diving for the rod. But remembering Nacho's bad habit, he stopped himself, allowing Hope to pull the rod from its holder as the line spooled off the reel in a blur.

"You got it!" he shouted.

"No!" Hope cried. "I don't want to hook a dolphin!"

"No!" Michael yelled, "Not a dolphin! Look!"

As his girl held tightly to the rod, it seemed as if the bowels of the ocean were being forcibly ejected to the surface, pushed ahead by a massive fish that surged up out of the boiling water, shook its head to throw off the heavy steel hook, then crashed back with a splash like a whale.

"Marlin!" Michael shouted. "A big blue! Hold on, Kiddo!"

Hope already had the butt end of the rod wedged down against her stomach and was holding tight with both hands as the fish ran north at thirty miles an hour. The taut line cut across the surface, sizzling like a hot iron immersed in water, and the heavy reel screamed in protest. Reaching over the rod, Michael switched off the clicker to silence some of the noise, but still the fish ran, stripping three hundred yards of sixty-pound line from the big Penn reel as if nothing were restraining it at all.

"What's he doing?" Hope yelled to her father.

"He's trying to figure out what's happened, testing his muscles on whatever's pulling at him to see if he can slip free."

"What do I do?"

"Keep your rod tip up and hold on. You don't have to reel yet—not unless he starts swimming at us. But if you feel any slack, you reel as fast as you can. Okay?"

"Okay," she answered through gritted teeth. It was almost all she could say.

"How much does this monster weigh?" Michael wondered. It was a big fish, the biggest he'd seen in twenty years of saltwater fishing. Six or seven hundred pounds of solid muscle—maybe bigger than that—and against it an eighty-pound girl who had never found a challenge she could not overcome.

The thing about a marlin, Michael knew, is that you can never be sure what will happen. A good fisherman hooked to a marlin half this size might get the fish alongside the boat in half an hour and, if he had any class at all, release it with no problem worse than sore muscles. But with the really big fish, all bets were off. Coop had told him more than once of the fourteen-hundred-pound marlin hooked by a teenager on a Buenavista charter. The fish ran straight out from the boat in one burst of speed, then died on the surface. A heart attack, Coop thought. On the other hand, some beefy football player from the L.A. Rams once tied into a twelve-hundred-pounder and fought it for thirty hours. The *Capitán* had to radio repeatedly for extra fuel, water, and supplies, and at one point a substitute crew came aboard so the first shift could sleep. But without another person so much as touching the reel, the big linebacker fought the whole battle on his own, only to have the fish slip the hook at the boat.

Those had been professional crews using swivel chairs and fighting harnesses on the decks of cabin cruisers with powerful engines to wear a fish down. Michael's twelve-year-old girl was tied to a fish nearly as long as their boat.

Twenty minutes after hookup, the fish was pulling harder than ever. Hope had shoved the base of the rod into the cup of the lightweight fighting belt that Michael strapped around her waist. Then she'd moved both hands forward on the rod, giving herself the maximum leverage as she held on for dear life. Somewhere out there under the surface, the big blue was turning on the power in little bursts, stripping eight or ten feet of line off the reel with every pump of its tail. As the line slipped further and further away, Hope looked grim but determined. Michael checked the reel and saw less than fifty yards of line left on the spool.

"Not enough," he thought. "Not nearly enough."

And at that moment the line ceased to go out.

"You stopped him!" he told her. "Now you've got to get some line back. Can you lift the rod a little, then reel down a turn?"

"I can try."

"I'll help you lift," he said, reaching to the rod.

"Don't help me!" she told him. "I have to do it on my own!"

Holding up his hands in surrender, Michael backed away. Then, with all the strength of her arms, shoulders, back, and legs, Hope lifted the rod to nearly vertical—though the tip bent down sharply toward the fish. Moving her right hand to the handle of the reel, she lowered the rod while reeling two cranks on the fish, bringing in one of the thousand feet of line strung across the ocean.

"That's the way," Michael told her. "Keep that up and you'll get him." Though he knew that most of the truly big marlin are female, somehow it seemed more appropriate to refer to the fish in the masculine.

It was going to be a long afternoon—a girl with grit and little equipment pitted against one of the most powerful creatures on earth. Hope prided herself on being tough—tougher than the teachers who wanted her to do things one way when she felt her way was better, tougher than most of the other kids she knew, boys included. Considering all the factors, Michael decided the fish might be in trouble.

There was little he could do to help. The marlin was pulling hard and it was not difficult to imagine the rod being yanked from her hand. Still, he had no intention of rigging anything to hold the rod to her. They could afford to lose the gear, but he was taking no chances of Hope going overboard. If the fish ran again, Michael could start the motor and follow. Or if the fish came at them he could use the motor to help her keep the line taut. Otherwise she was on her own.

"I couldn't have done it when I was her age," Michael thought. "No way."

The afternoon dragged on, and an unrelenting stalemate ensued. With three hundred yards of line out, the fish dove deep into cooler water, and neither Hope nor her marlin was able to gain on the other. As the sun burned down upon them in the boat, Michael's thoughts stretched back to one hot and hellish day of his own youth. Seventeen years old, he had fought the kind of fight Hope was waging now, but his was a battle that could never be won.

"Sit down, Mikey. Didn't your grandfather come with you?"

He was in the office of Bobby "Big" Bailey, president of the Junction State Bank. Bailey's son, Big Jr., had played with Michael on the Junction Panthers basketball team that had won the high school state championship just months before. That made this an onerous duty for the pudgy banker.

"Josh didn't come," Michael told him. "Something with his stomach."

"Well, if there's a better time."

Bailey's face was red, and beads of sweat were forming on his forehead.

"He ain't coming—now or ever," Michael told the banker. "So you better get on with it."

Bailey sighed and opened a manila folder on his desk. Michael was surprised how slender it was, how few papers it took to take someone's home.

"I want you to know we're all real sorry about this, Mike, but the ranch has been going farther and farther in the hole every year. Your grandmother was in the hospital a long time, bless her soul;

add in her medical expenses and there's no catching up."

"We just need some rain."

"We always need rain, Mike, but..." Seeing the glare on Michael's face, the banker stopped cold.

"How long 'fore we're out?" Michael asked.

"Well, technically—now mind you, I've requested an extension from the new owner. I mean buyer, but he hasn't..."

"God dammit! I said, how long?"

Mr. Bailey shut the folder. "Thirty days."

A bitter taste shot through Michael's mouth. He'd expected six months, a year. Little by little, his grandfather was dying, and Michael knew the old man wanted it to happen at the ranch.

"One other thing, Mike. The buyer asked if he could bring some people out for a look next week. You think that'd be okay?"

Michael walked to the door, then turned back to answer. "Tell him if he shows up before thirty days, Josh'll shoot him."

"Now Mike."

"And if Josh don't, I will."

It was hot outside and Michael's face burned with rage. Gone, gone, everything gone: Parker land and Parker water. Thirty days? God Almighty, where would they live? He was seventeen years old with two weeks left till he finished high school and two hundred dollars to his name. A few colleges had talked to him about a basketball scholarship—he'd hoped to get one at Texas A&M and study land management, but what was the point now? Spend his life running somebody else's ranch? Never.

For the time being he'd have to get a job and rent some crummy old house on the west side of Junction where the cedar choppers lived. Hell, when he was little, every Christmas he'd helped Gramma Parker bake turkey and dressing to take to the families in those houses—charity for those who had nothing. Now he'd be living in one of their busted houses, with broken-down pickups littering the front yards and rat-infested piles of cedar posts in the back. He was screwed, and everybody knew it.

From the bank, he walked across the street to the Dairy Creme and ordered an ice cream and a Coke. Digging in the pocket of his jeans, he found three quarters and dropped them on the counter.

"That's okay, Mike," Mrs. Nagel told him. "No charge. We sure were sorry to hear about your troubles."

Michael picked up the quarters.

"Yeah, thanks." He'd meant to sound grateful, but knew he had not. When he turned back around at the counter, everyone was staring at him. He took the ice cream over and set it in front of his pal Bugs. Then he took the soda, walked out to the truck, and drove toward the ranch.

"Thirty days!" he said bitterly. "They might as well take Josh out and shoot him."

THREE

"How you doing there, big girl?"

Hope could hardly answer. Her rod was still held high, but the tip was pointing straight down and her jaws were clenched tight. Two hours had passed since the big blue sounded, diving six or eight hundred feet into the cold water where the pulling would not wear so hard on the fish. With her feet up on the fiberglass gunwale, Hope's hands were frozen around the rod and every muscle of her slender body was rigid as steel.

"Maybe it's time for me to help," he told her.

Michael didn't know how much she could take, but he knew the marlin could dish it out for hours. Glancing around to check their position, he saw that Isla Cerralvo was barely visible on the horizon.

Just then the line slacked so suddenly that Hope nearly fell backward.

"You turned him," Michael said as he propped her up again. "He's coming toward us."

"What do I do?" Hope yelled.

"Reel!" he told her. "Reel as fast as you can!"

Moving the stiff fingers of her right hand to the reel, Hope begin to crank, slowly at first, then faster and faster, furiously trying to keep the line taut and the fish on the hook. Within a minute she'd gained fifty yards of line, but then the drag began to sing its warning that the marlin had turned again, this time to the north, farther into the heart of the Cortez. Pulling the rope to start the engine, Michael steered the panga to follow the fish.

Because he'd lost so much of what he loved as a boy, Michael had always wanted his daughter to have as much of what she wanted as possible. And one thing was clear: She wanted to catch this fish. But he also knew that with regard to Hope's safety, he had already crossed the line. They'd been out a long time, cooking in the sun and wearing their bodies and minds to the point that it would be easy to make a mistake.

"Drink some more water," he told her, holding the bottle to her mouth and tipping it in small sips till she'd had enough.

"I think you've almost got him," he said automatically. But then he realized he didn't have any idea if this fish was close to being beat. Maybe it was a mistake to hold out the possibility of false promise. Maybe it was a mistake to be there at all.

Half an hour later, Hope had gained no more line, but had drunk up a considerable quantity of their water. Then she saw the angle of the line begin to lessen.

"He's coming up!" she called.

As the big fish rose from the depths below, the angle of the line grew less acute until, two hundred yards from the boat, a large school of baitfish erupted from the water, then splashed down like a hailstorm. In the midst of this mayhem, the marlin surged up out of the ocean into the sky, blue on blue, a giant silhouette frozen for an instant on the horizon. Then the big blue collapsed with a giant splash among the smaller fish.

"What's happening?" Hope yelled to her father. "What's he doing?"

Scarcely believing what he was seeing, Michael watched the big marlin rise again and again in the school of fish, sending them scurrying in all directions while Hope did her best to keep the line taut.

"Dad! Tell me! What's he doing?" she pleaded.

Michael put his hand on his daughter's shoulder and spoke to her softly.

"He's feeding, Kiddo. He's getting something to eat so he can build up his strength."

After a moment she said, "Then I better eat, too."

"Man, she's tough," Michael thought. "Her grandfather would've been proud."

Listless and wan, Josh Parker seemed determined not to leave the old stone house he'd built overlooking the headwaters of the South Llano. Michael was beginning to wonder if the sheriff would have to use force to get the old man off the land. Michael had found an old rent house, but Josh refused to go see it. Only one thing motivated the old man to go into town, and that was to see his grandson graduate from high school at the head of his class of twenty-eight students. The whole town was there—not to watch Mike receive the valedictorian's certificate, which was given to him with little fanfare—but to witness the ceremony of raising five basketball jerseys to the highest rafters of the gymnasium. Soaring into the heights were the gold-and-white jerseys of five boys who had done the impossible, won the Single A State Basketball Championship without one substitute on the team. All five players had played every minute of every game for the entire season, and the celebration would not have been more stirring if one of them had been marrying the Queen of England.

When the grads finally tossed their tasseled caps into the air, Michael pushed his way through the other families till he stood before his grandfather. Staring for a time at his grandson as if he always wished to remember him in this way, the old man shook Michael's hand, man to man in a way that made the teen feel he had truly accomplished something.

"I'm proud of you, son," Josh told him. "Wherever you go—and I suspect you'll go far—I want you to remember the pride your grandmother and I took in you."

Unable to find words, Michael merely nodded his head in

acknowledgment.

The entire senior class then hopped into their beat-up pickups and headed to City Park at the junction of the South and North Llano Rivers where they got so uproariously drunk that the sheriff had to drive back into town twice to buy them more beer.

For a few days after, Josh seemed a little less resigned to his fate and just like old times, he and Michael passed the days seining minnows, catching bass, and generally cleaning the place up so that it shined as brightly as if Gramma Parker was still in charge. Rounding up what little livestock remained, they trucked them to the auction yard at Junction, then swept out the barn one last time. Two weeks later, every fence was stretched tight as piano wire, every gate hinged level, every windmill stood ready to pull the water out of the ground when the long-awaited rains finally came and the cavernous aquifers recharged with the gift of life.

As things often happen, the drought broke with two big rains in a row and the river came up in a roaring flood so that they had to go out once more to repair the fence gaps they'd stretched just days before.

Riding down the hill to check the springs on Contrary Creek, they forded the river by the mysterious whirlpool in the rock that took away the water as miraculously as it was provided just a few hundred yards upstream. Wading the horses up the creek-bed, they stopped below the Indian pictographs that marked the beginning of recorded time in this valley.

"What do they mean?" Michael asked his grandfather. "It must have been important or they wouldn't have gone to so much trouble."

Indeed, the paintings were thirty feet up the cliff face, with not the slightest hint of a ledge on which the artist could have stood.

"Well," said Josh, "I always wondered if the paintings meant that even in the worst of times, the water would eventually return, and so would the people who'd been blessed by it."

"You mean when the drought was over, the Indians would come

back home?"

"Why not? Maybe the Indians thought this was some sort of holy spot, a land blessed by the Spirit of the waters, and the paintings marked this as the place their spirits would return to after their bodies were gone."

"You mean heaven?"

"Why not? It's sure as hell where I'd like to end up."

With a flick of the reins, Josh rode on across the creek. For a time Michael stared up at the symbols on the cliff, then he spurred his horse to catch up.

That was their last day at the ranch. Sometime that night, while Michael slept fitfully and his grandfather slept none at all, Josh Parker had a heart attack. Not wishing to die elsewhere, the old man refrained from calling his grandson and simply lay in bed waiting for death to come. Finding no satisfaction in that department, he was still awake the next morning when Michael came to check on him.

Just finding Josh in bed after it was light outside was enough to tell Michael that something was wrong. Surprised at how light Josh's body had become, the boy carried his grandfather to the truck for the drive to Schreiner Hospital in Kerrville.

Three days later Michael knew he'd done the wrong thing. Though Josh had shown no more indication of dying, the doctors were unwilling to let him leave, and he was so upset at having been shanghaied into the world of medical quacks that he lay for long hours refusing to speak to his grandson.

Late one afternoon, the old man finally called Michael over to sit on the edge of his bed, then pointed to the window ledge, where a pigeon was perched.

"Damn bird's been sitting there for three days straight," Josh said.

"Why's that, you suppose?" Michael asked, almost afraid to hear the explanation.

"Well, these genius doctors said I had to take a re-laxative, but I just put them in their god-awful desserts."

"Sound like a good plan."

"But some nosy nurse—that's what they call these boys in white. One of these nurses found my laxative stuck up under my dessert, so now they say I have to eat the dessert, too."

"Are you doing it?"

"Hell, no! I slip the laxative in the pie and take 'em both over to the windowsill and leave it there for my pigeon pal."

"Why don't you just flush it down the toilet?"

"You know what's beneath that window?"

"I'm not sure I want to know."

"The driveway to the doctors' parking lot goes right under it. All day long that pigeon just sits there eating my laxatives and laying pigeon milt on the windshields of new Cadillacs. Yesterday they brought a heart specialist in from San Antonio. The bird and I nailed him right through the sunroof of his Mercedes! Serves him right for driving a German-damn automobile!"

The old man was beaming so proudly that Michael didn't know whether to laugh or cry. It's possible that he did both at once.

"Grandpa," he said, "you are never gonna grow up."

"Well, God bless you for your fine opinions, Mikey. And for everything else, too."

Reaching out to him, the old man felt the calluses and hard-earned leather toughness of the teen's hand.

"You keep working hard, son. Keep those hands tough, and you won't ever have any problems, not in this world or the next."

Still not saying anything, Michael began to rub one eye as if he had something lodged in it.

"You're the last one, Mike," the old man told him flatly. "The last person I ever came to love in the world, and the last one to say good-bye."

Michael nodded slowly to indicate he knew.

"You were the one that kept me going. I wanted to see you grow up, see what kind of man you'd turn out to be. If it hadn't have been for that, I'd have checked out the day my sweet Jean moved on. I know it's been hard being raised by old folks instead of the mother that loved you so, but I couldn't do nothing about that. You got your mom's goodness of heart, you know. And you got her eyes, too. I've seen the girls staring at you. It's okay to have some fun, but you be careful you're not thinking only of yourself. The trick isn't to find just any old girl; the trick is to find the right one. Can you remember that?"

"Yes, sir. I'll remember."

The two of them watched the pigeon for a while then his grandfather took a breath to finish what he'd started.

"Anyways, I got this far, so I got my wish. Now you get on out of here, cause I got to feed my pigeon."

Michael hugged the old man and somehow made it out into the hall without bursting into tears. He was downstairs in the lobby when it all came upon him. Sagging against the wall, he rubbed his hands hard across his face as if he were trying to keep something out, or something in. Just as he thought that perhaps he wasn't going to make it any further down this hall or anywhere else in life, two doctors stopped in front of him.

"Christ!" one of them said. "Did you see that?"

Michael lowered his hands for a look as the doctors started to walk away.

"Damndest thing I ever saw. God damn pigeon shit right on my new sport coat!"

With that last gift from Josh—and careful of which exit he chose—Michael came out into the bright Texas sun. That night, his grandfather disappeared from the hospital that had been named for Charley Schreiner—the Texas Ranger turned cattle baron who once owned most of the South Llano River and sold the headwaters to the one man he thought belonged there—Joshua Lacey Parker.

Josh was in his room when the nurse checked on him at midnight, but the next morning he was gone. When the sheriff asked around town, a waitress at a truck stop on the north side of town said an old man fitting Josh's description came in just before dawn.

"He ordered eggs and sausage and drank a whole pot of coffee," she said, repeating the story for Michael. "Then he said I was wearing a pretty dress and I oughta watch out about the company I keep."

"That's Josh," said Michael.

"I asked him what he meant by that, but he just smiled and said, 'Nothing, just watch out.' He didn't even have a car. When he left, I watched him go out to the highway and start walking out of town. I figured he must live out there somewhere."

A search by volunteers and Texas law enforcement failed to turn up a body or any more clues to his disappearance. Despite all their efforts, Michael knew that the old man, having said his good-byes with this world, had simply wandered out into the backcountry, found himself a beautiful hilltop and lain down beneath the arms of an old oak tree, full in the knowledge that he would never get up again.

Just a few days shy of his eighteenth birthday, Michael Parker was alone.

Four hours after hookup, the sun was finally hanging lower in the sky, but the heat in the open boat was no more bearable. All afternoon the fish had pulled on the slender line, and though Hope had managed to pump and retrieve a hundred or more yards, the marlin again found the strength to take back all that the girl had so painfully gained.

From time to time, Michael started the motor to pull against the fish or to help Hope gain line when she was about to be spooled, but their fuel supplies were limited, so he couldn't do much. He'd already switched the empty first tank for the second, which he was conserving for the trip back to Buenavista. Through it all, the powerful fish towed the boat north, nearly as fast, it seemed, as if they had been trolling with the motor. If he hadn't seen it with his own eyes, Michael wouldn't have thought it possible. But neither would he have thought his daughter could hang on past when most men would've given up in tears, and long past the point when the north end of Cerralvo Island completely disappeared from view.

Kneeling beside his exhausted girl, he gave her another drink of water.

"Honey," he said softly, pulling a few strands of sweat-dripped hair from her face and tucking them behind her ear, "I have to tell you something. Half an hour more is all the time we've got. It's after five, and we're a long ways from home. We have to be back before dark, and we have to start before we get beyond the range of our fuel supply."

Saying nothing in reply, Hope raised the rod and reeled down on the fish.

"Half an hour," Michael repeated. "Okay?"

Again she lifted the rod, biting her lip as she leaned back until the thick fiberglass pole was almost vertical. Then she reeled in another foot of line as she lowered the rod.

"A hundred more like that," Michael thought.

Half an hour later, Hope had reeled that much and more. Twenty feet out and twenty feet below them, the huge marlin was clearly visible as it swam left then circled right, turning on little bursts of power that made the girl cry out in pain. But still she continued to raise that rod and bring the fish closer.

Comparing the length of the marlin to the length of the boat, Michael figured the big blue was seventeen or eighteen feet long. Having only seen pictures of fish this size, he had to guess at the weight, but a thousand pounds was the figure that kept coming into his head. A thousand pounds—the words sounded terrible, like a warning that they should not have come this far. In any event, he knew there was no possibility or even a reason to boat the fish.

"Can you see him?" Michael asked. "He's huge!"

Hope leaned over the side and peered down at the marlin, a deep iridescent green and blue with the refracted sunlight dancing across its body like fire.

"He's so beautiful! We have to let him go!" she said. "I don't want him to die."

"Good," Michael told her. "Reel a little more. I'll grab the leader and get the hook out. If we swim him beside the boat to get fresh oxygen in his gills, he may live another fifty years."

But when Hope stopped reeling with the ten-foot leader just shy of the rod tip, Michael leaned over and saw that the fish was hooked not in the mouth but on the outside of its head, hooked deep near the eye. Trailing off in the current, a stream of blood stained the water.

"He's hurt!" Hope cried. "He's bleeding!"

"I've got to get the hook out," Michael told her. "If I do that, he may still make it."

There were no gloves in the boat, but he grabbed the monofilament leader anyway. Wrapping the line three times around the base of his fingers, Michael leaned slowly back, using his own weight to drag the marlin closer to the rail. He'd kept his hands tough just as Josh had told him, but not tough enough, for the line began to slice into his flesh.

"Dad, be careful!" Hope warned.

With the marlin in reach, Michael unwrapped the leader from his right hand and grasped the pliers that hung from his belt. Easing his bloody hand into the water, he closed the pliers around the hook, which was buried in the flesh and bone of the marlin's head. Summoning all his strength, he tried to back the hook out, working it left and right, up and down.

"A little more," he grunted. "I've almost got it."

Then a flash of movement caught Michael's eye and he jerked his arm back, dropping the pliers in the water. Again he saw the flash as it raced at them, a huge shark, closing on the scent of the marlin's blood, and of Michael's.

"Get down!" he shouted to Hope as he fought to unwrap the leader from his other hand so he could not be dragged from the boat.

Freeing himself from the leader, Michael grabbed the steel-pointed gaff that hung from the rail and swung it at the shark's head as he crashed by them. Seeing this new danger of the shark and the movement of the gaff, the marlin reacted with a huge thrash of its body, yanking the heavy rod from Hope's hand and jerking her onto the rail, where she teetered precariously over the ocean. She screamed, and Michael dropped the gaff and pulled her toward him.

Fifty feet from the boat, the shark turned and began to circle his prey.

Michael needed a weapon; floating next to the marlin was the wooden-handled gaff. Knowing that either the shark or the marlin could overturn them, Michael grabbed the second rod from the front of the boat and tried to drag the gaff within reach. Then he saw the shark coming again. Too late to reach the gaff, he raised the rod high, then speared the butt end hard upon the shark's bony head, shattering the fiberglass rod into a thousand pieces, but also turning the shark so that he hit the marlin only a glancing blow.

"Daddy!" Hope screamed, as the momentum of the shark carried both fish against the stern, a smashing blow that knocked Michael off his feet into the bottom of the boat with Hope. Now without any weapon of size, he lay there holding her tightly as she shook with fear.

It took all his nerve just to peer over the side and survey the water around them. The shark was nowhere to be seen. Fifteen feet away the big blue was floating just under the surface, his tall dorsal fin sticking straight out of the water.

"Is he going to be okay?" Hope asked her father. The fear had not gone out of her voice.

Looking out, Michael saw the marlin begin to swing its tail from side to side, pushing itself forward, slowly at first, testing its own strength.

"We've got to get farther away," Michael said. "In case the shark comes back."

Moving astern, he put the motor's gear selector in neutral,

primed the pump twice, and grabbed the starter rope.

"Come on, baby," he muttered. "We need you now."

Just before pulling the rope, he noticed a deep bloody gash on his left arm. Unable to feel the pain through his adrenaline, he gave the rope a hard pull and the motor roared to life. Never had he heard such a sweet sound.

"Look!" Hope said.

Hearing the dreaded motor that had plagued him off and on for hours, the marlin pumped its tail harder and began to move away. Then, with one last flash of blue, it streaked away to the depths of the ocean.

"We did it!" Hope cried happily. "He's gonna make it!"

Turning to her father, she hugged him tightly, the first time she'd done so in months. They'd lost two rods and reels, Michael was bloody, and both were sunburned and exhausted, but the boat was intact, the motor was running, and they were going to be okay.

"Yes," Michael said, his arms wrapped gently around his daughter, "we're going to be okay."

FOUR

Having lost all that he loved, eighteen-year-old Michael Parker decided it was wrong to have been through so much and still not "be a man," as his friends called it. To make matters worse, his girlfriend, a dark-haired Baptist girl with lustful eyes and pensive lips, had no intention of sleeping with him before they were married, a topic that Michael avoided at all costs.

A year younger than Mike, Jackie had moved to town when her father was appointed the minister of the Junction Baptist Church. Michael and Jackie's first date had been to see Dr. Zhivago at the Double Eagle Drive-in on a bitterly cold night during which snow flurries obscured the screen from the few cars in the lot. Michael didn't have enough gas to keep the pickup running and warm, which was a convenient excuse for the two of them to huddle under a blanket and begin an on-and-off relationship that would last for two frustrating years.

The frustrating part arose from Michael's eagerness to learn something about the mysteries of the fairer sex. This would have been easier if he'd been dating one of the cedar chopper girls, most of who were doing the hokey pokey well before they reached Jackie's age. But a Baptist preacher's daughter, that was something different.

By Michael's senior year, he and Jackie were the sweethearts of Junction High. Whenever the movie at the drive-in changed, the sweethearts returned for another go at the breathless kisses and groping hugs that had come to define their private relationship. In the long run, he learned more about movies than he did about sex.

Confused about the guilt she already felt from even simple acts like dancing—strictly forbidden in her Southern Baptist upbringing—she could not admit her own desire. Ultimately, it came down to her fear that she wouldn't know how to make him happy, and that once she'd given him what he wanted, he would move on.

With little else to do at night but sneak off and do what teens will naturally do if left alone in the dark, nearly all their friends had long since crossed over the forbidden line, making Michael and Jackie's relationship a source of frequent discussion.

"Why don't Baptists have sex standing up?" Bugs asked his classmates at the graduation night party. "Cause they don't want people to think they're dancing!"

Everyone burst into laughter, all but Michael and Jackie. That was the moment that Jackie, drunk on pink champagne, decided the time had come. It was nearly midnight when the young couple checked into the "Y" Motel, and only an hour before Jackie had to be home. In the drab room, she lifted her dress over her head, then draped it carefully on the single chair.

"Now, Michael," she said, reaching out to him. But then her arms dropped to her side and she passed out cold, falling across the rag-thin covers.

Being both a gentleman and pretty tired himself, Michael stretched out at Jackie's side to watch her sleep away that last hour. He awoke when the maid came into the room at ten a.m. His mouth and mind thick with the remainders of Southern Comfort and Lone Star Beer, he looked at the maid and said, "Oh shit!"

Jackie's father was waiting on the front porch when they arrived—half a day late and both looking like they'd spent the entire night doing what her parents would never believe they had not.

"I'm sorry, son," Reverend Jerrel said to Michael. "I know you been through a lot. But that's no excuse for what you've taken from our little girl."

"Daddy! Nothing happened!" Jackie insisted, though to be honest, she couldn't remember exactly what *had* happened.

"Jackie, go inside!" her father commanded. "And you go on home, son. Go home and don't be coming back."

"No!" Jackie pleaded.

Michael looked from father to daughter, knowing that if he pledged himself to her there and then, all would be forgiven. For a full minute he considered where that would take him—a job with the highway department or the telephone company, two or three kids in as many years, and the rest of his life living in a ranch town wishing he were a rancher.

"I better do like your father says," he told Jackie, his eyes fixed on a crack in the sidewalk that gaped as wide as Palo Duro Canyon between his former girlfriend and himself.

"No!" Jackie cried. "No!"

Feeling truly alone, he decided it was time to do something about the only thing he could do something about. So on the Fourth of July, the State Champion Junction High basketball team—Michael, Bugs, Big Jr., and the twins—all drove down to the border at Piedras Negras for a night in Boys Town.

Despite the irony of celebrating an American holiday in Mexico, hundreds of Texans streamed across the Rio Grande for the festivities. The boys started at La Macarena, a classy restaurant attached to the ring where the bullfights would soon begin. In his Tex-Mex Spanish, Michael said something to the maître d', who either misunderstood him or perhaps recognized him from several years of Fourth of July and New Year's Eve visits here with his grandparents. In any event, the boys were ushered through the crowded restaurant into a private room where the other tables were soon filled by well-dressed young Mexican men and their beautiful ladies.

"Shit-fire, Mikey," Bugs hissed, "those are the matadors on the bullfight poster. We don't belong in here."

Bugs rose to run as if the matadors intended to skewer him, but Michael restrained him and soon the boys were introduced to a different world. After a four-course meal with too many forks, they were invited to the stalls beneath the bleachers for a personal inspection of the day's bulls—an ugly lot that cowered under the stone arches of their pens. Though no fights had been held in the ring in months, the flies were thick and a smell of death hung in the air.

Then one ferocious bull, as heavy and muscled as any two of the others, came forward from the back and snorted what looked like white smoke. The youngest of the matadors pointed to him and gestured with great foolishness and even greater bravado.

"*Ya-ha!*" the young man shouted. "*Ya-ha! Arriva El Rey!*" The king has arrived.

The team stepped timidly to the rail for a closer look as the bull lowered his head menacingly.

"Shit, I wouldn't git in the ring with that thing for all the money in the world!" said Bugs.

"*Ya-ha!*" repeated the young matador, "Mañana los periódicos dirán que Antonio es el conquistador de reyes."

"The conqueror of kings," Michael thought. "I hope he's right."

There was never an explanation of the hospitality given to the boys. They did not know the Mayor of Piedras Negras was also the impresario of the bullring and an aficionado of basketball. Having recognized the Texas State Champion Junction Panthers from their pictures in the Del Rio Press, he was treating them to the honor he felt visiting dignitaries deserved.

Soon the boys were played into the ring by a loud and raucous brass band, then seated in a place of honor, not only in *la Sombra*—the coveted "shade" seating—but just one row back from the rail. Directly in front of them was El Mayor and his daughter, a beautiful girl about their age to whom the young matador, Antonio Valera, would dedicate the bull El Rey.

Of the group, only Michael knew much about bullfighting, all of it learned from coming here with Josh and from reading old LIFE magazine stories by Hemingway. Throughout the fight, Michael explained to his pals what was happening: the grand promenade bringing the brightly colored players into the ring, then the announcements from the *monosabio*. As the fights began, the first bull, looking weak and confused, was hit too deeply by the lances of the mounted *picadores*. Then the bull was pinned just as badly by two clumsy-footed *banderillos*, apprentices trying to learn their dangerous craft in a border town where few in the stands would know the difference between skill and survival. Severely wounded, the bull was unwilling to take the cape of an older matador, who could scarcely move forward because of a limp from some long-ago goring. After several rejected thrusts of the sword, the bull was finally put down and the bloody corpse dragged from the ring by a team of horses not fit for the glue factory. In the afternoon heat, a sullen mood came over the crowd.

"Sometimes," said El Mayor as he turned back to Michael, "the game of the bulls *es muy feo.*"

"Very ugly indeed," thought Michael, who had a bad feeling about the rest of the event and was beginning to wish they'd gone straight to Boys Town, done their business and headed home.

The second bull was not much better than the first, and when Antonio Valera took to the ring for the third, it was clear that only he could save the day. As the young man paraded around the ring with the crowd chanting his name, a violent pounding was heard, loud and terrifying like thunder on a hot and cloudless day. By the fearful reaction of those in the ring, Michael realized this was the sound of El Rey smashing his horns against the wooden gates that barred him from his prey. It took electric cattle prods to back up the bull for the gates to be opened. Finally the big bull came into the sun at the center of the ring, the dust rising around his sweat-covered body as his black eyes searched the ring for living flesh.

"Geez!" said Bugs in a whisper. "I never seen nothing like that before!"

The *picadores* rode in, looking small and scared on their blindered horses. The first jabbed his lance at the beast, but the sharpened point glanced off the bull's skin as if it had struck steel armor. Lowering his head and driving into the horse, the bull came up under the terrified animal, tearing through the padding that was supposed to protect it, and sinking his long left horn deep into the horse's soft belly. Pinned against the ring barrier, the rider tried for one long moment to push the bull away with the lance, then surrendered to his fear and climbed over the rail to safety. His load thus lightened, El Rey lifted the riderless horse completely into the air, tearing at the poor horse's underbelly then dropping him to the ground.

Having smelled the blood of his tormentor, the beast pulled free and began to search for another target. Astride a taller horse, the second *picador* fared somewhat better, sinking his spearpoint into the muscular topknot above the bull's shoulders and leaning all his weight on the lance to punish the bull. The crowd roared its approval. On the third and final *pic*, the bull chose to defend himself on a bloody patch of sand near the first horse's body, which had not been removed because of threats from the bull. This time the bull slipped down in the bloody sand, falling from under the *pic*, then rising up and tearing a hole in the *picador's* leather-armored legging. With an artery punctured and blood spewing from his leg, the man spurred his horse to escape the attack. Rescued by a flurry of capes that led the bull one way and another, the wounded *picador* received enthusiastic applause as he loped out of the ring, his leg bleeding and his face pale.

The terrified *banderillos* scattered their flags about the bull's body like a blindfolded game of pin the tail on the donkey. None were seriously hurt, mainly because none dared come within range of the long horns.

With the purpose of all that had come before—the weakening of the bull—having failed completely, young Antonio Valera stepped forward. Running to the devil with *banderillos* held high, he swerved abruptly in front of the wide horns, rose onto his toes, and planted the twin spears beside the single wound of the *picador.*

Returning to the ring wall for his cape, Valera then made a series of dashing passes. In the final of these—a breathtaking Veronica with his swirling cape painting a red carnation in the air—the bull scraped its blood and the blood of the horse and *picador* onto Antonio's suit of lights, but passed harmlessly in his pursuit of the cape, which wrapped around the young man's spinning body like a shroud around a whirlwind.

The cheers were deafening. When young Valera made his final glance to the daughter of El Mayor, Michael thought it the look of a man making a claim for her love.

Wanting the kind of performance that would make him an instant legend, Antonio decided to delay moving to the safety of the sword. Setting his feet lightly in the sand, the big cape directly beneath his chin, he called defiantly to the bull.

"Ya-ha! Ya-ha!"

"No, no!" shouted the senior matador with the limp, though his warning was drowned by the cheering of the crowd. The old man knew the bull had lost interest in the cape and was only out for blood, which he found on the next pass, hooking the left horn toward the smell of the horse's blood on the boy's suit. Sinking the horn into the flesh and bone of Antonio's thigh, the bull caught the boy, tossed him into the air, caught him and tossed him again. With the crowd screaming in horror, the older matador limped to the rescue, his cape flashing through the air at first, then finally thrashing at the bull as El Diablo tossed the boy like a rag doll, long since dead and now only the plaything of an animal fulfilling one of its two possible destinies, to kill or be killed.

The screaming and crying of the crowd seemed to last forever. Old men rent the hair from their heads in double fistfuls and the *mayordomo's* daughter, running to the aisle to jump into the ring, fell into Michael's arms with an insane look in her eyes. Michael would not let her go and she beat him with her fists, crying over and over, "Antonio! Antonio!"

Looking stronger and more triumphant than ever, the bull was distracted by other capes while the body of Antonio Valera, seeming too slight and too young to have been a part of this idiotic violence, was carried from the ring.

The older matador, crippled and without the skill or reflexes of the vanquished fighter, knew that he, too, was about to go the way of young Valera. Nevertheless, taking his sword and short cape, he stepped back into the ring. There were no cheers this time, only shocked silence that a man with nothing to gain could follow his ridiculous code to such a certain fate.

The *mayordomo*, on the other hand, had seen enough. His face a ghastly gray, his years and indulgences showing unkindly on his body, he rose in his seat and held up a hand to stop the old man. With a whisper to an attendant behind the barriers, El Mayor took the two large *pistolas* that were handed him. Stepping into the ring, he walked without hesitation toward the bull, who regarded him with a wary eye. This indeed was something new.

Waiting to be goaded into action, the bull stood his ground as the man reduced the distance between them to ten feet, then five. Stopping there, El Mayor raised both pistols and fired a dozen shots into the bull's brain, all twelve finding home before the bull hit the ground. As the smoke from the guns rose around them like a specter, the Mayor spit on the bull, turned, and walked away.

The people filtered out of the arena like the blood from the bull's bullet-ridden body. Despite the pall of grief that settled over the drought-stricken town, the Junction Panther basketball team still got drunk enough to pursue their original goal. With Michael's thoughts wandering to his grandfather's advice about avoiding mistakes, he steered them down a potholed caliche road to the decrepit outskirts of town, passing cardboard shacks with children playing in the dust. Atop a small hill with the dust-red sun setting into the west, they found Boys Town—an isolated block of unpaved streets and sad bars, each full of girls who might have been attractive enough in another time, but who on that night seemed both old and fat. Finally Michael found himself in the company of a girl about his age, not pretty but eager, and with hair that reminded him of the mayor's beautiful daughter.

Paying his five dollars, he climbed wearily up the stairs to a musty room above the bar. The girl seemed glad to have this handsome young gringo instead of a smelly Mexican ranch worker, but despite her best efforts, Michael body's could not accomplish the one feat it had done involuntarily a dozen times a day for the past five years.

She tried talking dirty to him, saying he was *muy hombre*, but Michael did not feel like a man, and eventually he pushed her away. When the girl began to curse him, Michael took another five dollars from his wallet, dropped it on the bed, and descended to the cantina below.

"Shit-fire! You weren't supposed to spend all night with her!" said Bugs, whose own experience had been more successful but lasted only a minute or two.

"Shut your face!" Michael told him. "Or I'll shut it for you."

Bugs did as he was told.

It was a long drive back to Junction beneath a starless sky. Michael dropped the others at their far-flung houses, and at first light drove out to the roadside park overlooking the ranch, which now belonged to someone else. Climbing from the truck, he stood through the dawn on the low rock wall by the stone memorial to the father he had never known. Despite the season, the stone was cold to his touch.

In his span of eighteen years, Michael Parker's entire family had left this earth, but the young matador was the first person whose death he'd actually witnessed. Sitting there while the light came to the valley of the South Llano, he knew he'd gone to Mexico on a fool's errand, and that he'd have to do better for himself. He had not known it was possible to be this tired, and he wondered if perhaps being a man would not be all that he'd expected.

FIVE

The late-afternoon light was gathering around the boat, but the outboard motor was idling smoothly and Michael was confident they had sufficient fuel and time to make Buenavista by nightfall. But as he slipped the transmission from neutral to forward, he heard a sickening grinding of metal and the motor shuddered to a stop. A wave of dread swept over him. Like that day in the bullring some twenty years before, Michael felt as if the life had been drained from his own body.

Tilting the motor forward on its hinge, he swung the propeller up and out of the water, revealing the entire mechanism, twisted like the trunk of an ancient madrone.

"It looks crooked," Hope said as she leaned over her father's kneeling body.

"Yeah," he replied, "she's pretty beat up. I guess the shark or the marlin must have slammed against it."

"What are we gonna do?"

Michael surveyed the horizon to their west, where the tops of the mountains were barely visible.

"We'll try to fix it," he told her.

"We better fix you first, Dad. You're leaking."

Looking down, he saw the blood on his arm where the splintered fishing rod had nearly run him through, and on his hand where the monofilament leader had cut into his palm.

"Okay," he said.

Tearing the bottom of his T-shirt into strips, he soaked them in seawater, then Hope washed the wounds and bound them up.

When the bleeding had nearly stopped, Michael opened the watertight hatch to the flotation compartment. Inside was the yellow emergency bag that contained the tools and parts that would send them back to Buenavista, where the story of Hope's incredible fish would be told for years to come.

But picking up the bag, he knew instantly that it was far too light. Yanking open the straps, he looked inside and found little of what they so desperately needed. There were two faded life jackets and a sealed pair of emergency flares, but the spare propeller was nowhere in sight. An extra water bottle and a glass Coke bottle were both empty and, worse still, there was no transponder. Without that vital piece of electronics, there was no way to transmit an emergency signal and summon help. Feeling as if he had been stabbed in the heart, Michael sank to the bottom of the boat, his face pale and eyes unfocused.

"Dad, are you okay?" Hope asked.

He did not seem to hear her.

"Here, take this."

At the touch of Hope's hand, her father jerked back to attention and saw that she was holding out a glucose tablet. Slipping it into his mouth, he felt his mind slowly return to action as his blood sugar found a more functional level. The onset of diabetes at an adult age had not been particularly difficult for Michael. While his grandfather's diabetes required a daily injection of insulin, advances in medicine allowed Michael to substitute twice-daily doses of Glucotrol, which stimulated his pancreas to secrete more insulin. But oral diabetes medicines work only when combined with a good diet, and Michael had broken all the rules: booze, dehydration, not enough to eat.

Realizing he'd been on the verge of hypoglycemia, he took stock of their situation. Only one liter of water remained, they had little food, and almost no chance of getting the motor running.

Besides his fishing knife, the only tools were a rusty pair of pliers and a couple of old screwdrivers. Using these, he removed the damaged prop, started the motor without it, and found that the drive still would not engage. Then came another sickening sound, the grinding of gears as the motor chewed through its chain and sucked it into the cylinder, dragging forged metal links through the aluminum motor body, reducing it all to useless junk.

On the ocean that had occupied so many of his dreams, Michael and Hope were adrift.

"That sounded bad."

Michael did not respond.

"Is someone going to find us?" she asked.

Turning to face her, he took her hand.

"Sure they will, Champ. But it may take a few hours. It might even take till morning. So while we're waiting, I know a game we can play."

"A game?" she said. "Gimme a break, okay? This isn't a game. We're in deep shit!"

Shit? This was the first curse word he'd ever heard from his 12-year-old daughter. He wanted to say, "Watch your language," but he knew she was right. They *were* in deep shit.

"Shit is right," he replied, "but we might as well make the best of a bad situation—you know, try to have some fun."

"Yeah? How do we do that?"

"We could pretend we're not gonna be rescued."

"Yeah, that's sounds great!" she replied, her sarcasm turned up loud.

"No, it will be. But we can't just play the game for a few minutes. We have to play it all the time, okay?"

Hope thought about it, unsure whether she was being talked down to by a father who couldn't see she was nearly grown, or whether she was still a little girl who needed to rely upon his every word. After a bit, she grudgingly said, "Okay."

"So, what do you think would be the first thing we would do if we were stranded at sea?" Michael asked.

"*If?* Dad, we *are* stranded at sea!"

"So what should we do?"

"Check our water supply."

"Exactly."

"And our food. We should check that, too."

"See? You're gonna be good at this."

As they talked, Michael laid out the bottle of water, the rest of their lunches consisting of one orange and one sandwich, and the pill bottle with his last Glucotrol tablet—none of which would suffice if they weren't found soon.

"When do you think somebody will rescue us?" she asked.

"Well, it's hard to say exactly. We're pretty late already, so Coop is probably watching for us now. Even a fast boat would take a couple of hours to get to us, though, so they might not find us till tomorrow morning."

"So we're stuck for the night?"

"Not necessarily. A fishing boat from La Paz or a freighter could come along any time. But if we do have to spend the night, it'll be a heck of an adventure to tell when we get back home."

"I think it's creepy. My arms hurt, my shoulders ache, and I'm hungry."

"I know you are, Sweetheart. But if we're gonna play this adventure game, we've got to do it all the way. And even though someone will probably find us in the morning, part of the game is to pretend they won't."

"Yeah, but if we're pretending they won't find us the first day, then we should save some of our food for the next day, too."

"See, you've got the hang of it now. Even if we get really hungry and thirsty, we still have to save some of the food and water. Tell you what, if they haven't found us by the time it gets dark, then we'll have two bites of sandwich and two sips of water. Okay?"

By the standards of most games, this one just plain sucked, but

Hope didn't know what else to do. Her only comfort was for her father to be right.

"Dad," she told him, "I'm sorry my fish got us in trouble."

The long battle and the hours in the sun were beginning to take their toll on her. Seeing that she was close to tears, Michael took her hands and pulled her close.

"Don't say that, Hope. You're the Heavyweight Champion of the World! Don't ever think that you got us into this, not even a little bit. You did a hell of a job with your fish."

"You really think so?"

"I never saw anyone do better. And that includes grown men who've been fishing for years and years."

"Thanks, Pops. We really did it, didn't we? We caught the biggest fish in the ocean, and then we set him free. I bet not many girls can say that!"

Drawing her legs up to her chest, she laid her head in Michael's lap and wrapped her arms tightly around his waist. A gentle breeze curled around the two of them as small waves lapped softly on the hull of the boat. Michael knew he had things to look after, but instead he sat there watching the sun sink behind the jagged peaks of the Sierra Gigante Mountains as Hope let her eyes fall closed.

Checking his watch, it took him a moment to realize that it read barely six o'clock when it was probably after eight. Then he realized that the watch Kate had given him on their tenth anniversary had also been broken in the fight with the shark. An ironic smile came to his face. "You wanted time with you daughter," he thought, "and now you have it."

As the boat drifted further from shore and the earth spun them further from the sun, Michael sat motionless so as not to disturb his sleeping girl. With his eyes on the west where he hoped some boat would appear, he watched the sky parade forth a dazzling show of expanding pink and blue rays, refracted light and shadow, shadow and light. Beneath that radiant sky, his weary mind pondered how all the moments of his life could have come so quickly to this—a man with not enough insulin in his body and a girl with too much faith in her father.

It had been years since he'd thought back to Hope's first moments on earth. Kate's gentle pregnancy had not forecast the fury of the birth that awaited them. The panic of that day had long since faded, though, and what remained was the nurse passing the pink-scrubbed, bawling newborn to Michael, who took her tenderly in his arms. In that immortal moment when their eyes first met, Hope gazed up at him, then quieted almost instantly. With a look that said, "I am yours, and you are mine," a bond was forged that he had sworn would never be broken.

"So full of hope," he said softly to his newborn. "I love you, little girl. And I promise that I'll be there for you, to care for you, provide for you, and watch over you for all of my days."

And with those words, his baby girl had closed her eyes and slept, slept in his arms as she slept now, far out on the Sea of Cortez.

And what of my promises, Michael wondered. Weren't they the same promises he had made to Kate? Hadn't he now failed Hope as much as he'd failed her mother? If there were any doubts about whether he'd failed Kate, they were now fully erased. Breaking down on the open ocean with Hope as his charge would be the crowning failure atop the other strikes against his marriage. It wasn't as if he hadn't tried to make Kate happy again after they lost their second baby, but trying and succeeding are two different animals. And two years makes for lots of trying—perhaps too much, he'd finally decided.

"So you're flying off into the wild blue yonder the way you always do?" Kate pressed when he suggested a long stretch of work in Mexico.

This wasn't going the way he'd planned, but he was determined to press his point.

"Come on, Kate. You know we need the money."

She looked at him like he was accusing her of something. They needed money because Kate had walked away from an art school teaching position, a choice she was sure they'd made together.

"Kate," he said softly, "we've spent a long time going round and round whatever's wrong. And we're not getting any closer or any further away. We're just in some endless holding pattern. Maybe it's you, maybe it's me; maybe we just need to miss each other."

"Maybe you just don't want to be around."

For a long moment Michael stared at her, thinking that whatever he said would only make it worse. With both of them seated at the breakfast table of the little house he'd built on the banks of Lake Austin, Michael watched as his wife's gaze wandered across the water to the steep cliff on the other side.

"When I'm not flying," he tried to explain. "I'll lease the plane for a lot more than I get in the States. Bill's got it all set up."

"So it's already settled?" she said. "You arranged it without talking to me."

"I'm talking to you now."

"This is gonna be hard on Hope."

"I'll pick her up when school's out and take her to Cooper's just like last year."

"Gone till summer," she said.

But the part left unsaid was the most troubling, the nagging thought that it wasn't about work; but separation. After thirteen years, was he leaving her? There had become too many unknowns in their lives. The one thing Michael did know was that Kate could end this mess with three little words. Did she love him, or not?

But Kate said nothing, and her gaze continued to wander aimlessly across the rocky bluff.

"What does she see there," he wondered. "What is she searching for?"

At home in Austin, Kate Parker thought about her husband and daughter on their grand vacation in Mexico. She'd been sitting at the dining table for half an hour, the meal in front of her untouched as she thought it all through for the ten thousandth time. For months, she'd been trying to rouse her emotions and do something to save her marriage, but she'd been seized by an emotional lethargy. Two years grieving a baby she'd never known wasn't too much or too little. It just was. And Kate knew she had to get through this in her own time. It had taken her months to simply quit crying at any or all hours of the day, and months more to reach the point of having one good day. Even then the loss could rush back upon her like a flood, suffocating her so that she thought she would die. And when her breath finally returned, with it came more tears until she was ashamed to be seen so weak. When Michael thought she was getting better, she was only crying in secret so that no one would see that she was losing her mind.

That was what really worried her; she thought she was losing her mind. At any time of the day or night, she might feel Jamie kicking in her womb. From the next room, she'd be certain she heard him crying. Sometimes he smiled at her as she cradled him in her arms.

When the tears and phantom emotions finally began to lessen, they were replaced with anger and with resentment toward anyone who didn't share the depth of her loss. Deep down inside, she knew that Michael had also suffered, but all too soon that inevitable Michael smile found its way back to his face. That smile seemed so out of place to Kate. Or was he only trying to give her strength? She didn't know what to think.

"Oh, Michael!" she suddenly said to no one.

From the moment Michael gave her the news that he was leaving till the day the cab picked him up for the airport two months ago, Kate had known she could stop all this madness by simply opening her heart and saying that she loved him, and needed him and always would. But somehow she couldn't cut through the fog that isolated her from everything and everyone. Nothing scared her more than the truth. And the only truth she knew was that she would never be the same.

"Just waiting for them to call is unbearable," she'd told her friend

Rachel earlier in the day. "Michael says he's leaving and what do I do? Make a cup of tea."

Since Kate and Rachel had become friends in junior high, Rachel had basically never stopped talking. She had an opinion about everything and everybody, and she wasn't afraid to share them. Now, for the first time in all those years, Rachel had nothing to say.

"What?" Kate asked.

Rachel shook her head slowly. There was too much at stake for her to venture what was best.

"Maybe he's right," Kate said for her friend. "Maybe it's better this way."

Rachel still said nothing.

"Or maybe he's being selfish and inconsiderate," Kate went on. "I mean, what kind of husband just walks out on his family? Not that I didn't give him plenty of reason to leave... or none to stay... oh, hell, I don't know. All I do is go around in circles."

Reaching over the table, Kate grabbed Rachel's hand and held it tight. "What should I do, Rach?"

Rachel had known Michael since the day he and Kate met. In those thirteen years, Rachel had dated more men than she could remember, perhaps two or three of which she now considered smarter than a pile of owl shit. What she wanted to say to Kate was, "Call him. Tell him you love him. Beg him to come back." But she also knew the decision was not hers to make.

"You're asking complex marital questions of a ditzy redhead whose longest relationship to date is three months," Rachel said. "He's a good man, Kate. Do you love him or not?"

Deep down inside, Kate felt sure that she did. The question for her was, why had it become so hard to say, even to herself?

At the end of their visit, Kate said she was fine, but she knew otherwise. Instead of painting or swimming laps at Barton Springs, she spent the afternoon looking out the window at the lake and the steep bluff beyond. When they'd learned they were going to have a boy, Michael joked that any boy of theirs would soon be scaring them half to death by trying to climb that bluff. That's the way things were now. Everything she saw brought Kate back to her sweet baby Jamie. There was no place to hide from her loss, no way to make it go away.

As the afternoon wore on though, for the first time in months it occurred to her that there remained still more that she could lose.

"I wish they'd call," she said to no one.

And then the phone rang.

SIX

When she'd dropped Hope at the private terminal in Austin, Kate sent her daughter inside with her bag, then waited in the car to see if Michael would come out to say hello. Ten minutes passed before Kate realized he wasn't coming. Running to the flight apron, she got there just in time to see Michael's twin-engine Cessna taxiing down the runway.

Now it would be two more weeks before they'd have a chance to sort things out. And though she still didn't know what she'd wanted to say to him, no sooner had the wheels of the Cessna left the ground than it suddenly seemed unthinkable to endure two weeks with both of them gone.

Where had the years gone? Hope was almost a teenager. Her childhood had flown away—as Burroughs put it—like wild horses over the hills. It seemed like only yesterday that Kate first spoke to Michael in that bar in Cancun; now their daughter was nearly thirteen—hormones raging, mad at her father for being gone so long, mad at her mother for continuing to insist that he'd be back soon and everything would be normal again.

"Normal?" Hope pushed her mother. "What's that supposed to mean?"

Kate knew she was right; it'd been a long time since things felt normal.

Once upon a time, Kate and Michael had been the couple that

everyone pointed to as having the perfect relationship, the one marriage that would never fail. They loved each other and stood side by side against whatever problems the world threw in their path. With Michael often gone on charter flights, they had frequent opportunities to miss each other and forget their petty differences and rekindle their desire.

Even when they learned after Hope's birth that it was impossible for Kate to conceive again, impossible to have the baby boy that Michael had always wanted, they still found refuge in each other.

"We've been blessed with one perfect girl," he told her. "What more could we want?"

They had never felt closer. But nine years after Hope was born, the inconceivable occurred.

"You're going to have a boy!" Dr. Ward told them.

Kate was jubilant, triumphant, stunned.

"Oh my God!" she said. "How is that possible?"

"Well, we could choose to say that your tubes were only partially blocked, or we could simply call it a miracle."

Their lives became a flurry of excitement. Hope made long lists of prospective names for her little brother. Michael added a bedroom to the cabin he'd already built in place of Kate's old Airstream trailer on the banks of Lake Austin, and Kate painted fanciful pictures on the walls of the nursery, a peaceable kingdom populated by a hundred different animals.

After she lost the baby, all their efforts seemed so wasted. Michael's patience with her depression was a comfort at first, but at some point his patience began to wear on her. And soon enough, he began to ask when she would feel like her old self again.

"It's not the kind of thing you bounce back from," she told her husband.

When the phone rang she knew it was him, both of them, her husband and her daughter, calling to share some fabulous account of their day. For one instant, the fog lifted from her mind and she thought that everything was going to be okay.

Precisely at the end of the second ring, she snatched up the receiver.

"Michael," she said softly.

There was a long silence, then a somber voice.

"Kate, it's Coop."

The room was swimming around her; it couldn't be Coop—he never calls the States. No, there was only one reason Coop would phone.

In a thin voice Cooper related to Kate the same news that he had just given their friend Bill Frazier. The boat was missing. Probably nothing more than a fouled spark plug, but perhaps she should come down.

"Bill's taking off at six a.m. There's no point in leaving earlier because customs won't be open at the border."

Trying simply to stay on her feet, Kate said nothing.

"You think you can make it?" Coop asked.

"I'll be there," she said in a weak voice.

"I mean the little plane. You think it'll be okay?"

"I said I'd be there."

Her voice was impatient now, though she knew he was right to ask.

"Who else have you notified?" she asked.

"Everyone—the harbormaster, Mexican Coast Guard and Air Force. We'll all be out there at first light."

The silence was longer this time. What was there to say?

"Cooper, don't let anything happen to my daughter."

"I've never lost a boat," he reassured her. "I don't intend to start now."

An hour early, without the slightest glow on the eastern horizon, Kate Parker pulled into the lot at Austin Aero. Looking out at the flight apron, she saw Bill already walking around his plane, clipboard in hand as he made his preflight inspection. Nearly thirty years her senior, Wild Bill Frazier was like a father to Kate. An almost mystic bond had grown between them, a bond that negated the need for small talk and let each of them save their energy for things that mattered. He'd called right after Coop to reassure her it would all turn out fine. Despite his advice that it was important to get some sleep, she'd lain awake kicking herself for letting Hope get into this situation, cursing Michael for taking their girl to Mexico, and trying all the while not to think about climbing into another small plane.

Putting her bag into stowage, he waved for her to climb in the plane.

"Coop said we'll get to the border before customs opens."

"We're not stopping at the border," Bill explained as he warmed up the engines. "Straight to Monterrey, then over the mountains to Baja. I made some calls."

The air between them was saturated with her fear. Michael had taught Kate to love the sky, and had even taught her to fly. If anything were to happen to him on one of their family trips, God forbid, she wanted to be able to land the plane. But it had taken only one incident to erase all that she'd gained, and Kate had sworn she'd never fly in a small plane again. As if to test her resolve, Bill revved the engines. With the brake still set, the plane shuddered uncomfortably.

"You're not nervous about flying?" he asked.

"I'm not flying," Kate told him. "You are. Now let's go."

Thanks to Bill's connections, the customs stop two hours later in Monterrey was little more than a touch and go. They landed and taxied toward immigration where a Mexican aviation official walked quickly to the plane and took the papers that Bill handed him.

"It's all there," Bill told him. "Aircraft title, license, medical, passport, insurance—*todo.*"

"*Buena suerte,*" the official said as he passed the papers back without even looking at them.

Half an hour later, they topped the nine-thousand-foot peaks of the Sierra Madre. Clearing the last peak, they had their first view of the Sea of Cortez, an eight-hundred-mile swath of deep blue sea.

"Look," Bill said softly, pointing at the wide expanse of blue. "Clear sky, calm water. That's the most beautiful sight in the world."

"Michael and Hope are going to be the most beautiful sight," she said as she dug the binoculars out of Bill's flight bag and began to study the water.

"We're too high," she told him. "Go down."

"I'm going lower for the crossing, but we're headed straight to Buenavista to draw up a search plan and lay out a grid."

Kate checked the instrument panel.

"We've got plenty of fuel. I don't want to waste time on the ground."

"Kate, listen to me. We don't know which way the wind's blowing or how the currents are running. We don't even know which way they started. Our best chance is to gather information and follow standard search procedures."

Reaching over, Bill laid his hand on hers.

"They're down there, probably out of gas or with motor problems. We'll sort it all out and then we'll find them."

Pushing on the control yoke, Bill started their descent and turned the plane slightly to the south. Just before the banking plane raised the focus of Kate's binoculars from the sea up into the sky, she thought for one moment that she saw a boat on the horizon to their north. Lifting herself in her seat, she quickly panned the surface with the binoculars, but this time saw only water.

"Dad! Wake up!"

Lying in the bottom of the boat, Michael stirred uneasily. His stomach was knotted in cramps and a terrible thirst raged in his throat. For most of the night he'd sat up watching for any sign of boat or shore, all the while considering what he could do to increase their chances of being found. Waking with the sun, Hope had relieved her father on watch, and he'd fallen into a deep sleep.

"Wake up, Dad! I think I hear a plane."

Coming to his senses, Michael sat up and began to survey the sky. Holding one finger to his lips, he silenced Hope, but the only sound was the lapping of the waves on the boat.

"I don't hear it," he said after a while. "You sure it sounded like a plane?"

Hope sagged back down onto her seat. "No. I guess I imagined it."

Checking the height of the sun, Michael saw that he'd slept a couple of hours, longer than he'd intended.

"You okay?" he asked.

"I'm bored. I was really hungry, so I had two bites of sandwich like you said, and two sips of water. Now it's your turn."

"I'm not hungry," he told her. "Maybe later."

Hope pushed the rest of the sandwich on him anyway. "You better eat some before it goes bad."

Knowing he'd be no help if he went into diabetic shock, Michael took his two bites, then handed the last piece back. Reaching forward for the water bottle, he spread his feet to steady himself in the rolling swells. But as he tried to push himself to standing, his swollen arm collapsed beneath him.

"Your arm looks bad," Hope said, helping him back onto the seat.

Untying the bandage, he inspected the gash made by the fishing rod. The lacerations had closed and scabbed over, but the flesh was puffy and discolored. His left hand, which had been cut by the line, looked better but felt worse.

"Did you see anything while I slept?" he asked as he rinsed the bandages over the side.

"I saw some flying fish. One flew into the side of the boat and I tried to catch him, but he got away. Cooper's gonna find us this morning, though, right?"

Rubbing his forehead, Michael tried to coerce his mind into action.

"Sure, he probably will. But we should keep playing our game anyway. Even if we're hungry and thirsty, we should still play the game, right?"

Hope just stared at him. It was not a look of confidence.

"So, we've got three problems," he said as he surveyed the horizon. "Food, water, and sun. The sun is the easiest. We wear sunscreen and hats, and stay below the sides of the boat anytime we can. Water we can't do much about except go easy on what we've got. That leaves food. Got any ideas?"

"The sea, Dad. It's full of fish."

"Yeah, but how are we gonna catch 'em? We lost both our rods."

"We've got the casting net."

"That might work, but there's not many baitfish out this far."

Looking in his tackle box, he found an extra spool of line and a box of hooks, then began to rig a hand line. "With the bait left over from yesterday, maybe we can catch a dorado. If we don't catch anything, we can eat the baitfish. They're just sardines without all that nasty oil in the can."

"Dad, there's no bait left."

"Of course there is," he told her.

Moved forward to the bait well, he stood motionless, his eyes glazing over as he tried to fathom what he saw. He'd suspected the sardines might be dead, but he was astonished to see not one fish, live or dead.

"I don't understand. Where'd they go?"

A pensive look came over Hope as she worked up the nerve to explain.

"I fell asleep for a while this morning. When I woke up there were two seagulls on the front seat."

"Seagulls?"

"I think they ate our bait."

Though he said nothing, Michael mind was racing. His girl's life was on the line, and he'd made a critical mistake.

Seeing the look on her father's face, Hope was stricken to the core. "I'm sorry," she said, her voice about to crack. "I didn't mean to fall asleep."

"Oh, no, it's not your fault, Sweetie," he told her. "I should've spread the net over the bait. Besides, we can make do without them. So, Swabbie, are you ready to get this old tub shipshape so we can hold our heads up high when they find us?"

In a flash, her look went from guilty to downright surly. They were in a tight spot and her father was treating her like a baby. Seeing her reaction, he took a different tack.

"Hope," he said flatly, "I know it sucks. And I'm the one that screwed up, not you. I screwed up big time. I'm sorry about it, and I'd give anything to undo it, but I can't, so let's just..."

"Awaiting your orders, Captain!" she interrupted. "Under one condition, Sir."

"Which is?"

"Don't call me Swabbie."

"Okay. Whatever you say."

"Or Sweetie or Sweetheart, and especially not Kitten."

"I thought you liked Sweetie."

"Five years ago."

"What about Kiddo? I'd hate to give that up."

She thought about it for a moment.

"Okay, Kiddo's fine. But if you say Pookie or Angel Puss, I'll slug you. Now what do I do?"

"Get the scoop, then bail that salt water out of the bait well. I'll fix up a hand line with a lure. Before long we'll be having a fresh fish lunch."

"Wait a minute!" she said, looking at him suspiciously. "How do we cook the fish?"

"Cook it? We'll eat it Japanese style—sushi!"

"You mean raw?"

"Better than no fish at all," he told her. "Now start bailing."

As Michael held the scoop out to her, he noticed a tremor in his hand. Hope noticed it, too, but said nothing. Knowing his blood sugar was out of control, Michael wondered if he should take his last pill. Deciding to wait as long as possible, he patted the front pocket on his fishing shirt just to make sure the medicine bottle was still there. And then he let out a small laugh.

"What's so funny?" Hope asked.

"This is my lucky fishing shirt," he explained. "Get it? My *lucky* shirt—makes you wonder what would have happened if I'd worn an unlucky shirt."

"Yeah, that's a laugh riot," Hope told him. "How much other lucky stuff have you got?"

"I don't know, but let's find out. We checked our food and water, so let's see what else we've got. Help me lay everything out. You never know what might make the difference between getting found and..." Glancing up, he saw the look on her face and knew he'd made another mistake.

"Between being found *today*," he corrected, "and not being found till tomorrow. So whadaya got on your end?"

There wasn't much.

From the bow, Hope produced their empty water bottles, a bit of sandwich, most of a liter of water, and the casting net.

From the emergency bag, Michael pulled out the life jackets, pliers and screwdrivers, two flares, a hundred feet of nylon rope, and the empty Coke bottle.

From his tackle box, he retrieved a map of the Southern Cortez, sunscreen, a fishing knife, a spool of monofilament line and assorted hooks, weights and lures, plus a small pad of paper and a pencil.

"We've got this stuff," he said, "plus two gas cans—one with gas, but no motor to use it in—a broken watch, and my wallet. Too bad there's not a store in the neighborhood."

"You're cracking me up, Dad."

"Come here, you," he said, lifting his good arm so she could lean close. "We'll give Coop till midday. If he hasn't found us by then, we'll build a nuclear submarine out of this stuff and cruise back in style."

Hope rolled her eyes, but she also looked a tiny bit amused. "In the meantime," he added, "it's your turn to rest."

As Hope stretched out next to him, Michael remembered that he'd been dreaming during his long nap. In his dream, he was young and unafraid. Climbing to the top of the San Saba Railroad trestle as he had one night at age fifteen, he had leapt off into the black void below. The real fall, he remembered, seemed to last only an instant, but in his dream, the free-floating fall through darkness went on and on as if he'd fallen off the edge of the earth.

Doing idiotic things for no other reason than to beat back fear itself had been a rite of passage for the Junction boys. After a big rain, they would swim through the corrugated steel pipes that carried surging water beneath the low-water crossing on the South Llano. The pipes were only thirty feet long but barely wider than his shoulders, and the water rushed through them like a rocket, passing over jammed tree limbs that grabbed at Mike's body and clothes until he freed himself and was catapulted out into the sun from that dark place where all his fears seemed to lie in wait.

So perhaps it was not that he had been without fear, but only that he had thought it important to laugh in its face. Teens will risk their lives because they feel they have everything to prove and nothing to lose. But the older you get, the more you cherish what you have. That's when the fear starts to rebuild inside you.

By the time Wild Bill Frazier first crossed Michael's path, a child's worst fears had already come to pass. Michael's father had been killed in Korea, and his mother, unable to deal with her grief, had driven off a bluff on the Junction highway. She'd been drunk, Michael later concluded, though he was only five at the time and remembered her more as the idea of a mother than anything else. Raised by grandparents almost sixty years his senior, young Michael Parker found his solace on the banks of the river.

Without siblings or close neighbors, his usual companion was Blue, the horse Josh had given him on his seventh birthday. A dappled mare of sixteen hands, she'd been born with the cord wrapped around her neck, coming into the world as blue as the deepest sea and with just as little oxygen. Young Michael took the cord off the foal's neck and got her circulation going by rubbing her skin with a towel, while Josh Parker blew air down her windpipe with a blacksmith's bellows until she snorted and choked out her first breaths. In the ensuing years, she'd regained some of her inherited color, but she always retained a pallid blue in her coat as if you could see right through to her veins.

One sunny Saturday morning when Michael had just turned sixteen, he and Blue headed west from the barns, paralleling the river on the abandoned county road which had long ago been replaced by an asphalt highway built further from the river to protect it from floods. Horse and teenage master were riding on the old caliche road through a mesquite flat when both perked up their ears at the sound of a distant motor. Not knowing the source of the sound, both glanced around nervously.

"I hear it, too," Michael said softly to Blue. "Sounds like an old car."

Then he saw it coming over the horizon, a faded biplane sputtering down the river valley and headed straight for them. Barely clearing the tops of the trees at the far end of the flat, the pilot obviously intended to land on the same narrow road currently occupied by horse and rider. Glancing around, Michael confirmed what he already knew; the gates at each end were too far to reach in time and both sides of the road were lined with barbed-wire fence. Beyond the fence lay a solid wall of mesquite limbs and thorns that formed an impenetrable barrier. Beneath him, Blue began to shift uneasily.

With nowhere to run, Michael pressed his right heel gently into Blue's flank as he eased back on the left rein, causing the horse to sidestep until her left side pressed lightly against the fence.

"*Eeea-sy,*" he whispered as he laid his head alongside hers and gently wrapped his arm over her eyes.

By now the plane's wheels had bounced for the second time and the plane was rolling toward them at fifty miles an hour. Michael's first hope had been that the wings would pass over them, but as the plane rushed closer, he saw that the wings were too low.

"Damn!" he said just loud enough to unnerve the horse even further.

He wished he'd hopped off and pulled Blue down in the old

cavalry fighting dismount Josh had taught him, but it was too late for anything now except to pray that the wings were not wider than the makeshift landing strip. As the plane came upon them, Michael could already see the pilot struggling to hold it straight, fighting the bumps in the old road, trying his damndest to save them all.

Seeing at last that the lower wing was slightly shorter than the upper, Michael used his own weight to lean the horse and himself at an angle against the fence and posts. Then the plane was upon them. Just as the lower wingtip whipped past them, the upper wing snatched his favorite hat right off his head. Sliced almost in half, the hat fluttered in the wing wake like a giant butterfly. Through it all, the horse had barely moved.

As soon as the plane passed, horse and rider were again upright and off in hot pursuit. Thirty feet before the road ran out, the pilot suddenly spun the plane around so that it skidded to a halt facing the opposite direction from which it had come.

"Holy cow!" the man hollered as Michael rode up alongside. "I thought we'd all bought the farm that time!"

Yanking off his goggles, the pilot lifted himself straight up out of the cockpit and hopped onto a solid strut of the cloth-covered lower wing.

"Son!" the man hollered. "That was the finest piece of horsemanship I ever had the pleasure to witness, though I don't believe I'd care to see it again."

Hopping off the wing, he held out his hand to the still-mounted rider.

"William Frazier's the name, though you may call me Wild Bill."

"Michael Parker," the boy said. "And I got half a mind to punch you in the nose. What the heck are you doing landing on my ranch?"

Wild Bill grinned at the boy. "Your ranch, huh?"

"Well, it belongs to my granddaddy—Joshua Parker—and you better get that thing out of here before he gets back or he's liable to use it for firewood and windmill repairs."

"I'll be damned!" said Wild Bill. "You're Marvin's kid. God, you look just like him."

Michael stared at the man suspiciously. "You knew my father?"

"I had the honor of flying on his wingtip—in Texas and in Korea."

"How come I never heard of you?"

"Well, let's just say your grandpa don't have a high opinion of me. How is the old goat?"

"Not so great since Gramma died."

"I heard she passed and I'm sorry," Bill said, taking off the leather flyer's helmet in respect. After a brief moment of silence, he added, "Damn, son. You're running out of family. One of these days, you gonna be the last Parker standing."

"I know that, Sir. What's your point?"

"No point; I just happen to admire your family."

All through their talk, Michael was circling the plane, feeling the varnished cloth on the wings, the polished wood of the propeller, and the taut wire struts that held it all together.

"How old is this heap of junk?" he asked.

"Younger than me," said Bill Frazier, "if it's any of your beeswax. Think you could help me find this fuel leak, then ride me down to the barns for some gas?"

Michael said nothing.

"Pay you cash money for the gas and ten dollars for your trouble."

For the first time, Michael noticed that the plane had an open second cockpit just ahead of the main.

"I don't want your money," Michael answered. "And I'll *give* you the gas."

"Ah, the Parker clan..." said Wild Bill, sounding if he was about to wax eloquent.

"I'll give it to you..." Michael interrupted, "*if* you give me a flying lesson."

Wild Bill thought about the offer, scratching the back of his neck all the while.

"Jesus Hubert Christ," he finally said, "your grandpa may kick my bo-hind half way to Rocksprings, but what the hey, you got a deal."

They rode double to the barn and drove back to the plane in the ranch pickup, a rusted old Ford that rattled like a wagonload of nuts and bolts on a cobblestone road. When they had the leaky fuel line replaced and the plane refueled, Bill Frazier hopped up on the wing. As he started to climb into the back cockpit, Michael grabbed him by the ankle and held on tight.

"Hey! What about that lesson?"

"Now?"

Michael just looked at him.

"Hell, son, I don't even know if this old plane'll get off this crummy road."

"Don't bullshit me, sir! You owe me a lesson."

Nodding his agreement, Bill climbed into the pilot's seat, flipped a few switches, and gave Michael the high sign to spin the propeller. Michael gave it a whirl, then jumped back to safety as the motor fired, misfired, then fired again. Flames and black smoke spewed out of the holes in the cowling, and the propeller began to pull at the air.

"Well," Bill Frazier asked him, "you coming, or you just gonna talk about it?"

"Can't be worse than getting kicked by a mule," Michael said as he scrambled onto the wing. But as he lowered himself into the open front cockpit, he remembered that he'd never been kicked by a mule.

"What are the pedals for?" Michael shouted back.

"Shut up and keep your big damn feet off 'em!" Bill hollered over the roar. "How many of those phone poles you got from here to that wall of mesquite at the end of the road?"

"Thirteen!"

"You sure?"

"I'm sure. We race horses here. They're fifty feet apart, and thirteen times fifty is an eighth of a mile."

"Okay, count 'em and holler out as we pass. We plow into that mesquite jungle and they'll be pulling thorns out of your butt for a month."

Revving the engine, Bill released the brakes and the plane leapt forward. As they passed the poles, Michael shouted over the roar of the engine.

"Three... four... five!"

Hitting a rock in the road, the plane bounced hard, sending Michael momentarily airborne.

"Seven... eight... nine!"

At the tenth pole it still seemed like they were traveling much too slowly to get off the ground.

"Eleven!! Twelve!!!"

Before he could say "thirteen," Michael's head was tossed back as they jerked up into the air. By the time he had righted himself, they were well into the sky and banking over the sparkling waters of the Blue Hole.

"This is great!" he shouted. But if Wild Bill Frazier heard him over the wind and the motor, the man gave no indication.

As they climbed, Michael tracked their location by landmarks below. When at last he took his gaze from the land and looked out upon the blue sky, he knew he would never again see the world in quite the same way.

"Wow!" was all he could say.

Five minutes into the flight, his reverie was interrupted by Wild Bill clapping him on the shoulder.

Michael twisted around to answer. "What?!"

"Your shoulder belts!" Bill hollered. "Are they on?"

Michael nodded, and at that moment, hoping to shake some of that boyish enthusiasm out of the lad, Bill jerked the wheel to the left and executed a perfect barrel roll, the twisting momentum thrusting Michael hard against the side panel, then hard against the other side when the roll jerked to a stop, again at perfect level.

"How you feel?" Bill shouted forward, expecting the boy to turn around green in the face and begging to get back to the ground.

"Yee-hi!" yelled Michael, his eyes wide as saucers. "Do it again!"

"I'll put the bugs in that grin," Bill Frazier muttered. "Lesson two! Crop dusting!"

Diving down toward a field of alfalfa, Bill began to skim his wheels through the seed heads, scaring up thousands of fat grasshoppers, which were chopped up by the propeller and thrown back onto Michael in the front cockpit.

"Cool!" Michael shouted as he used his hands to protect his eyes from the bug juice.

"Last lesson!" called Bill, who was beginning to realize his plan to scare the boy might have been poorly conceived. "Navigating in fog."

Dropping down on Highway 377, Bill flew the last couple of miles back to the ranch at an altitude of approximately three feet, the plane hugging the curves of the road as if it were a race car. When they passed *under* a set of power lines, Michael turned around with another of his goofy grins, only to see a wide-eyed look of terror on Bill's face.

Puzzled, Michael turned back to the front just as they jerked up and over a semi-truck and double-decker cattle trailer coming straight at them.

"Cripes, I nearly dirtied my diaper that time!" Bill hollered.

Finally lining it up on the paved highway in front of the ranch house, Bill Frazier eased off the throttle and set it down in the middle of the road. When they coasted to a stop, they were right at the main gate.

"Thanks!" Michael called as he hopped down from the plane. "That was more fun than pissing on an electric fence!"

"Son, there's more to flying than fun and games," Bill cautioned as he sailed a business card down to the boy. "Come see me over in Kerrville sometime. I'll give you a real lesson."

"Okay. You can buy me a new hat."

"Here," Bill told him, "you can have mine."

With that, he took off his flyer's helmet and tossed it down to the boy. Michael stared at the worn leather hat in his hands as if he were holding the Holy Grail. Then Wild Bill, his shaggy hair blowing back behind his head, swung the plane around to take off into the wind.

Twenty-five years later, as Bill Frazier lined up his nose on the sand and seashell runway of Buenavista, he remembered looking down at the young Michael Parker standing there by the road, the helmet in the boy's hand as he waved good-bye. Now Bill would have given anything to see Mike waving up at him from the dirt strip below.

"Damn, boy," he muttered. "Where have you gone?"

SEVEN

"Not good," Michael thought. "Not good at all." It was pushing noon and getting seriously hot in the open boat. With the little information available to him, he was trying to figure their position.

"Thirty miles out, maybe more," he mumbled. "Forty miles north. They're looking for us but Cooper thinks we went south. Gilberto knows which way we started but he's gone to the island with his radio turned off cause his scientists don't like to be disturbed."

To make matters worse, they were drifting further and further north. Along the west coast of the Cortez, the current runs from north to south, pushed from the north by giant upwellings of deep water that fuel the sea's rich marine life. So many microorganisms thrive in these blue waters that the entire sea sometimes blooms in a vast red tide like an ocean of pale blood. The Vermillion Sea, the first Spanish explorers called it. But move far enough from shore, and the current doubles back to the north. Trolling the day before, Michael had crossed over the scum line that separates the two currents. Pushed by the sea and the south winds, they were moving steadily north and decreasing their chances of being found by any boat from Buenavista.

One way or another, they had to reduce their drift.

"Hand me the rope," Michael told Hope. "We need to set an anchor."

Crouched in the narrow shadow of the gunwale, Hope looked at her father like he'd lost his mind.

"Dad, we don't *have* an anchor."

"I know that. Just hand me the rope."

"Even if we had an anchor," she said, "the ocean's like two miles deep. I don't think the rope's gonna reach."

"Now hand me the yellow bag," he told her.

Hope shrugged and passed the waterproof emergency bag to her father, who took out his pocketknife and began to cut a series of holes around its opening.

"What are you doing?" she asked.

"Making a sea anchor. It's like a parachute in the water. The boat pulls it along as we drift and the sea anchor tries to hold us back... if it works."

Cutting four short pieces of rope, he tied them to the holes he'd made in the bag, then secured the four leads to the seventy feet of rope that remained, Michael slipped the whole thing into the water at the side of the boat and began to play out the line.

"You remember how to tie a bowline?" he asked.

"I think so."

"Then tie that end to the cleat on your side."

He'd been teaching her different knots for years, but never really thought she'd need them to save her life. Soon after she had the knot tied, the bag reached the end of the line. But instead of popping open and dragging against the boat, the bag only flopped limply on the surface. Grabbing the tethered line, Michael pulled the bag toward him a bit, then let it play back out, but it still wouldn't open.

"Nice try," Hope told him.

Ignoring her, he continued jerking on the line, still without success. He was about to give up when the bag floated up on a small swell and suddenly popped open. Immediately, both Michael and Hope felt a tug on the boat.

"It's working!" Hope cried out. "I felt it."

But as Michael watched the open bag in the distance, a frown came to his face.

"What's wrong?" she asked.

"It's spinning. If it spins too much, it'll kink up the rope and tear itself up."

Pulling in the line a few feet, Michael tried to maneuver the bag to stop the spinning. If anything, he made it worse. By the time the twists accumulating in the rope had backed all the way to the cleat, he'd seen enough and began to pull in the bag.

"I've got an idea," Hope told him as she dug into the tackle box. "We've got fishing swivels. Let's put one on the line."

Taking the heavy black swivel, Michael examined it closely.

"I don't think it's strong enough," he concluded.

"Come on, Dad!" she wheedled. "What have we got to lose?"

"If the swivel broke, we could lose the bag," he told her. "It's a bright color; we might need to wave it to get someone to see us."

"If it breaks off, I'll swim for it," she said brightly. "I'm hot, anyway. The water would feel good."

Seeing no fault in her logic, Michael re-rigged the bag by cutting the nylon rope and splicing the two ends back to the little wire loops at each of the swivel. They were both holding their breath when the new rig reached the end of the rope. This time the bag opened to the water almost immediately and again they felt the jerk of its pull.

"It's still spinning!" Hope said dejectedly.

"The sea anchor's spinning, but the rope isn't," he told her. "The swivel's working."

Holding up his hand, he exchanged a high five with Hope. Their elation had hardly subsided when Michael saw the rope slacken as a larger swell passed beneath the bag. After a beat, the line snapped back to full tension. As the process repeated itself, Michael realized they were gliding up one small swell while the sea anchor was sliding down the back of a different one, which caused the line to alternately tighten and slack. He was reaching for the line to shorten the trailing distance when a larger swell shoved the boat forward, yanking the rope tight. For a moment, it all held, but then they heard a loud snap and the fully stretched rope shot back toward them.

Pulling in the loose line, Michael examined the broken half a swivel, then looked to the bag, now floating up and down on the swells fifty feet behind the boat.

"I'll get it!" Hope yelled.

Before Michael could stop her, she'd moved to the rail.

"Don't!" he yelled, but it was too late. She'd already made a beautiful dive into the sea.

"It feels great!" she called to her father when she surfaced not far from the panga. Then she turned and swam quickly toward the yellow bag about thirty yards away. Hope had been swimming in Lake Austin and at Barton Springs since she was tiny, and like her mother, she had a strong kick and a powerful stroke. These swells were no match for her grace in the water, and within moments she'd reached the bag. Grabbing it, she turned and waved to her father.

"Come back," he called to her. "Right now."

Despite having to drag the bag along behind her, the return trip seemed even easier. She was moving with the current now, instead of fighting it. But about halfway back, she stopped swimming forward and began to tread water.

"Can I stay in a while?" she asked.

"Quit messing around!" Michael ordered.

"Come on, Dad. It feels great!"

"I mean it, Hope," he told her. "I want you to get back here right now." He knew the swells weren't big enough to cause any real problems, but every time she slipped out of sight, Michael's heart leapt into his throat.

Then he saw something else—a fin cutting through the water just a few swells behind Hope.

"Shark!" he called out. "Behind you!"

Hope turned to look, but saw nothing. Paddling hard, she started toward the boat anyway, but the emergency bag slowed her down.

"Drop the bag!" Michael shouted as he glanced around in search of some weapon.

But Hope would not drop the bag. Then he saw the fin again, circling just one swell behind her. This time Hope saw it too.

"Daddy!" she screamed.

Taking his knife from the tackle box, Michael stepped onto the rail and was about to dive in when he noticed the rope, still tied to the panga, with the other end trailing on the water near Hope.

"Grab the rope!" he ordered. Doing the same from the boat, he began to pull furiously, dragging her hand over hand toward the boat. Just ten feet remained between them when the fin came up behind her, slicing through the water till it was at her heels. Then she suddenly shot forward, propelled almost into her father's arms by a powerful thrust.

Grabbing her wrists, Michael dragged her aboard, expecting the worst. But as he pulled her over the rail, instead of gashes or blood on her body there was only fear on her face. Looking again to the water, they saw the explanation as the fin came out of the water, revealing, not a shark, but a large dolphin, mottled gray with a long scar on one side.

Both amazed and out of breath, Michael and Hope stared at the dolphin as he turned and sped away.

"I guess I was wrong," Michael said, as he reached over and pulled the yellow bag back into the boat. "There wasn't a shark."

"No," Hope said, "I saw the shark; the dolphin chased him away."

Shaken, Michael sat down heavily on the seat, every muscle in his body trembling from the exertion he'd made and from the scare. Knowing he could wait no longer, he took the medicine bottle from his pocket, opened it, and swallowed his last pill. Then he hugged his daughter tightly.

"I was scared," he told her. "I was so scared."

After a hasty planning meeting at Buenavista, Kate and Bill were already back in the air and headed south—Kate with a nautical chart unfolded on her lap and Bill calling out course and direction for her to mark the progress of their search. They were not the only ones crisscrossing the Sea of Cortez. Every fisherman from Pulmo to Pescadero was on alert. The Mexican Air Force had even sent out its aging Mirage fighter trainers from the base in La Paz. Not long after dawn, the two French-made jets—painted with desert camouflage as if the Mexicans expected to fight a battle over the mountains of Baja—had roared over Buenavista on their way to the transition waters where the Cortez met the Pacific. If Michael and Hope were still in the Cortez, Coop figured, it might take a day or even two to find them. But if the panga got caught out in the Pacific current, they might be swept far to the west and never be found, so logic dictated using the fastest craft the furthest away.

The southern Cortez, from Buenavista south to Pulmo, was to be covered by Bill and Kate—two sections before they had to refuel, then two more in the late afternoon.

A pilot himself, Michael's pal Cooper wished he was in the air, too, but his plane was in the States for annual service and Michael's twin-engine Cessna had been leased for the week and was already somewhere on the mainland. That meant Cooper was grounded, relegated to coordinating the search from the office at Buenavista.

"I need better charts!" Bill had insisted at the planning meeting that morning. The dining room at Buenavista had been filled to capacity, with Cooper and Bill Frazier standing in front of a large table facing a room full of captains and deckhands from Coop's place and two other fishing resorts in the area. The harbormaster, both local policemen, and the mayor were also present. It's bad business to misplace two American tourists. Standing at one side and feeling useless, Kate alternated between surveying the room and looking at her watch, muttering to herself all the while, "Come on, come on! Let's go, let's go!"

But Bill was unhappy because there was no clear consensus as to whether a disabled boat would have drifted east or southwest from Cabo Pulmo.

"I want to know the tides, the currents, the shipping lanes, where there's fishermen, where there's not. And I want to know which way the wind has been blowing for the past twenty-four hours," he said. "Christ Almighty, Cooper, these charts don't show much more than ocean depths. Twenty-five years down here and this is the best you can do?"

"I've never had a single boat lost more than a couple of hours," Coop said defensively. "And if they were in one of my boats instead of that junker they borrowed, they wouldn't even be lost. I'd never have let them go out in that rusty bucket of Nacho's."

Seated in the front row, Nacho was shaking his head from side to side. He knew the blame was on him, and he wasn't taking it well.

"If they'd been in one of my boats," Coop continued, "they would have called on the radio and I'd have picked 'em up last night."

"Then why weren't they in one of yours?" Bill challenged. "And why weren't you there when they left?"

Cooper's face paled to gray as he reminded himself for the twentieth time that he wasn't there because he'd still been drunk from all the tequila the night before, just as he'd been drunk every night since his father died three months ago.

"Bill, you think I'm not blaming myself? I've sent a car to La Paz for newer charts, but it's gonna take a few hours. So until then, get off my butt, please."

Bill didn't like it that he'd gotten mad at Coop. Sometimes showing your temper, can get things done, but he hadn't acted with purpose; he'd acted out of frustration and nerves, even though he'd known that Coop would hold up his end.

Seeing the pensive look in Bill's eyes, Kate reached over and touched his hand on the yoke of the plane. "Thanks for doing this," she told him.

Most men Bill's age were enjoying their retirement, and there was a frown on his face that worried her.

"Where else would I be? Especially after I blew it the last time he needed me."

"Don't even start with that," she scolded. "You've been there for him a hundred times, for more than half his life. And you still blame yourself for not being there once. If there's anyone to blame today, it's me. I'm the one who's been feeling so sorry for myself that my husband came to the conclusion he'd be better off as a crop-dusting bum in Mexico than he would be at home with his family. And I'm the one that let Hope go off on the dangerous vacation from hell!"

"The two of them had a little say in it," Bill told her, "so you stop being so tough on yourself."

"I figured we might need a little tough."

"Maybe I like your attitude more than I realized," he said.

Turning to Kate, he saw her binoculars fixed on a point of the horizon where a dark mass was barely visible on the horizon.

"What's that?" she asked, adrenaline coursing through her body. "What's that on the water?"

For a long, hopeful moment, Bill focused his gaze on the spot, then the corners of his mouth turned downward.

"Turtle," he said.

"That can't be a turtle. It's too big. Besides, if it was a turtle, you couldn't possibly tell at this distance."

"Try the other binoculars," he told her.

Setting down the wider-sweeping 7 x 35 binoculars, she raised the big Leica 10 x 50s and started working the focus wheel to bring the object into view.

"What is it?" he asked.

"Still can't tell. Let's go see."

Bill banked left and they rolled into the turn. As they dove closer to the water, Kate's heart raced with the accelerating engines.

"Hope," she whispered softly. "Please be Hope and Michael."

In a matter of seconds, they were over it, a big Ridley's sea turtle, three feet long and paddling slowly north with the current. Powering into another turn, Bill headed back to their previous track.

"Good eyes," he said. "Keep it up. That's how we'll find them."

Switching back to the smaller binoculars with a wider field of view, she again began to sweep the surface of the water. A frown on her face, Kate listened to the drone of the engine as her thoughts flew back to the day that began it all.

Once upon a time, they'd been strangers in the same small city, and yet they found each other a thousand miles away. In her journal she wrote of that meeting,

He smiled at me, and I looked into his eyes and saw a window on my future. It felt as if my whole life had been pointed toward that moment.

In the summer of 1978, Kate and her friend Rachel decided they needed a break from Austin and found a cheap flight to Cancun—a new beach destination on a pristine stretch of Mexico's Caribbean coast. The two *gringas* made a good pair in Mexico because Rachel, with her flaming red hair and personality to match, was everything that Kate was not.

Rachel was making eyes one night at their waiter, a young Mexican man with flowing black hair and dark eyes set against a white shirt and shorts that showed the lean muscles of a long-distance runner.

"He looks like a Mayan god!" Rachel gushed.

"A *gay* Mayan god," Kate corrected, causing them both to burst out laughing.

But the waiter proved Kate wrong when he brought a round of margaritas, compliments of the house, and smiled at Rachel as he set them down.

"Hasta la vista, Big Boy!" Rachel said as he walked away. With a little tequila in her, Rachel was not one to be shy.

"Jesus, Rachel, control yourself!"

"Kate, how many times do I have to tell you? You see something you like, you gotta go for it. Your problem is you're always waiting for Mr. Right to pull a dozen roses out of his butt and start singing love songs. Loosen up, girl."

"Better Mr. Right than Mr. Right Now."

"Ha-ha. But did you ever think that maybe you'd find both?"

By the next margarita, Kate was starting to catch a little of Rachel's wild air.

"Just for argument's sake," said Kate, "do you get to pick this dream date for me, or do I get a say?"

Glancing around the room at the mix of drunken college boys and sad, expatriate Americans, Rachel's eyes came to rest on a guy in a beat-up straw hat who'd just come in the door.

"Hey, cowboy!" Rachel called to him. "Over here!"

"Jesus! Let's don't embarrass ourselves too much," Kate said under her breath.

"Lighten up, Sweetie. It worked, didn't it?"

Just as Rachel's cowboy arrived at their table, Kate looked up from his tall, lean body to his tentative grin and deep blue eyes, and her mind flashed to the first time she'd seen him.

She'd even dated the page in her journal: *"July 2, 1977."*

Every day after her swim—two long laps up and back at Austin's famed Barton Springs—she would fill exactly one page in the journal, writing about kids playing in the shallow end or sketching the noisy black grackles that squawked from tree to tree. With no intention of showing the book to anyone, she was free to fill it with whatever caught her fancy. She was twenty-two years old, an art school dropout with the simple ambition of learning to paint a little better.

On July 2, she was just finishing a rough sketch of a chubby eight-year-old boy trying to work up his nerve to do a cannonball off the high diving board. Later she would be unable to remember if the boy had ever jumped, but in her second drawing, he made a tremendous splash.

It was one of those perfect days at the Springs, the kind of day that twenty years later the old-timers would talk about with wistful smiles and sad eyes, a time when Austin was more friendly than big, the water clear and clean, and life so easy. Glancing up from her notebook, she saw him standing at the front gate. He was about her age, she guessed, but half a foot taller. His skin was tan and he was wearing cutoffs and a Day of the Dead T-shirt with a slender skeleton curling from his waist to his shoulders. In his hand was an old cowboy hat.

Coming down the steps to the pool, he peeled off his shirt, kicked off his *huaraches*, and dropped the hat. Peering around as if he were looking for someone, his eyes finally came to rest on Kate, still staring at him from the tree-shaded bank on the far shore. For a long moment their gazes locked, and then he flashed her a smile and dove into the water.

Kate watched for him to surface, watched and waited, but didn't see him come up. Perhaps he was going to swim all the way across to her side. A long time to hold your breath, she thought.

Thirty seconds passed and still he hadn't surfaced. She stood to get a better view. There was a lifeguard on a tower not far away, but he was paying no attention.

Her eyes darted around, searching the pool to see if he had come up elsewhere, and squinting through the sun's glare to see if he had sunk to the bottom. Hurrying to the water's edge, she was about to dive in when she looked to the far end of the pool—two hundred yards away—just as he burst into the sunlight and air.

"Okay, showoff. If that's your idea of a joke," she mumbled, "I guess I was wrong about you."

Gathering her things, she started up the slope to the south gate.

At the top of the hill she turned back to glance at him, but he didn't seem to have noticed her exit. Instead, he'd pulled himself out of the water and was lying back on the warm cement bank, oblivious to all as his body drank in the warm sun.

And then he said, "Hi."

Nearly spilling her drink as she snapped to, Kate's face flushed red.

"I'm Michael," he said, taking off the straw cowboy hat and brushing the shaggy hair back from his face. "I don't know one person in this silly tourist town. Can I join you?"

Rachel looked to Kate for the answer to that question but found her friend almost in a daze.

"Sit, sit!" Rachel told him as she kicked Kate under the table to bring her to her senses.

"Kate," she said, introducing herself. "Not Katherine or Katie or Kitten, okay? Just Kate."

He liked that. Kate.

Fifteen minutes later the three were laughing and telling stories like they'd been friends for years. All being from Austin seemed a wonderful coincidence, so a thousand miles away in Mexico, they found themselves talking about their favorite clubs, restaurants, and swimming holes back home. Saying he usually didn't drink, Michael had one margarita anyway, though he steadfastly declined to go out on the dance floor.

"I had a Baptist girlfriend in high school," he explained, "and I never learned to dance."

"I bet I could teach you!" Rachel said coyly.

Rachel was obviously having second thoughts about setting Kate up with this one. When Rachel whispered something in Michael's ear, he laughed in surprise.

"I'll be back in a minute," Kate said sharply as she stood to walk to the rest room. But then she wheeled back and leaned close to Rachel.

"If you ever want me to speak to you again, keep your hands off him!"

It was a joke, sort of.

When she came back into the bar, the music hit her like a wall of noise. Looking to their table, she saw that—despite the warning—Rachel had that hungry-cat look in her eyes that could mean only one thing.

"Now or never," Kate said to herself.

As Rachel continued to buzz away in Michael's ear, his eyes were focused on Kate coming straight across the room, the dancers seeming to part before her. Walking up to the table, she paused and looked down at him as he smiled up at her.

"Rachel, the waiter asked to dance with you," she lied. "Go find him."

Happy to have emboldened her shy friend, Rachel went off to dance with her Mexican waiter, nearly causing a fight when she winked at a blond surfer who tried to cut in.

Not far away, amidst the loud music and shouts for tequila, one couple sat together in the eye of the storm. Inches apart in order to hear each other above the noise, they talked about everything and nothing at all. Kate told Michael that she lived in an old Airstream trailer on what was left of her mother's land on Lake Austin. Michael told her that he didn't really live anywhere.

Then without the two of them having any idea how long they'd been talking, the music stopped, the lights came on, and people began to head for the door.

"Time to go," he said.

Kate nodded in agreement, but Michael had not suggested where. For the first time, she realized he wasn't going to invite her back to his room. Perhaps nothing was going to happen at all. She'd been acting like some silly flirt of a schoolgirl, which she now realized was exactly the wrong thing to do around a soft-spoken man who probably thought she was as easy as her red-haired friend.

"How about your pal?" he asked. "She gonna be okay?"

Though the music had stopped, Rachel was still dancing with her Mexican waiter. As the pair spun slowly around, Rachel waved behind the waiter's back for Kate and Michael to go on without her.

In the lobby of the Hotel Playa Blanca, Michael and Kate both tossed fifty centavo coins into the fountain and made their own private wishes. Taking his hand, Kate turned to him, wanting to invite him to her room but unable to find the words.

For a long and unknowing moment, each looked into the other's eyes, searching for something that might or might not be there. Then exactly as he leaned down to her, Kate raised on her toes, and they kissed. It was a kiss no longer than a sweet good night, no more searching than a glance into a darkened room, but with that kiss their lives were forever diverted from two tracks unknown to one path forged on the wishes of two Mexican coins in a pink stone fountain.

"Bill," Kate asked as he came out of a long, sweeping turn and set a new heading for the reverse track, "mind if I ask you something?"

"Sure. Unless you want to know how come I never got married."

"No," Kate laughed. "I just wondered if you have any idea why we all do such stupid things. I mean, how could I get everything I once wanted and still not have it be enough?"

"You're talking about you and Mike, right? You want to know how things went wrong."

When she didn't say no, he continued.

"Well, for starters, I'd have to say you're asking the wrong guy, 'cause if you look at my life, you'll see I made a mess of it all. But if you want me to venture a guess, I'd say it's because we forget."

"Forget what?"

"That part's up to you," he said. "I just think that people tend to forget the best parts of their lives and for some reason they let the hard times call the shots."

Glancing at her, Bill saw that her gaze was still sweeping the endless rows of blue swells below, but her head seemed to be moving almost imperceptibly, slowly nodding in agreement.

EIGHT

Floating mostly below the surface and finning steadily to the north, the big Ridley's turtle raised its head to take in the shape of the panga. For a long moment, its deep, dark eyes locked with the gazes of Michael and Hope. Then without breaking the rhythm of its paddling, the turtle slowly submerged and passed directly beneath the boat, the kind of turtle-submarine that may have inspired Jules Verne to imagine traveling in boats to the mysterious depths of the ocean.

"Wow!" Hope said as she leaned over the side to look down at him. "He's big!"

"Bigger than the two of us together," said Michael. "And older still."

Surfacing on the north side of the boat, the turtle continued on its way into the distance.

"Dad, the turtle found us and he's really slow. How come Cooper can't do the same thing?"

"I don't know. Coop may be looking in the wrong place. But if he doesn't find us, and the Mexican Coast Guard doesn't either, I know who will."

"Who?"

"Your mom."

Michael had calculated over and over how long it would have taken for Coop to get the word back to Austin and for Bill and Kate to fly to Baja.

"Your mom and Uncle Bill."

"Really?"

"Where else would they be? The two of them are in a fast plane with charts unfolded while Bill sweeps back and forth across the ocean. One thing I know about Bill is that he always comes through."

After losing both the ranch and his grandfather, Michael spent four years working for Wild Bill's Flying Service, doing everything from washing dishes and sweeping hangars to working on engines and hydraulic systems. All the while he studied flight manuals, took lessons, and flew with Bill to a hundred places from Mexico to Montana. When he had enough hours to get his own commercial license, Michael started flying for Bill instead of with him. In search of enough business to support two pilots, they moved to Austin, where Willie Nelson and Jerry Jeff Walker were changing the face of Texas music, and where there was always a band that needed to fly to a concert, a legislator going home for the weekend, or a fisherman with an itch for open water.

"Bill has always been there for me, Kiddo. He taught me to fly, he gave me my first plane, and because of that plane I found your mother."

Looking up, Michael saw his daughter staring at him.

"Something you want to ask me?"

"Were you in love with Mom then?"

Then. The inference was like a knife to his heart. But perhaps, Michael thought, this was not the time to delve into their troubles.

"Yes," he told his daughter, "I was in love with her. Right from the start, before she even knew me."

All those days he'd watched her at Barton Springs, He never had the nerve to introduce himself. She sat on the south side, some kind of sketchbook in her lap, and he longed to touch the illuminations she placed upon its holy pages.

"Patience," Gramma Jean used to tell him about almost anything.

"Your day will come."

In Cancun, he knew his day had come. After saying good night in the lobby of Kate's hotel, Michael lay awake for much of the night, both from excitement and from worry that he would oversleep the snorkeling date they'd set for the next morning. Strolling back into the lobby at eight a.m., his heart leapt just to see her waiting for him.

"Aeropuerto," he told the cabdriver out front.

"We're flying?" Kate asked.

Michael just smiled. At the entrance to the airport, they passed the Quonset hut that served as the private terminal and drove directly onto the tarmac toward a sleek twin-engine plane.

"Wait a minute!" she told him. "You said you were a pilot, but I didn't think..."

"Oh, come on! You're not afraid of small planes, are you?"

"No, no," she lied. "Of course I'm not afraid. You just caught me by surprise."

He could almost see her mind racing back. "You ever flown in a small plane?"

"Once," she said. "It was... fun."

Only in this case, Michael felt certain that "fun" was another word for "terrifying."

"No sweat," he reassured her. "I've taken up plenty of white-knuckle passengers and I've always managed to get them excited about flying—not in a big jet—but real flying, in a small plane that takes you exactly where you want to go."

Early on, Bill had taught him that the trick to calming nervous flyers is to show them how things work, familiarize them with the controls and the gauges, and with the reliability of the equipment.

"What if the engine quits?" she asked as she cinched herself in so tight she could barely breathe.

"Airplanes don't fall out of the sky when the engine stops. They glide, and while they glide you have time to look for a place to land. Besides, we've got two engines, and this baby flies great on one."

She still looked unconvinced.

"Look, I've logged thousands of hours and I haven't had one problem... I mean, so far, I haven't."

He flashed her a mischievous grin and something in that look and his obvious love of flying put her enough at ease that the hammer-lock grip she had on her armrests began to relax.

"You ready?"

"Yeah. Let's go before I change my mind."

With the engine running smoothly, he radioed the tower, revved the engine and eased out to the runway. Getting a final clearance at the north end of the strip, he released the brakes with his feet as his hand pushed the throttle, and the Cessna jumped forward. As they accelerated down the runway, he saw Kate glance to the air speed indicator, which was already moving past eighty. Then he pulled back on the wheel. As they pointed up to the sky, the nose gear came off the tarmac, the rear wheels just naturally followed along, and the roughness of the ground fell away. On Michael's side, the terminal passed below them, then suddenly they were over the unbroken canopy of the jungle.

"You okay?" he asked.

Peering ahead of them, she could see a long strip of the white-sand beach and the clear aquamarine waters of the Caribbean.

"It's beautiful," she replied.

They flew straight down the coast, passing over the sparkling bay of Xel Ha, then over to the seaside ruins of Tulum, where he took it down to fifteen hundred feet and banked right to give Kate a better view.

"Take a look at that," he told her. "Looks like the golf course of the ancient Mayans."

"The colors are incredible! I've never seen so many different blues and greens in one place—sky, water, trees, grass. Do you think it looked like that when the Mayans were there?"

"The Mayans are still there, from here to Guatemala—five million of them. Their lives aren't much different now than a thousand years ago—same forests, same food, same houses. Look over there on the horizon. Can you see the little hills?"

She nodded.

"They're not hills. They're the peaks of pyramids overgrown by jungle. Last winter I flew some archaeologists to a new strip at the ruins out there. They say there are five thousand ancient Mayan structures hidden under the vines."

"What happened? Why did they abandon their cities?"

"I don't know. Maybe it all just quit working. Maybe people got tired of living so close together, working their whole lives for someone else, always told what to do and when to do it. Maybe they just said, 'Chuck you, Farley,' and went back out to the life that their ancestors' stories had taught them about."

"Sounds like you'd like to do the same thing."

"If I could afford the right piece of jungle, I'd do it in a minute."

Continuing down the coastline, the sandy roads became farther and farther apart. Only half an hour into the flight, it occurred to Kate that, for the first time in her life, she could see no sign of civilization.

"Where are we going?" she asked. "Unless my high school geography was a waste, we're about to run out of Mexico."

"British Honduras," Michael told her.

"I can't go to another country! I don't have my passport."

"Nobody checks passports where we're headed."

"All this just to snorkel?"

Michael pointed to the back seat at a parcel wrapped in brown paper.

"I'm making a delivery."

A hundred miles from nowhere with a guy she didn't really know, and he was delivering secret contraband to a place she'd never heard of.

"Are we doing something illegal?"

"Relax. There's nothing to worry about. On my honor."

"But are you honorable?"

Easing off on the throttle, Michael trimmed the plane level, and double-checked his gauges. When he was satisfied with the new course, he turned to her.

"I don't think it's up to me to judge if I'm honorable. But I was raised to be, and I haven't screwed up too bad yet."

"Okay. But if you get me in trouble, I'm gonna kick your ass."

"You've got a deal. Any trouble and you can kick my ever-loving ass."

Over the water again, a series of slender islands began to pass beneath them, one with a town but no paved roads, most with little or no signs of human habitation. One after another, Michael passed them by until only one remained, a tiny dot on the horizon. When he finally lowered his landing gear, the island didn't seem to have grown much larger. All Kate could see was a few low buildings and what seemed like a very short landing strip.

"Should I be nervous?"

With a Cheshire grin on his face, Michael set the plane down as light as a feather with a hundred feet of the sandy strip remaining.

"No," he finally answered. "You don't need to be nervous. Welcome to Lighthouse Reef."

As he cut his engines by a small group of buildings, a man came out to greet them.

"Hey, Mikey!" the man hollered, waving the big white palm of his hand that stood out like a signal flag against skin so dark that it was impossible to determine whether he had once been white and was burned to a crisp by the tropical sun, or whether he was black, Creole, or some mix of all three.

Mike flopped the door open and stepped out onto the wing.

"O-scar!" he yelled, "I didn't come all this way to look at your ugly mug. Where's your beautiful wife?"

In answer to his question, out stepped a stunning woman with skin like café au lait and silky black hair so long that it was tied into a knot behind her shoulder blades.

"Mikey, I'm not caring how you sweet-talk me," she called back.

"I'm not cooking no conch for your lunch."

Behind Michael, Kate stepped into the door of the plane and he lifted her down lightly.

"Lord God Almighty!" the woman proclaimed on seeing Kate. "O-scar, I believe our Mikey's in love."

Both Kate and Michael tried not to blush at this. Introductions were made all around, then Oscar moved things to business.

"Quit joking my head here, Mikey. I'm standing in the hot sun, and still you don't tell me. Did you bring it?"

Pulling out the wrapped package, Michael held it above his head. Oscar reached for it, but Michael had the height advantage and held it higher.

"Nunh-unh! Not until I see some greenback dollars. It takes a lot of gas to get my twin engines down here."

Removing a rubber band from a fat wallet, Oscar began to count hundred dollar bills into Michael's hand. "One, two, three... Mikey, you bandit, eight, nine hundred, one thousand."

Again Oscar reached for the all-important box, and again Michael pulled it away. "Come on, Oscar, you short-counted me, that's only nine hundred."

Flashing his pearly teeth, Oscar forked over the final hundred. "Now open it up. I want to see if you got the real stuff."

The group moved to the shaded front porch where Michael unwrapped the mystery package and lifted off the lid. Almost afraid of what she'd see, Kate peered over his shoulder at the box of hand-tied fishing flies.

"Fishing lures?" said Kate. "You flew all the way to deliver fishing lures?"

"Not lures, Miss," said Oscar. "Feathers, wet flies—hand-tied by Mister Bob McCurdy in Austin, Texas. These the only flies in the whole world those picky-damn bonefish are going to eat. Mister Sada and Mister DelaRosa be in a terrible mood if they don't get their flies."

"Yeah, well, since I saved the day," Michael said, "loan us a boat so we can go to the atoll."

"No problem, I give you Elena Dos. She's a pip!"

Half an hour later, Michael and Kate entered the world of Half Moon Caye, a perfect crescent-shaped sliver of sand surrounding a coral reef with deep, blue water and visibilities of two hundred feet. As they snorkeled, reef fish by the tens of thousands swirled around them on invisible currents—spadefish, tangs, schoolmasters, and jacks—each group more colorful and more curious than the last about these two strange creatures that had joined their domain.

"Oh, my God!" Kate said as they waded back to shore. "It was beautiful! I could see forever, and there were fish everywhere. What were those long ones with the big teeth? There were hundreds of them."

"Barracuda," answered Michael.

"And those tiny ones all lit up with yellow and blue stripes like neon. What are they?"

Michael laughed. "I haven't the slightest idea. Oscar says there are six hundred species down there. I just like to watch them swim, especially the ones that use their side fins the same way I use the flaps on my plane."

With Michael almost everything came back to flying. But this time he had swum along at Kate's side and seen the ocean in a different light. Floating on the surface, he listened to the sound of the air from his snorkel rushing in and out of his lungs, and when he took a breath and dove down into dense schools of fish, he could hear the sound of his own beating heart. Through it all, his eyes kept turning back to Kate, the muscles in her long legs stretched taut as she kicked against the currents. When she raced to catch up with a school of angelfish, she locked her legs and kicked like a mermaid, her whole body moving like a wave through the water, her arms and hair trailing behind like Poseidon's own daughter.

Spreading a blanket on the beach, Kate slipped her hand into Michael's and they plopped down to catch their breath. Looking around, she saw that the entire atoll was theirs and theirs alone.

Turning onto her side, she peered into Michael's blue eyes—so beautiful and calm, but tinged by some sadness that she did not yet know—and was almost overcome with her desire to make love to him.

She wanted to tell him that she loved him, that she was sure she would always love him. But afraid she might ruin everything, she said nothing, and instead her eyes began to glisten. Since her mother's death, she had felt very much alone. And now that feeling was suddenly gone.

Leaning toward her, Michael kissed both her eyes, drinking in her tears.

"How you doing?" he asked softly.

"Sorry," she said. "It's just so beautiful here... with you."

For most of the afternoon they made love under the hot sun, resting at times to talk and laugh and eat the wonderful lunch that Inez had made them after all—fried conch, crispy brown on the outside and juicy white within, along with fresh papaya and pineapple that they fed to each other in moments of perfect passion. At times they tried to nap, but even on the edge of sleep they found their hands reaching out, fingertips touching, then slowly entwining, pulling each other closer till again their lips met.

When Michael opened his eyes, he knew that he'd been dreaming, reliving the day that had most changed his life. Looking forward, he saw Hope standing on the bow of the panga as she drew in the empty casting net and carefully gathered its folds for another throw. He had no idea how long she'd been at it, but one look at her expression told him all he needed to know. Each time she drew back the rope, the salt water slipped through the woven hemp, and the net came back empty. Now with her arms cramping as they had the day before with the marlin, even the strong-willed Hope had to admit that on open water she could not catch a fish with her tiny net.

"I can't do it!" she said bitterly.

"Hey," he consoled her. "Even Gilberto couldn't net anything out here."

"Yeah," she replied, "but if Gilberto was here, I bet we wouldn't be lost."

Then she saw the look on her father's face.

"I'm sorry, Dad. I didn't mean that."

"No," Michael told her. "You're right. And when we get back, there'll be hell to pay with your mom."

Michael made an attempt to smile, but it was halfhearted at best. This was one situation that wouldn't allow him to bull his way through with a grin and foolish determination. In a few more hours they'd be spending their second night on the ocean. And the longer they were out here, the greater the chances that they were drifting out of the search area.

Digging for a soft cloth in his tackle box, Michael began to rub it in circular motions on the small aluminum box in which he kept his favorite lures.

"What are you doing?" Hope asked.

"We need a signal mirror. This box is pretty dull, but if we rub it enough, it might do a good job of reflecting the sun."

"And someone could really see that?"

"If they're close enough. Because we're down low," he explained, "we can only see the surface for a distance of maybe three miles."

"That's not very far."

"I know. But it sounds better if you take the area of the whole circle around us. How do you figure area?"

"What are you, my math teacher?"

"Do you know or not?"

"Okay... it's pi R squared."

"Right, so the area we can see is about 3.14 times three miles squared. That's almost thirty square miles."

"So if another boat is in our thirty square miles, we could flash them with the mirror, right?"

"If the sun's out and the mirror is good enough, yeah. Or at night we could use one of the flares."

"That's cool," she admitted.

"But it gets better. A person on a bigger boat is higher up—maybe twenty feet; and if they're on a ship they could be fifty feet above the water. That makes four times the area they can see."

"What if they're not looking?"

"Then it's up to us to get their attention. That's why one of us has to watch all the time, especially at night. A big ship goes fast, and they could come over the horizon and run right by without ever seeing us."

"Okay, okay," she said. "I'll watch. I'll watch until I see something."

An hour later, Michael's rubbing the metal surface of the lure box didn't seemed to have changed it much, but he could feel the heat coming up through the cloth to his fingers and had to trust that he was making progress.

The sun beat down, and they both had two more sips of water and the last of their food, prompting Michael to ponder how his system would react when his diabetes medicine had played out.

High blood sugar or low, the consequences were equally bad. For the first thirty-eight years of his life, Michael had thought he'd missed inheriting his grandfather's diabetes. But only a couple of years ago he'd started having problems—frequent thirst, weight loss, sluggishness. It didn't take long for his doctor to determine that his pancreas wasn't producing enough insulin to burn the sugars and fats in his diet.

Running out of insulin for the first time since he'd gone on regulation, he was unsure what the results might be. He knew his blood sugar was likely to soar, while ketones—the toxic by-products of all the stored fats he'd be burning—would accumulate in higher and higher levels until ketosis began to poison his body. Unless he received insulin soon, a worsening parade of symptoms awaited him: nausea, abdominal pain, thirst, infection, drowsiness, coma... death. How long it would take to progress from the early symptoms to a final outcome was guesswork.

In the meantime, there was little he could do other than find some way to put additional food and liquids in his body. He could not make it rain, so all depended on one thing—to catch a fish.

God, he had caught so many fish. In Northern Alaska, one late summer day—Michael and a doctor from San Antonio had strapped on chest waders and stepped into the icy waters of the Chandalar River. With fly rods whipping bamboo arcs against blue sky, hand-tied lacewings were lofted to the ravenous gulp of powerful Coho salmon, their bodies fat from long months at sea. On that final desperate journey up river to the place of their birth, time after time the giant salmon felt their bodies snagged and turned from their destination, pulled toward some terrible unknown.

As the lengthening shadows reached out to him from shore, Michael's heart had raced with every salmon's attack—their flashes of silver sunlight shooting through his eyes and his arm at the same frozen instant like a perfect painting of a man in a perfect place that had not yet been touched by civilization's multitude of imperfections. After each long battle, Michael drew unto himself a fish both stronger and more beautiful than he could possibly have imagined. After releasing one, he'd somehow hook another that was stronger still. Each of the big salmon fought for their manifest destiny, battling not just for their lives (which would end soon anyway), but for the continuation of all life; fighting to lay their pink, round eggs and perfect milky seed in the shallow gravel where their journey had begun; fighting back toward the very reason they had been spawned.

Though Michael knew the will of the salmon was stronger than his determination to catch them, time after time the moment came when he slipped his hand into the water and lifted the powerful, trembling fish into the cradle of his arm. Over his shoulder, he carried a wicker creel lined with wet ferns on which to lay the fish that would be his dinner. But with each fish, he found himself removing the hook, then easing the fish back into the water. Time after time he watched them swim away, slowly at first, then shooting up the river in a flash toward their beginning and end.

So many times did he cast his spell and draw them in, then cast them back upon the waters, that the day had seemed to last forever. Despite this sorcerer's spell, the sun did eventually touch the horizon. Almost at the Arctic Circle, Michael would always remember that simultaneous gathering twilight and coming dawn as he watched the last salmon slip from his fingers. Then he drew in his line and made his way downstream to where his plane on its pontoons was anchored to the shore. There he found the doctor in a state of exhausted ecstasy, his fishing having been equally fine so that he, too, had come back with a creel as triumphantly empty as both men's stomachs.

Knowing that in a thousand trips to a thousand streams, they could never find a better day, they gorged on peanut butter sandwiches and camped upon that shore, illuminated by a dancing aurora borealis while both men dreamed of fishing that was not nearly so good as what they had actually known that day.

Two months later, the phone rang at the hangar in Austin, bringing the sad news that the good doctor from San Antonio had died from the cancer he'd known would soon kill him, but which he'd never mentioned to Michael. All he had wanted was one perfect day of fishing. And that was what they'd had.

To catch a fish, thought Michael. It cannot be possible that I, who have caught so many fish, cannot catch just one for a girl as great as Hope.

Even with her teenage attitude and the blame Hope laid on her father, he thought she was an incredible girl who was beautiful, passionate and curious. He and Kate had been truly blessed. And here before him, sunburned in this open boat, was the very hungry proof.

It would have been so much simpler if they still had one of the rods. Instead Michael had only a spool of twenty-pound test line, from which he cut fifty feet.

"No reason to chance losing the whole spool over the side," he reasoned.

Tying a yellow and red albacore feather to one end, he wrapped the other end of the line around his unhurt palm and tossed the lure out into the water.

"Like that's gonna work," Hope muttered just loud enough for her father to hear.

Though the sun was approaching the horizon, it was still hot as hell in the open boat, and Michael felt that he deserved whatever she needed to dish out. He could take it. All that mattered was getting this girl back, alive and well, to her mother's arms. All that mattered was Hope.

NINE

They were flying back to Cancun, returning from that perfect day at Half Moon Caye, and Kate could not help but notice that the man with whom she'd fallen so completely in love had sunk into silence. With the sun about to touch the horizon, she wondered if she'd done or said something wrong.

On the beach, they'd made love and made love again, then Kate kissed him quickly, jumped up and plunged into the ocean. Pulling hard against the surge of the surf, her legs swung easily from her hips and the motion flowed down and out through her fins. As she came to the reef, she took a deep breath and plunged beneath the surface.

She stayed under a long time, hiding perhaps from what seemed too wonderful and easy with him. Or was she merely trying to pay him back for scaring her at Barton Springs?

"Probably never noticed me then," she thought. "But I remember, and that's what counts."

He watched her until she waded into the shallows, her body vibrant and so alive, then his eyes fell closed. When he awoke, she was seated near him, cross-legged with her pack open, a sketchpad in her lap, and a charcoal pencil in hand. Instead of drawing, she was staring out to sea.

"Hey." His voice sounded soft and happy. When she turned to him, he was smiling.

"Hey," she answered. "Nice nap?"

Michael stretched his arms above his head. "Yeah. What'd you draw?"

She turned the pad to reveal a pencil drawing resembling one of Michelangelo's working sketches. Only this drawing was of Michael, asleep on the beach. Holding it like a mirror, he studied it in wonder.

"Wow! You really are an artist. But with all this beautiful ocean, why a picture of me?"

"You mind?"

"I'd rather have one of you."

Kate frowned.

"I say something wrong?"

"No, I've just never done a self-portrait—got myself kicked out of art school over it."

"So I guess that begs the question. Why?"

"I don't know. I guess I didn't want to look at myself that closely."

"Yeah, well, you ought to think it over. You might like what you find."

Kate looked off into the distance.

"My grandmother was a painter," Michael continued. "When she had the time. Sunday afternoons, after the dishes were done, she'd say, 'I believe I have just enough time for some art.' Then she'd get out her old wooden easel and her paint box, and she'd set up under the oaks in front of the house, or anywhere the wildflowers were blooming. For an hour or two she'd forget about how hard she always worked, and she'd paint a field of bluebonnets or a carpet of leaves. When I was little, I liked to watch her mix the colors till she had them just right. To her, color was the most important thing."

"Color is hard," said Kate. "I guess that's why I do so much with charcoal and pencils."

"So what's the most important thing to you?" he asked.

Kate took the sketch and studied it a moment, then turned to him with a smile.

"The subject," she said. "Definitely the subject."

Rising to his hands and knees, Michael moved toward her, stopping only when their lips were pressed together in a kiss that seemed much like their first kiss the night before.

In love like she'd never dreamed was possible, Kate was trembling from head to toe. When their lips parted, she was about to say, "I could stay here with you forever." But before she spoke, Michael turned to look at the late afternoon sun and said, "It's time to go."

An hour later, he'd hardly spoken a word to her since they left Oscar's little airstrip on Lighthouse Reef. With his silence, Kate was falling back into her old insecurities, wondering if what she'd hoped was a beginning would also be the middle and end? She thought she'd found the person for whom she'd been searching, but already she found herself searching for him again.

"What are you thinking about?" she asked, silently kicking herself for sounding so trite.

He turned to her, looking surprised to find someone else in the plane.

"I was thinking about a promise I made."

This did not sound good. "A promise to whom?"

"To myself. As long as I can remember, I didn't want to do anything in the world but grow up, fall in love, raise a family, and run my grandfather's ranch."

"And?"

"It didn't work out like I planned."

"What happened?"

"We lost the ranch—right down to the scorpions and the stickers."

"And you promised you'd get it back someday?"

"Yeah, that's about the gist of it."

Kate thought about how a young pilot could raise enough money to buy a ranch, and then she thought about the men who'd put up so much cash for the delivery of those precious fishing flies. They'd been waiting when Michael and Kate returned from the atoll— Mexicans or South Americans, she thought—but dressed like mail-order sportsmen from some overpriced catalog.

The oldest—tall and gray-haired with long, elegant hands—seemed to be a friend of Michael's. The two hugged and Michael said something that made the man laugh. A second man also joined in the laughter, but the third neither laughed nor smiled. All her life Kate had converted real faces into pen-and-ink drawings, an endeavor that made her an expert on deciphering the character behind the visage. Watching their conversation from near the plane, she wondered if this man was perhaps incapable of smiling.

"The men back at the Caye," she said, "they made me nervous."

"They're in a nervous business. The older guy is Victorio. He's a friend of my teacher, Wild Bill Frazier."

"And this guy, Wild Bill, what did he teach you?"

Michael's face lit up at the memories.

"Among other things—how to fly. I went to see him when I didn't have anyone else. He took me in, taught me everything he knew, helped me get my private license, my instrument rating, my commercial. And he set me up with Victorio to fly his friends around Mexico."

Kate had her doubts, but said nothing.

"Look," he explained, "if you're worried about me—and it feels sort of nice to think someone might be worried about me—let me tell you something. Wild Bill set only one rule. No drugs. I swore on my honor and our friendship that no matter the circumstances, I would never fly a plane with drugs on board. Okay?"

"Okay. But isn't it funny to worry so much about someone you hardly know?"

"Oh, I'd say you know me very well."

Perhaps the thing she liked most about him was his radiant smile. With Kate blushing happily beside him, he banked the plane toward the west and a glorious setting sun.

"Is it always so beautiful?" she asked.

As the sun touched the horizon, what looked to be an unbroken layer of clouds beneath them began to show large holes. The single vanishing spot of the sun refracted up through the holes, filling them with brilliant red as if Michael and Kate were flying above and toward vast lakes of fire.

"No," Michael answered. "It's never been this beautiful."

Still sweeping her binoculars across the surface of the ocean, Kate was momentarily blinded as her gaze passed across the setting sun. Rubbing her tired eyes, she was surprised to see that they were running out of daylight. All afternoon she'd alternated a direct visual search with a methodical horizon-to-horizon sweep at ever-increasing angles with the binoculars, pausing only to mark the time and track on the chart when Bill banked into a new course. For much of that time—with a sense of failure growing about them—the constant buzz of the engine was the only sound.

"One more pass," Bill told her. "Before it gets dark."

"Bill, a long time ago I promised I wouldn't ask you about some thing, but I have to ask you now—did you know a man named Victorio?"

"Victorio Abriz Santiago DelaRosa."

"That's a lot of name."

"He was a lot of man."

Shifting in his seat to ease his sore muscles, Bill settled into the story, trying to fill the void created by their fear.

"You know I went to Korea with Michael's father as my wingman. When I came back solo, the ghost of Marvin Parker haunted me wherever I went. There was hardly a town in Texas where we hadn't danced with the old ladies and kissed the young ones, and hardly a street I could stroll down that someone didn't ask me about my pal Parker.

"People said I was a war hero, but I knew better. The heroic thing would have been to send Michael's father back to Texas to answer questions about my absence, not the other way around. Running from it all, I bought an old biplane and flew down to Mexico. Nobody knew me from Adam, and I got to fly to places where the locals had never even seen a plane. I'd just pick a village, land on the road, and give airplane rides for whatever they could afford to pay. Once I got paid with a live pig. Nobody would buy him from me, so I strapped him into the passenger seat and flew him to the next town.

"When I landed, a big crowd came out to see the *gringo loco* with the *puerco gordo* in his biplane. I got to admit, it looked pretty funny. And out of the crowd of dirt-poor farmers and Huichol Indians steps this tall man in a white linen suit and Panama hat. In crisp English, he invites me for drinks and dinner. For five years, I slept in his hacienda, parked my plane in his fields, and flew the two of us to meet every rich rancher in the country."

"Sounds like fun."

"It was more than just fun. Victorio's mission was to tell our hosts how great a country Mexico could become if only the people had education and better roads, decent medical care and a little more grub in their stomachs. One by one, he convinced each of these men to give his solemn promise that a portion of the new wealth Victorio brought them would go to improving conditions for every Mexican."

"That's a great sentiment, but I don't get it. How was he going to make them all this money? Drugs?"

"Drugs were nothing then. No, he did it by bringing them together. Deal by deal, he introduced them to each another, tying one man's assets to another's needs, one man's ideas or energies to another's capital or workers. You can't imagine how backward Mexico was in the fifties. I watched him build the framework of a modern country from practically nothing. The government was nearly overwhelmed with problems, so the men with the money did what needed to be done. And I felt privileged just to witness it all, to know such a man I could call my friend."

"And?" she asked.

"Two friends turned into three. Her name was Yesencia. I called her Jessie."

"Beautiful?"

"Too beautiful. I knew from the moment we met that she was the girl for me. Unfortunately, she was just as certain that Victorio was the man for her. I stayed long enough to see them get married, then went home to Texas, bought myself a brand new Piper Aztec and started a real charter company. A couple of times a year, Victorio would call me with a job to ferry a few guys from point A to B. Before or after the job, I'd stop off at their hacienda on the mountain for a few days, but sooner or later I always had to pull myself away from Jessie. It's a hard thing to love someone you can't have."

With the sun now below the horizon, Bill put the plane into another long turn and set a course back to Buenavista. With both of them thinking of lost love, they flew along in silent failure.

"Dad, can we have some water?"

All afternoon Hope had tried to hide from the ever-persistent sun. When the burning rays finally began to cast a shadow across the gunwales of the boat, Hope huddled there, trying to protect her already painful skin. Now that the sun was down, she was awake and thirsty.

Moving toward her, Michael was surprised by how much his joints ached.

"Two big sips," he said.

He passed her the bottle and she drank thirstily, two long mouthfuls. Then Michael took the bottle back and started to tie it back in its place.

"What about you? You didn't drink."

"I already had mine—about an hour ago—drank so much I'm about to wet my pants."

"Very funny."

Tying off the fishing line he'd been stringing out behind the boat all afternoon, he picked up a scrap of paper from the tackle box and began to write in small, neat print.

"What are you doing?"

"Updating our position. Trying to keep track of where we are."

She moved closer.

"How do you do it? We don't have a compass or anything."

"I'll show you. Know what this is?" he asked, holding up a round piece of cardboard.

"Sure. That's the back of your spool of line."

"Well, it used to be. Now it's a compass."

Tilting it, he showed her the lines he'd drawn for the cardinal points—north, south, east and west—with smaller lines indicating the divisions in between.

"But there's no little magnet. How do you know which way to point it?"

"I don't know, not exactly, but I'm pretty close. Last night after sunset, I pointed the line for north at Polaris."

"Which one is it?" she asked, looking at the stars, which were just beginning to show.

Michael pointed to the sky in the north. "There's the Big Dipper – *Ursa Major*. The two stars at the end of the Big Dipper's cup are called the pointer stars because a line between them points straight to Polaris."

His finger traced a line to a star hanging well above the horizon. "That one."

"I thought Polaris was supposed to be bright."

"Not bright, *constant*—always in the north. And once I know where north is, I can mark the card where the sun went down."

"And where it comes up, too, right?"

"Yeah, plus I use it to note which way the waves are running. Wave directions change pretty slowly, so even if it gets cloudy, I can still tell which way is north by looking at the waves. And if I watch something floating on the surface I can also figure out the current's direction and speed. Then I write down the hours we travel with how much wind and put it all together. It's called dead reckoning."

"I don't like the name," Hope said, as he wrote in another line of figures, and made some calculations.

"So where are we?" she asked.

Michael unfolded his map of the southern Cortez and showed her the succession of short lines, each indicating their relentless drift to the north and east in the thirty hours since she'd hooked the marlin.

"Yesterday I estimated we traveled about seventy miles north by northeast. Today we drifted maybe fifteen miles from current, and another fifteen from the wind. That puts us fifty miles northeast of La Paz."

"It doesn't seem very accurate. Too bad we don't have a computer."

"A computer? Hey, I'd settle for a two-way radio and a cooler full of sodas, but since we don't have any of that, I'm just doing the best I can with what we do have. I'll show you. Stick your arm straight out and hold your hand sideways like this."

Hope just stared at him. She was tired and didn't see how sticking her arm out was going to accomplish much.

"Just try it," he told her.

Humoring her father, Hope held her hand out toward the horizon.

"So what's that supposed to do?"

"I want to double-check how far north we traveled since last night by figuring our change in latitude. If you're at the equator— zero degrees latitude, Polaris is right on the horizon. If you're at the North Pole..."

"Ninety degrees latitude," she said.

"That's right—then Polaris is straight overhead, so the angle between Polaris and the horizon is your latitude."

"That's cool."

"If I hold my hand at arm's length, a star just on top of my hand is five degrees above the horizon. Right now, Polaris is one, two... five hands, or twenty-five degrees above the horizon. How about for you?"

Hope began to stack one hand above the other.

"Eight hands," she said. "Does that mean forty degrees?"

"No, that means smaller, more accurate hands. Your hands are closer to three degrees each. We're in the tropics, so one degree of latitude is equal to sixty miles. Tomorrow night at dusk, if we're still out here—which I don't think we will be—you hold your hand to the horizon. If Polaris is half a hand higher, we'll have gone a degree and a half, or ninety miles farther north. Got it?"

"Yeah. But what good does it do us? We don't have a radio to tell anyone, so we're still screwed, right?"

"Screwed?" he asked.

Hope rolled her eyes. If they were going to be stuck out here, at least he could let her talk like an adult.

"Look," he explained, "I think we're in a tough spot that requires us to do everything we can to increase our chances of getting home... sooner. But I don't think we're screwed."

He lifted up his arm for her to come closer.

"I'm sorry," she said as she leaned close. "It just doesn't seem like there's anything we can do."

"I know, Kiddo. But whatever we do, at least we can do it together."

He laughed as he closed his arm around her. "Isn't that what you wanted? Spend some time with your pop."

Hope laughed too. "Yeah, some adventure!"

The breeze was blowing steady now, and in just a few short minutes the heat of the day had shifted to the cool of the evening. Hope huddled against her father and together they watched a million stars fill in the holes of the sky.

When she spoke again, her voice sounded so soft and sweet that Michael felt as if the two of them had gone back to when she was five years old.

"Dad."

The sound hung in the air about them.

"Dad, there's one thing you forgot," she said, giving him a serious look as if he'd made some grave mistake.

"What?"

"You forgot to make a wish."

From age two to age six, when her world was mostly fantasy and imagination, Hope had spent hundreds of such wishes on her fervent desire to see a dragon, a flying horse, or just a plain a fairy or sprite. For one year straight, she'd wished for a hundred baby unicorns—no modest ambition. And shortly after reminding her dad of what she'd wished for, she usually remarked that she'd been making this wish for a *long* time and it STILL hadn't come true.

Michael had also wished on those same first stars and thrown many more coins in fountains after that first fifty-centavo piece with Kate. But after Hope was born, he had wished only for her, wishing for happiness to find her, or for her to find it. That was it: for the two of them—Hope and happiness—to embrace each other as lifelong companions. It wasn't until the last couple of years that he'd begun to wonder if he should have saved a few more coins for Kate and himself.

"Star light, star bright," said Hope. "First star I see tonight."

She paused and nudged her father to join in. When they'd finished the rhyme and made their wishes, Michael hugged her softly.

"It's been a long time since we did that."

"Too long," she said. "I miss all those things we used to do when I was little."

"Like what?"

"I dunno—the way you used to tickle me, and do baby quakes, and throw me way up in the air and catch me."

Knowing she liked a quick surprise, Michael grabbed her ribs and began to tickle hard, but he was too fast for a girl on the edge of fear.

"Ow! My sunburn!" she wailed. "Stop it!"

Releasing her, he held up his hands in surrender, but the damage was done. Hope gave him the kind of look a dog gives to someone who once kicked it.

"I'm sorry, Kiddo. I don't mean to treat you any different than I used to. It's just that you seem so grown up now. You're nearly a teenager—almost as tall as your mom—and you act like girls a lot older than you. Besides, I thought you *wanted* to be treated like a grown-up."

"But I don't want *everything* to change!"

Now he pulled her back to his side, wrapping his uninjured arm around her shoulder.

"Listen, some things are gonna change no matter what you do. You just have to hold on to the things that matter. And whatever happens, you'll always be my little girl, and I'll always be your Papa. Even when I'm a very tired papa."

Throughout the day, whenever the heat or her exhaustion from the battle the day before made her drowsy, Hope had slipped off into sleep. Her father, on the other hand, had been awake for all but two of the past thirty-six hours, and sleep was falling on him with the darkness.

"You be the captain for a while," he told her as he lay down in the bottom of the boat. "I'm going to rest my eyes and work out a plan."

Hope almost laughed out loud. As long as she could remember, her father had taken a nap on Sunday afternoon, invariably saying he was going to "rest his eyes for a bit," shortly before he began snoring loudly.

"Go to sleep, Swabbie!" she told him. "And that's an order!"

With his cracked lips trying to form a smile, he closed his eyes and soon fell into a restless sleep.

He'd always had plans. He'd had a plan to save the River Ranch, but it failed. He'd had countless plans to get his family's land back, but they'd failed too. When he met Kate in Cancun, he was in the middle of the most promising and most dangerous of those plans. Ten years after losing his family home, the ranch finally came up for sale. The Pennsylvania steel magnate who'd bought the

River Ranch with dreams of being a Texas cowboy had brought in architects from Dallas and ag experts from Wyoming. Despite spending a small fortune, he soon discovered that ranching the high Hill Country of Texas is no simple task. The first year, his high-dollar engineer built two large dams and a concrete bridge across the river. All three washed away in one spring flood, a thirty-foot wall of water caused by a deluge of biblical proportions that fell miles farther up the long, dry portion of the stream bed.

"Of all the luck," the steel man complained. "It hardly even rained here!"

Next, the cows and horses he brought from the Great Plains proved too tender-footed for the rocky country, and the sheep he imported from New Zealand died in the summer heat. A million dollars in losses later, he finally found a local foreman who claimed to know the trick. For three years, the man eked a profit off the land by covering it with Angora goats, which were sheared twice a year, producing a veritable mountain of valuable mohair, one of the finest clothing fibers known to man.

One of Michael's favorite childhood memories was shearing time, when a crew of Mexican men arrived at the ranch in an old bus pulling a shearing trailer that looked like the world's wackiest sewing machine. After each animal was sheared, the fleece was tossed up and over into a giant burlap gunnysack suspended from an eight-foot-high frame. Standing inside the sack, it was little Mikey's job to stomp the fleeces down tight, a high-stepping dance that continued for hours at a time. When the shearing was done and the bags full, owners and shearers alike settled down to a *cabrito* dinner—young Spanish goat grilled to perfection over mesquite coals. Michael was usually so tired by then that he often slept right through the celebration, but Gramma Jean always made sure to save him some *cabrito* for the next day.

Sheep and goats in moderation did well on the land, but knowing the definition of moderation was a fine art. Double the number of goats and you double your profits. At some point, however, the profit comes at the expense of the land, for goats take their own toll, eating the grass and every other speck of green right down to the bare earth, exposing the roots to the spring rains, which wash away the thin soil till little remains but rock and cedar. With no grass to absorb the rain, and with the water-robbing roots of the cedar taking over the draws and canyons, even the most reliable of the springs quit flowing.

As had happened with so many ranches in the Hill Country, the land and the water of the Parker River Ranch were soon used up. After nine years, the steel mill man put his tail between his legs and went back to Pittsburgh, cursing Texas all the way.

But Michael knew that good land management could bring back the grass and the wildflowers, that the grasses would eventually rebuild the soil, and that by cutting back the cedar, he could enable the springs to flow again as they had in his youth.

Even in its depleted state, the ranch was priced at half a million dollars. That was more than Michael could save in a lifetime of charters to Mexico and Alaska. There was only one way to fulfill the promise he had made to himself and that would be to break another promise, the one he had made to Bill Frazier the day he took possession of his first plane.

"Mine? This baby is mine?" Michael asked in astonishment as he circled the twin-engine Cessna.

"Signed, sealed, and delivered. Title's in your name," said Bill Frazier. "And there's only one rule."

"Don't smash it up?" Michael asked with a grin.

"Okay, two rules, smart guy. Don't smash it up and don't carry any drugs."

"No problem." Michael was so busy inspecting the plane that he was hardly even listening.

"I ain't fooling around here," Bill told him. "It's a dirty, dangerous business. I've known twenty pilots who got chewed up flying drugs. If you don't crash on a night landing or take a forty-five hollow-point in the back of the head, you get caught by the law. If you're lucky, you get busted in the States and leave prison fifteen years later, wondering what happened to your life. God help you if you get caught south of the border. So when I say no drugs, I mean NO DRUGS. You have to promise."

Peaking into the interior, Michael gave Bill an absentminded, "Okay."

"Well, say it then, damn it!"

After years of work and study, with Bill's help and generosity, Michael had now achieved a prop pilot's ultimate goal; he'd passed all tests of character and knowledge, he had an instrument rating, a commercial license, and now he had his own plane. The sky was literally the limit. Turning to his mentor, Michael gave Bill a huge bear hug. "Thank you," he said. "Thank you for everything."

"And?"

"And no drugs," Michael said solemnly. "I promise I won't fly any drugs on my beautiful plane. I won't screw up and I won't let you down."

But even in the face of honor, old dreams die hard. The vision of the Indian paintings was like a mystic map to the land from which Michael had sprung, and the bubbling sounds of Contrary Springs called to him with their mysterious, unknowable word.

With a little bulldozer work, Michael could turn the old county road on which Wild Bill had first landed into a first-class private strip. Then he'd have the land, the water, and the sky. He could spend the rest of his life keeping that promise to Bill, or he could do something about the hole in his soul he'd lived with since the death of his grandfather.

Flying back to Cancun with Kate, he thought about the foolish deal he'd made that began this mess. Bill's old friend Victorio had been party to the deal, which made Michael somehow think it was okay. And it wasn't cocaine or something worse, it was marijuana. Who the hell cared about marijuana? But the clincher, Michael had reasoned, was that the dope wouldn't be in his plane. He would only be the decoy.

In the middle of the night from a dirt strip in the jungles of the Yucatán to another in South Texas, Michael would fly nose to tail with an old DC-3, a stripped-out gooney bird carrying five tons of marijuana. With the two planes making one blip on the closely watched U.S. radar screens, he'd radio a flight plan and request customs for San Antonio. But coming off the Gulf into Texas, he'd declare a failed engine and request an emergency strip. There was only one. Both pilots would line up for a landing on the darkened strip, and at the last minute the DC-3 would go down to the trucks that awaited it and Michael would pull up, swearing on the radio about cows on the runway. The most likely chance of failure was not in getting caught but in getting killed. The prop wash of a DC-3 is no place for a small plane, and landing in the dark with only one engine in San Antonio would be no picnic either, but success would mean a multi-million-dollar haul for Victorio's friends, 10 percent of it to Michael.

Then something happened to change his willingness to risk all. He met Kate.

"I can't do it," he told Victorio DelaRosa and Alberto Sada when he and Kate returned to the strip at Lighthouse Reef.

Sada did not take the news well. He argued and cajoled, and called Michael a liar, a coward and a son of a whore, all to no avail.

"There are other pilots, other planes," Michael told him. "Lots of them. The plan is the key and you can have the plan as my gift, the concession of my cowardice."

On the way back to Cancun he made another plan: take Kate back to her hotel, then get himself and his Cessna out of the country without delay. He'd heard stories about people who had crossed Sada. Now he was one of those people.

Just before midnight, having promised to see Kate in Austin, he again lifted off the strip at Cancun, but this time he banked north for home. Right away he knew there was something wrong. He could feel it. Not enough power. He'd have to circle back and land. But then it dawned on him. His engines were fine, he was just heavy, maybe a thousand pounds heavy. There was only one explanation. While he'd been kissing Kate good night, Sada's men had filled his baggage compartment with drugs. If customs searched him when he landed in Texas, he'd lose the plane and go to jail. If not, Sada would have someone waiting to unload them and deal with this rebellious gringo pilot.

"Think," he told himself. "Can't go to Texas; can't go back to Cancun. They'll be waiting both places."

To complicate matters, he was no doubt being tracked on radar by both Sada to the south and U.S. authorities to the north. Taking it down to three hundred feet, he looked up and saw that the clouds were thin enough for the moon to illuminate both clouds and the ocean below. Dropping lower still—beneath everyone's radar—he skimmed above the waves, pointed not north to Texas or south to the Yucatán, but west to the mainland of Mexico.

At two a.m., he saw a few scattered lights along the mostly deserted coastline ahead. Climbing to bank right at the beach, he headed north along the coast and waited for a break in the clouds. He'd almost given up hope when, coming over the southern reaches of the Laguna Madre, the clouds parted and the white sands below shown brightly beneath the full moon. Making two passes to check the longest stretch of beach, he lined it up a third time, lowered his gear and landed in the hard, wet sand, which had only recently been uncovered by the receding tide.

The takeoff from the wet beach would have been impossible if Michael hadn't off-loaded a thousand pounds of marijuana, all of it sealed tight in the white plastic bales that soon dotted the beach and surf for fishermen to find at dawn.

Back in the air, he steered a course for San Antonio, his conscience clear, but knowing he would never again fly into Sada's Yucatan territory. As soon as he landed, though, it all went to shit.

"Michael Parker?" the customs agent asked. Michael noticed the man's holster was unstrapped.

"That's me," Michael answered, holding out a hand, which the agent declined to shake.

"Got a tip that says you're carrying marijuana. Any objection to our searching the plane?"

"Go right ahead," he told them, his face a picture of innocence but his stomach twisting into knots. "I got nothing to hide."

Surprised to find the cargo hold empty, the agents soon discovered a half-pound of marijuana where Sada's men had stashed it beneath the copilot's seat in case Michael did something clever like dump the rest of the load. In stunned silence, Michael realized that all of Bill's warnings had come to pass.

"What was I thinking?" he asked himself. "I'm completely and totally screwed!"

TEN

Far out on the night-black waters of the Sea of Cortez, with the stars wheeling clockwise across the sky in their graceful pirouette, Michael's body had already begun to surrender its strength to the acids building in his bloodstream. His joints ached like fire, and his stomach clenched periodically like the fist of a vengeful god. Worst of all, he knew that his mind would soon become as weak as his body.

Having resumed the watch from Hope, he thought back on the long day spent sharing every mite of information she might need to carry on without him. Having little control over his own destiny, Michael's chief purpose now focused on getting his girl out of this terrible situation, to save her—body and soul—for whatever lay beyond the horizon of her future.

Through much of the day he'd polished the aluminum lure box that he hoped to turn into a signaling mirror, keeping constant watch on the horizon for a sign of possible rescue. But now—as the three-quarter moon rose slowly—the box fell to his side and his focus turned inward. While there was time, he wished to think about the things he'd once wanted in his life, the things that he still wanted, and whether it would be possible to do something toward that end.

With regards to Kate, his desires were little changed since they first met— to wake beside her, to spend countless hours beneath the sun or stars in her company, to bathe in the light that shone from deep within her when all was well with her world. The memory of her love was burned into his heart, as was the pain of the later realization that his presence was no longer enough to turn on that light.

"I just want things to be the way they were," he told her before he left for Mexico.

"But *we're* not the same," Kate explained. "We've both changed. It may not be for the better, but I'm a different person than before." Before what, she could not bring herself to say.

Michael tried to find a response to the notion that his wife had become someone else, but in the end all he could say was, "I see that now."

She looked so sad and vulnerable, the ghosts of tears always haunting the corners of her eyes. Two months later, lost in body and thought on the darkened ocean, Michael reached out his hand to catch her tear. But suddenly his arm was pulled straight by some unseen force. Traveling in his thoughts, he'd forgotten his attempt to catch a fish.

With the line wrapped around his hand, he'd been determined to stay ready for the strike of a fish, but then he'd allowed his attention to drift. In any event, he would have been unprepared for the fierceness of the attack. Regaining his balance, he pulled back on the fish, but this only caused it to pull harder. A tug-of-war ensued, with Michael struggling to gain two feet of line, then the unseen fish pulling harder and drawing him back to the rail. Leaning back on the middle seat, he was raising his leg to the rail for leverage when the line suddenly broke, sending him tumbling backward, where he landed on his wounded arm.

"Shit!" he called out in pain and frustration. "Shit, shit, shit!"

The fish was gone, and the lure with it. Little by little, their opportunities were slipping away. "What could have cut the line so easily?" he wondered. "Barracuda, wahoo, maybe another shark."

Pulling himself upright, he began to stow the fishing gear. From now on he would have to fish only during the day.

Though he knew he needed sleep, someone had to keep the watch and be ready with a flare. Unwilling to wake Hope, he rested his head on a life jacket and watched the red light of Mars sink into the west while the white solar mirror of Venus followed the moon higher in the east. From somewhere in the distance, he listened to the rhythmic, rushing breath of a whale that passed them in the night. The whoosh of the whale's exhalation filled the darkness then slowly faded away, to be replaced a few moments later by another massive gasp of air.

In the sound of the whale's breaths—just as in the sound of Contrary Creek during his youth—he thought that he heard some message, some insight into what his life had been for and about, a clue as to how he fit into the essential whole of this miraculous creation. As his journey fell into parallel with the whale's, Michael's mind fell in sync and carried him to uncharted depths and distant seas known only to this whale who had come so far to help him understand his place on the infinite arc of time. Approaching the horizon of human comprehension, he moved ever closer to deciphering the secret coda. For one moment he almost had it, but then the whale moved further away, its slow breaths growing more and more faint, and the message slipped away until Michael and Hope were once again alone.

In his cell in San Antonio, Michael lay in the darkness wondering if Bill Frazier would come to his rescue. Bill had helped the feds in dozens of air smuggling cases and could have easily figured out what happened to his protégé. If Michael had phoned and begged forgiveness, Bill would likely have granted it, but Josh Parker had raised his grandson to take his licks when he did something wrong. How could that lesson possibly apply more than now?

To make matters worse, the San Antonio district attorney was up for reelection and needed a high-profile case to guarantee a win. An arraignment followed soon after Michael's arrest. Too ashamed to phone either of the two people he loved, Michael accepted a court-appointed lawyer with no experience and a great deal of fear that some evil drug cartel would have him waxed if things went badly for their pilot.

"Don't worry..." the lawyer stammered. "We'll g-g-get you off."

"How?" Michael asked.

"How?" the lawyer repeated like an idiot, his eyes darting around the empty interrogation room as if searching for some means of escape.

Having been taught by Josh Parker that the secret of horse-trading was to know what was going on in the other man's mind. Michael knew immediately that his lawyer was a fool.

At the arraignment, the man stammered uncontrollably. "My client will p-plead n-n-n..."

Since his arrest, Michael had been haunted by his own words to Kate when he told her he was an honorable man. Wanting to prove that he was—and unable to take the farce of his lawyer's ineptitude—Michael rose from his seat. "Your Honor," he interjected, "I plead guilty as charged."

"What's that?" the judge asked, lifting up his glasses to get a better look at this young man who looked so little like a drug smuggler.

"Guilty," Michael repeated. "I don't want to put you to the trouble and expense of a jury trial. I didn't know that marijuana was there, but I should have. And I'll take what you give me."

"You mean you want to plea-bargain?" the judge asked.

"Yes, sir," Michael answered.

Neither the assistant DA nor the extremely relieved attorney for the defense had any objections, so within an hour Michael was on his way to the federal penitentiary in Bastrop to begin serving a three-year sentence. His last act of freedom was to hand an envelope to his lawyer.

"Mail this for me," Michael instructed. "Then find a new line of work."

Dinner at Buenavista is normally considered one of the prime reasons for staying at the little hotel on the beach. The old iron bell is rung and everyone gathers round the long dining tables for plate after plate of home cooking, all of it passed around *la familia* style until the overstuffed diners begin to call out, *"No más!"*

During the meal, one can generally hear all kinds of fish stories, most of them sounding like outrageous fabrications, such as the time that a striped marlin was feeding so close to shore that it got stuck on the rocky point just in front of the hotel bar. Seizing the day (and the fish), Elvis the bartender leapt out the open window, waded into the water, and wrestled the hundred-pound marlin to the beach. After having his photo taken with it, Elvis then filleted the fish, made ceviche for his patrons at the bar and took the rest home to his family. Sounds impossible, but it really happened.

The wonders of the Cortez have been attracting adventurous *Norte Americanos* since the fifties, large numbers of them to Campo Buenavista, where the pictures of fish that adorn the walls from the early days appear to have been doctored like some tourist postcard of a small trout that looks larger than a car. But at Buenavista, the fish sometimes *were* larger than cars. Hearing such tales, tourists came in steadily increasing numbers. Over the years, the numbers and size of the quarry dropped dramatically, but much of that was due to overfishing from commercial long-liners and gill-netters who seemed determined to vacuum the ocean clean, no matter the consequence to their own jobs.

With fishing having declined from the good old days, Cooper was already under a financial strain when a tropical storm the year before dropped thirty inches of rain. Since then, business had basically sucked.

"It's all this bad press," Coop often explained. "We get one little storm and people in the States act like we've been wiped out."

Now, with Michael and Hope lost somewhere on the hundred thousand square miles of ocean separating Baja from the mainland, the only diners were those who had spent all day searching for them. Not too surprisingly, the mood was somber. With the exception of Gilberto, who was still out with the dolphin experts, all of Cooper's boat captains were there, as well as the *capitans y pangueros* from the other hotels.

"We covered everything within thirty miles," Cooper said as he spread out the new charts that had been brought from La Paz. "That means they've drifted out of range of the small boats. Tomorrow we're going to shift our focus."

Having flown three thousand miles from before dawn to dark, Kate could barely hold her eyes open. But thinking she might miss some essential piece of information, she refused to go to bed until everyone had related the details of their efforts. Finally, Bill drew things to a close.

"Coop's got the assignments," he told them. "The smaller boats to cover the same areas we went over today in case we missed them, the faster ones covering new territory farther out."

Kate didn't think she'd ever been so tired. Could it really have been just twenty-four hours since that phone call from Coop? Opening the door to room number three, she was greeted by two beds—both unmade for some reason—and by Michael's and Hope's bags lined up like orphans on the window seat.

Knowing she needed to sleep and build her strength for the coming day, she fell onto one of the beds without even undressing. Her head slipped back onto the pillow and sleep came upon her, but then her eyes opened wide as the unmistakable smell of Michael swept in from all around her. It was everywhere, permeating the pillows and bedspread, reaching into her mind and body. It had been two months since she'd seen him, much longer since they had shared a bed with any of the passion that had once been the driving force in their lives.

"Two months," she thought. "The same as after I met him. Two very long months."

In the dog days of the summer that she thought would never end, Kate remembered glancing up again and again from her easel to check the slow progress of the hands on the clock. Just past noon, she dropped her charcoal pencil back into the box from which she had picked it up at nine, stared a moment longer at the still-blank vellum paper, then stepped out into the heat.

Walking up the drive to the mailbox, she barely noticed the last of the summer's wildflowers or the big doe and spotted twin fawns watching her from the deep shade of the pecan trees. An odd sensation had come over her, the feeling of being somewhere outside her own body—just beyond the touch of her own fingers and hands. Could that single day of desperate love really come to nothing?

The day she returned from Cancun, she'd hoped for a phone call from Michael or a message on her answering machine. Instead, she found only a headline in the paper—*Pilot Jailed on Drug Charges*. She tried repeatedly to contact him, but the feds wouldn't allow it.

Fear was upon her like the heat of the day. Fear that he would never be hers; fear—worse, *certainty*—that in all her life she would never feel this way about any man but Michael; fear that in his sense of shame, he might have already locked her out of his life, if only because she had been a small part of what went wrong, a reminder of his fall from grace.

Like a wild dog, this fear gnawed upon her, growling its message that once he had closed his heart to her, he might never open it again. Fear was in the mirror she held to her life. Would it still be possible to be just Kate alone, as she had been since the death of her mother? Or had Michael become a piece of her, now a missing piece that left a gaping hole in her heart?

In the following days, she maintained only the motions of life, moving through her tasks by habit, walking to the mailbox, not because she cared what was there but because she had done it so many times before. Once she'd loved these simple moments enlivened by the ever-changing beauty of her mother's tiny piece of Texas, three acres of spring wildflowers, burnt summer grasses, and fall's golden show. But what once had formed the colors of her palette had now faded to a dull gray.

Dull, dull, everything dull, the colors of her life faded and worn like old jeans that even the Salvation Army would not take. The brilliance of the blue jays and painted buntings had flown, leaving behind birds without hues and wildflowers without their coats of many colors.

Even her cherished swims at Barton Springs had fallen away. For the simple truth was that since that brilliant day on the shores of Half Moon Caye, the Springs no longer belonged just to her, but to the both of them. At the Springs she had first admired him from afar. Now that memory lent a joint tenancy to the place that made it impossible for her to go there alone, knowing that she would search all the while for him at the top of the stairs, his eyes sparkling brighter than the light on the water that day when he had changed her life forever by smiling toward some unknown girl on a distant shore.

At last her feet presented her body to the misshapen mailbox, dented by some teenagers' drive-by baseball-batting. Retracing her steps as she flipped dully through the bills and wasted advertising. Then suddenly she stopped and the clutter that had come into her life that day fell to the ground like confetti, leaving just one letter clutched tightly in her hands. With trembling fingers, she peeled back the flap and withdrew the dangerous cargo within.

Unfolding the note, she took a breath, then read the three words he had written, *Wait for me.*

Somehow the water always seemed to stand between them: from the opposite shore of Barton Springs—where she had nearly dived in to rescue a man who did not need saving—to the endless nights of his incarceration, when Kate had dreamed again and again that he was drowning. Through the long nights of her uneasy sleep, she'd fought against current and tide, struggling to reach the source of the water, where she sensed that he was trapped, unable to breathe. Only she could save him, that much she knew, but he was so far away, and the water so wide.

In her bed at Buenavista, with the waves rolling up the beach outside her window, she found herself separated from him again, this time by a vast, indifferent ocean whose only purpose seemed to be the testing of her love. Pulling hard against the water, she cut through the waves, but the night was black, and her only guide was the faint sound of Michael's beating heart, calling to her across the gulf of sadness and blame that had replaced long-shared dreams with some invisible weight that seemed to constantly drag them down.

ELEVEN

Lost in sleep, Kate could hear a distant knocking, a warning perhaps, or was it the sound of someone rapping out the dots and dashes of Morse code? When her eyes finally came open, she realized the sound was coming from nearby, that someone was pounding on her door.

"Oh my God!" she said, leaping to her feet and seeing it was fully light outside. But pulling the door open, she found no one there, just a woodpecker banging noisily on the porch beams.

"Shit!" she told the woodpecker. "We should've left an hour ago!"

In the office, she found Cooper working the phone, arguing with someone in rapid-fire Spanish.

"What's going on?" she asked Wild Bill, who reached out and took her hand.

"Kate, The Mexican Coast Guard's calling off their search. Air Force too. Their policy is no more than thirty-six hours after the first missing-at-sea report."

"They can't do that!" she protested. "Michael and Hope are still out there. I know they are!"

"You know they're out there. And I know it too. But these boys don't know nothing except what's in their book. They say they've done all they can do."

"Cabrones!" Cooper exclaimed. "They're more interested in drug

interdiction than search and rescue, 'cause that's what the DEA pays them for."

Kate felt her body go limp as the news began to sink in.

"What'll we do? One plane's not enough."

"I've already been on the phone," he told her, "calling pilots in Austin and San Antonio, some more in Phoenix. We're lining up five or six teams. They'll all be down here tonight, ready to go out tomorrow morning," he told her. "If we still need them."

Kate threw her arms around him. "Thank you, Bill," she whispered. "Without you, we'd all be lost. Now let's go."

Through most of the night, Michael had lain awake, searching for lights of ship or shore and studying the brilliant stars in the sky. Drifting toward the dawn, the panga rolled gently on the waves, rocking Hope in her dreams as she lay cradled in her father's arms. When the first glimmer of light began to show in the east, he was sure Kate would be preparing to take off with Wild Bill.

"Today, Kate," he murmured. "Make it today."

As the sun began to rise, the entire sky was filled with an almost blinding light. Within seconds Michael felt Hope stir in his arms. Seeing that her eyes were open, he finally allowed his own eyes to close. At first Hope had no idea where she was. She wasn't even certain *who* she was. All she knew was the terrible empty feeling in her stomach and in all her body. Then she saw her father asleep at her side and it all came back. Only now—for the first time—there was the new knowledge that she might never see her mother again. The two of them—she and her father—might die somewhere on this lonely ocean.

How long could they live without food or water? She'd read stories of people lost at sea for weeks at a time, but only if they had fresh water. Besides, her father was sick and she felt sure he couldn't last long without insulin. Even in his restless sleep, his eyes were puffy and black. More than anything else, she was scared for him.

Having seen the chasm that had opened between her parents,

Hope had lived these past months in fear of her life being turned on end. She'd seen plenty of kids whose parents lived far apart—physically or emotionally—and those kids always seemed disconnected, not just from their parents, but also from themselves. The fear of that happening to her suddenly seemed meaningless compared to what faced her now. Worst of all, Hope thought, would be to lose her father and be left alone on this unforgiving sea.

"Please don't die," she said to her sleeping father. "I can't make it without you. Not here, not anywhere."

Through the depth of his sleep, the soothing sound of her voice reached out to him. For a few moments, the tensed muscles in his face relaxed enough for him to rest easy, but all too soon she saw the strain return. Even in sleep, he could find no rest. Laying her head down near her father, she began to sing softly to him, as he had sung so many times to her.

Pack up all your cares and woes
Here I go singing low,
Bye bye blackbird.

Where somebody waits for me
Sugar's sweet, so is he,
Bye bye blackbird.

When he awoke two hours later, Michael pulled himself upright and rubbed his eyes to get them working. As they began to focus, he saw the fuzzy shape of what seemed to be a huge bird just before him. He blinked, and blinked again. And then he made out the looming figure of a large brown pelican perched just before him on the bow of the boat.

Jerking back in surprise, he startled the pelican, which spread its huge wings and hopped to the boat's prow.

Hope touched her father's shoulder, then spoke softly.

"He's been here an hour. Does it mean we're near land?"

He scanned the horizon, searching for shore or for other shorebirds.

"Maybe, maybe not," he said softly. "Pelicans don't like to land on open water. Too many sharks. He may have just gotten tired and needed a place to rest."

"Oh.

Hearing the disappointment in her voice, Michael mentally kicked himself for being too straight with her. Then he noticed that the pelican was staring into the water near the boat.

"Look at that!" Michael said in an excited whisper. "He sees something!"

Just then, the pelican leaned forward and dove straight down off the front of the boat. Landing with a splash, it came up with a fish about eighteen inches long, the tail extending well out of its mouth. Spreading its wings, the bird flapped back onto the bow.

Taking two quick steps, Michael dove forward and grabbed for the pelican.

"What are you doing?" Hope shrieked.

Seizing the pelican by the wing, he made a grab for the fish, but the bird managed to suck the fish into the vast pouch beneath its bill and began to flap its huge wings in Michael's face. Instinctively raising his arms to protect himself, Michael let go his hold, allowing the bird to yaw into flight, taking the fish with him.

Pulling himself upright, Michael watched them go.

"That fish was going to be our breakfast," he explained.

"I'm sorry, Dad. I should've helped you."

Then it dawned on him. "Look over the side!" he told Hope as he dug in his tackle box for the spool of line and a lure. "Are there more fish?"

While he tied a lure in place of the one he'd lost in the night, Hope leaned over the rail and stared into the water.

"No," she said, "I don't... Wait! I do see them. There's little ones in the shadow of the boat, and some bigger ones cruising by!"

This time Michael wrapped his line around the empty soda bottle that Nacho had left in the emergency bag. Michael had fished many times with Mexican kids and their old *abuelos*, fished from piers and beaches and tiny rowboats with fishermen whose most complicated piece of equipment was a line wrapped around a tapered bottle. Not only could you hold the base of the bottle and fling your arm forward to cast your bait or lure, you could also wrap the line back on the bottle as you fought your fish.

When all was ready, he slid quietly to the rail then flung the lure twenty feet out. The silver spoon flashed in the sun as he retrieved it by winding the line onto the bottle. When the lure was halfway back to the boat, Michael felt a hard yank and held on tight. It was not a big fish, but it fought hard, and he hadn't been so thrilled at fighting a fish since the first one he pulled in at the Blue Hole with Grandpa Josh thirty years before.

With increasing excitement, Hope watched as her dad brought the fish close to the boat. Sliding his right hand down the line, he got a firm grasp around the fish's body, then lifted it into the boat—a four- or five-pound bonito, fat like a silver bullet.

"You did it!" Hope yelled. "I knew you could catch one, I knew it!"

Flashing her a smile, he dropped the fish into the bottom of the boat, and turned to cast again.

Fifteen minutes later, they had three of the fat little tuna in the boat, with Michael stopping only after a big bull dorado grabbed the lure, leapt into the air with a flash of brilliant gold and green, then broke his line.

Now comes the real test, Michael thought, pulling his knife from the tackle box.

"Okay, Hope. You ready for breakfast?"

"Do we really have to eat it raw?"

"Afraid so. We've got no other food and almost no water, and the flesh of this fish has both. This fish is practically a gift from heaven."

Michael had already killed one of the fish, and was now cutting off thin slices of the best filet.

"Listen," he told her. "I've been to sushi restaurants in Los Angeles where people paid twenty dollars for the tiniest little servings of raw fish not nearly as good or as fresh as this."

He handed her a small slice and kept one for himself.

"You ready?"

Hope nodded, then they both took small bites and began to chew slowly. Suddenly Michael burst out laughing.

"What's so funny?" she asked.

"Your face. You're making an old lady face!"

"Am not!" she protested, but he could see her beginning to smile as she chewed.

"You should see yourself," he insisted. "You're making a face like an old lady in an elevator after somebody cut the cheese."

"Dad!"

"Well, you are."

"Oh yeah?" she dared. "Show me!"

Michael handed her another slice of the fish. Then he popped a second bite into his mouth and made the most prim and disgusted face he could manage.

"That's not it!" Hope laughed. "You're making a worm-eating face!"

"Am not!" he said in the same tone she had used.

As he offered her another slice on the blade of the knife, the boat pitched on a small swell and the little filet fell to the deck. Staring at it for a moment, they both came to the same idea.

"Ten-second rule!" they called in unison. In a flash, both dove to reclaim the bite.

Whenever Kate was out of the house, Michael and Hope had used the ten-second rule to judge the cleanliness of food dropped on the floor. Snatching the bite before her father, Hope quickly brushed it off and popped it into her mouth.

For the next few minutes, they ate bite after bite of raw fish, imitating all kinds of people eating all kinds of things they really did not wish to eat. Finally Michael held out yet another slice, which Hope declined to take.

"No, please!" she told him, now acting the dowager. "I couldn't possibly eat another bite, dear man. But do give my compliments to the chef."

Considering that they had not eaten in over twenty-four hours, and very little then, it was no surprise that the two of them felt stronger after filling their shrunken bellies with fish. Their water situation was no better than before and Michael knew that their thirst would seem nearly unbearable in the hot sun of the afternoon, but for now Hope was less scared and more optimistic. And that was worth a lot.

"I had a funny dream last night," Michael told her as he filleted the other fish and laid the strips out in the sun to preserve them by drying.

"Me, too," said Hope, "lots of them. First I dreamed I was fighting the big marlin, and then I dreamed that Mom was swimming through the ocean to rescue us. The next thing I knew, she was in the boat with us and everything was okay."

"Well, you had better dreams than me."

"What was yours?"

"I think I fell asleep when I was watching for ships. But in my dream I was still awake, and I saw one—a big cargo ship. It was so close, they were bound to see us."

"What happened then?"

"I woke up."

"Before they rescued us?"

"Yeah. I woke up and I thought 'what a funny dream.' And then I looked up and I saw the ship for real—at least I thought it was for real."

"It wasn't?"

"No. It wasn't real. I was just seeing things."

By now he had spread all the fish out in the sun on the aft seat of the panga, then covered the slices with the casting net to keep birds from stealing them.

"Maybe it was a ghost ship, Dad. Like we read about in <u>Moby Dick</u>."

"Maybe, but more likely my mind was playing tricks on me because I haven't been taking my insulin."

She thought about this as he rinsed the knife and his hands in the salt water over the side. Setting the knife in its place, he took her hands in his.

"Hope, it's important for you to know that when I don't get my medicine, my diabetes may make me see things that aren't really there."

"Like an hallucination."

Michael laughed at himself for talking to her as if she were still a child.

"Yeah, like an hallucination. So if I say I see something you can't see—I want you to tell me. Okay?"

"Yes, sir," she said.

He'd tried to teach her to say "Sir" and "Ma'am" to her elders, and sometimes she even remembered to do it, but he'd never gotten used to hearing it in reference to himself.

"Now, what do you want to do today?"

"Duh," she told him. "Get rescued."

"I mean *until* we get rescued. You want me to tell you a story?"

For a moment there was a flash of excitement in Hope's eyes. But just as quickly the glimmer was gone, replaced by the suspicion that her father was patronizing her.

Michael didn't mind her attitude, for he felt the heart of their relationship was built on storytelling. Since Hope was old enough to understand them, Michael had told his daughter stories that revealed who he was and who they were; through stories, the two of them had been united as one. And no matter her reluctance, she always came around.

"Seeing things last night reminds me of a story about Nacho's cousin, Hernán."

"Wait a second. This isn't scary, is it? This trip is scary enough."

"Now lemme tell it, okay? About five years ago, Hernán was

out in his brand new panga—a twenty-three-footer with a big outboard and twin gas tanks."

"You mean like this one, but it didn't suck?"

"Exactly. And it was summertime, like now, and he was cruising around doing something really terrible."

"What was it?"

"He was catching sea turtles. He'd race around the ocean, looking for green sea turtles swimming into the Cortez on their way to laying their eggs on the beaches where they'd hatched. And every time he found a turtle, he roped it and pulled it into the boat. He was going to take them home and lock them in a pen he'd built on the beach. After they laid their eggs, he'd sell the eggs, then kill the turtles and sell the meat, too."

"But sea turtles are endangered. Why would anyone eat them?"

"People down here have been eating turtle eggs and turtle soup for a long time, and they don't change their ways very easily. Anyway, Hernán is racing across the ocean just before sunset, standing by the motor when one of the turtles in the bottom of the boat bites him really hard on his bare foot. He screams, of course, and when he jerks his foot away, he loses his balance and falls right out of the boat."

"What happened then?"

"Well, he comes up to the surface just in time to see his new panga racing across the water, headed full-throttle straight out to sea with no one aboard except a bunch of turtles. So what can he do? He looks to shore, and sees by the silhouette of the mountains that he's about five miles out."

"You said it wasn't scary."

"It isn't. Hernán did the only thing he could do. His jeans were heavy in the water, so he peeled 'em off and started swimming. It was almost dark when he started and it took him hours to swim across the current and reach the shore."

"Wait a minute," she interrupted. "He swam to shore? Why don't we put on our life jackets and swim for it?"

"We're too far out, and there might be another shark. Our best chance is to stay with the boat. Anyway, when Hernán got home, he'd been out all night and didn't have any pants—which probably didn't look too good to his wife. But when he came in, she just glanced up from bed and said, "How was the fishing?""

Michael thought this story was hilarious, but Hope just stared at him.

"I don't get it. Did he find his boat?"

"No. That's the weird part. The boat should have run out of gas in a couple of hours at the most. People kept looking for it, but they never found it. About a month later, a man was out night fishing and he said he saw a panga race by with no one driving it. Other people began to see it too, though I think most of them were drinking at the time. Coop thought he could use the story to scare people into leaving the turtles alone, so he started telling the fishermen that the turtles had stolen Hernán's panga, and if anybody was catching turtles, the turtles might get their boat too."

"Did the story work? Did people stop killing turtles?"

"Maybe some of them did. Sometimes you just have to settle for whatever gains you can get."

"But you always tell me I'm not supposed to compromise; that I should fight for what I believe in. Which one is it?"

Michael had to laugh at that one.

"I guess I don't know the answers any better than you do. But I do know one thing. I know I love you. And despite this huge mess I got us into, I love the ocean, too."

"But you say the same thing about the sky when you fly. And you said it about the River Ranch when we went there."

"And I mean it about all of them. I loved the ranch because it was my home. I love flying because it's the ultimate freedom. And I love the sea because it has a perfection all its own. All its creatures have adapted over the ages to fill some essential part in the way it works."

"Then that's what we should do," Hope told him. "Adapt."

"Exactly. And we have to remember that the sea is not against us. It's just there. When we love something—like the sea or flying or the ranch—we can only show that love through our stories."

"What about when we love someone? Is that the same?"

"Now you've got it," he told her. "Love also has to be shared. What is anything without its story?"

TWELVE

Two hours later than they'd intended, Bill pulled back on the yoke, and he and Kate soared into the air over Buenavista. On top of the loss of the Mexican Navy's jets—both of which were faster than Bill's Beech Bonanza—the weather was now threatening to interrupt the entire search.

By the early nineties, though detailed weather forecasts were practically a national obsession in the States, reliable forecasts in Mexico were almost impossible to obtain. Coop had long ago discovered that local fishermen generally knew what was headed their way better than the meteorologists a thousand miles away in Mexico City. Unfortunately, this time both fishermen and scientists agreed they were in for a blow. Far to the south off the coast of Acapulco, a low-pressure system had started moving north. The meteorologists first thought the storm would steer to the west, missing the Sea of Cortez completely, but the locals were battening down as they had for Hurricane Beatriz a month earlier. You could not be too careful.

For Bill, as for Kate, it had not been a good morning. Both from worry and from all the coffee he had drunk the day before, Bill had lain awake much of the night. On top of that, his neck was stiff and his butt sore from too many hours in the plane. This was a young man's test of endurance, and he was not a young man.

As Kate diverted her eyes from the water below, in one glimpse she saw that long-forgotten pains were creeping back into Bill's mind and body.

"I'm tired," she said. "How about you?"

"Okay—just impatient to find them. Like I said before, I don't want to let him down again."

"Bill Frazier," she scolded. "You've got to quit blaming yourself for something that was Michael's fault. You told him you wouldn't help if he got in trouble with drugs, and he did it anyway, just like he took my daughter out to sea in a leaky old boat! This is his fault and I'm never going to forgive him for it!"

"Kate, that's what I told myself when he got busted. And I've never quit regretting it. Listen, he didn't know this fishing trip would be trouble any more than he knew there were drugs on that plane. Half a pound of pot—what a joke! He was set up and I knew it. I could have straightened it out, but for some fool reason I told myself it would do him good to be scared for a bit."

"So you got mad. I'm more than a little mad myself."

"I didn't get mad, I got drunk. And I stayed drunk because I wanted Michael to love flying, even though deep down inside I knew he'd always love that damn ranch more. Hell, I was passed out in a cold bathtub with an empty whiskey bottle in my hand when Medilift called to say they needed me to fly that kid to surgery. I figured, what the hell, I'd be back before dark, and the next day I'd head down to San Antonio for Michael's arraignment."

"I know the end of this story," she reminded him. "Among other things, it ended with the two of us meeting."

"You got someplace you have to be?" he said. "No time for me get to the point? Things don't just happen all of their own accord. Everything we do in life is tied to things that came before, and those things to what came before them, all the way back to the beginning of man."

"That sounds pretty wise for an old grouch."

"I wasn't always a grouchy old man, you know. You may not believe it, but there was a time when I was a grouchy young man."

For a moment, Kate actually smiled. Then she checked and rechecked her map, shifting in her seat to make holding the heavy binoculars more comfortable as she settled in for what Bill called...

The Story of What Went Wrong

David San Luis was eight years old and brave as they come. Those were Bill's estimations as they dodged around the scattered thunderstorms that cast dark shadows on the Texas coastal plains.

"Can we fly through a cloud?" David asked. "I want to see one from the inside."

"Oh, I don't know, son," Bill told him. "It's pretty rough in those thunderstorms. I don't reckon your mom'd want me to bounce you around too much."

The boy's mother, a Hispanic woman with three other children and probably as many jobs, had waved a tearful good-bye from the tarmac at the Goliad Airport.

"Please!" the boy wheedled. "I've never been inside a cloud before. Mama says clouds are where the angels live."

"Sounds right to me," Bill told the boy, "but I can't say I've ever seen one."

David stared off into the sky, his face showing more disappointment that he wanted. Bill had flown kids like David before, and the ones he remembered best were the ones who never made the flight back home.

"But then again," Bill continued, "I'm usually paying such close attention to the flying that I don't get to do much sight-seeing. Maybe you can help me look."

With that, Bill banked the plane toward a soaring cumulus group—white on top and black beneath—with occasional flashes of lightning on its eastern edges.

The plane passed from light to dark, and when the first wave of rain slammed into the windshield, David held on tightly. Wide-eyed and electrified, he rode the roller coaster as they hit an air pocket that dropped them two hundred feet then thrust them back into the air like a giant hand playing with its toy glider. The thunderhead wasn't big enough to offer any real danger, but Bill couldn't help but think of the old pilot's saying, "If you keep looking for trouble, you'll find it."

He was just beginning to doubt the safety of his judgment when they burst back into the bright blue sky.

"Did you see her?" David yelled. "Did you see the angel? She smiled at me!"

Bill smiled at him, too. "Wow! You're a lucky kid. I've been flying for years and I've never seen one angel. Now you see one on your first flight. That'll bring you blessings and miracles, you know."

"Boy, I can't wait to tell Mama," David gushed.

The boy's face was full of life, all his pain forgotten.

"Bright before me," Bill whispered to himself, a flyer's mantra that had been passed to him by Michael's dad Marvin Parker, and which had brought him through so many difficult times.

After dropping little David with a medical team in Houston, Bill refueled at Hobby and took off for home. It had been a good day. He'd remembered that he would rather fly than drink, and that meant he didn't have to drink anymore. He'd remembered a thousand things Michael had done right, which helped push away the one thing he had not. And Bill had realized how lucky he was to have found Michael at all.

Then a voice came on his radio, the voice of another boy—a boy who was in trouble.

"Hello! Can anyone hear me? My name is Buddy—Buddy Marucci. I think my father had a heart attack!"

The boy did not say that he was alone in an airplane that he was unable to fly, but the fear in his voice told all. Bill was the first to answer the call. Within seconds he had the kid calm enough to check his altitude and fuel supply. Together they discovered that the autopilot was already engaged when the boy's father collapsed, and that the plane's fuel tanks were half full.

"Buddy," Bill radioed to the boy, whose plane was nowhere in sight. "I'm gonna teach you how to fly that plane. And I'm gonna teach you

how to land it. Okay?"

By this time a dozen other pilots and the controllers at Mueller Field in Austin were listening intently. Finally a small voice was heard by all.

"Okay," Buddy said. "Tell me what to do."

Bill had the boy switch on his transponder. Within a minute, the tower in Austin relayed the plane's location and heading to Bill, who cut a quick course to intercept. Over the years Bill Frazier had taught hundreds of people to fly, and in the next forty-five minutes, as he flew alongside the other plane, he added one more student to that list. Explaining yaw and pitch, ailerons and rudders, altitude and attitude, he soon had Buddy capable of flying the plane in any direction Bill told him to go. Then together they turned both planes toward Austin where emergency crews awaited their arrival.

"You're doing fine, Buddy, just fine," Bill told him when the airport came into sight. "There's only one thing we didn't talk about, and that's getting out once you roll to a stop. Do you know how to open the latch on the door?"

"Yes, sir," Buddy replied. "But it's kind of hard."

"You'll manage. Sometimes it helps to pull on the door as you turn the handle. Now do you see the main cutoff on your center console? It's a big red switch."

"I see it."

"Good. When the plane rolls to a stop. I want you to cut off the main switch, then open the door and get away from the plane."

"What about my dad?"

"Oh, there's guys on the ground who'll get your dad out, but I don't want you to wait for them. The best thing is for you to get out of their way."

"Baker One," radioed the tower. "The runway's clear, but be advised of crosswinds from the southeast at twenty to thirty."

"Well, there's nothing I can do about that," Bill told them flatly. Ahead of the two planes, the airport was now in sight.

"Okay Buddy, here we go. Remember the landing gear lever? Pull

back and down on it now." Bill's voice was calm but his throat was dry as sand. "Perfect! Your wheels are down. There's one other thing I wanted to ask you, son. How old are you?"

"Eleven," the boy said. "But in three months I'm gonna be twelve."

"Christ!" Bill muttered to himself. "I thought he was older."

Angling down with the boy, Bill kept his own plane just behind and above the other as Buddy lined it up almost on the center stripe, his wings tilting, then overcorrecting, then tilting again.

"You're doing fine," Bill told him as they flew over the first third of the strip. "But you need to push the wheel just a little bit forward, son. Easy, not too much."

Dropping quickly, Buddy's plane bounced hard on all three wheels and hopped back into the air.

"Don't pull back!" Bill said firmly. "Hold it right there."

The boy did as he was told and the plane touched down again, first on two wheels, then on all three. The battle was half won.

"Okay now, cut the throttle, son. Pull it all the way back."

Buddy was rolling at ninety miles per hour. Still flying just behind him, Bill knew the boy's hands were frozen on the wheel as he tried to steer down the runway as if he were driving a car.

"Buddy, you've got to slow down. Ease off the throttle, and I mean now!"

As the plane rolled past the emergency equipment parked on the apron, the boy still did nothing.

"Buddy, listen to me! Take your right hand off the wheel and put it on the throttle. Now pull the throttle back slowly. That's it. All the way back."

"Good," Bill told him, all the while thinking 'bad, bad, bad.'"

"Now you've got to use the brakes, remember? Remember how you practiced sitting forward so you could push the brakes with your toes?"

"Yes, sir."

"Do it! Do it now! Stand up if you have to, but push hard on those brakes."

"I can't! It's too hard!"

Suddenly the stall warning in Bill's plane began its buzz. Buddy was running out of runway and Bill was running out of sky. Pointing his nose down, Bill swerved to the edge of the pavement and dropped all three wheels in a perfect greased landing. They were both doing seventy knots, and the end of the strip was rushing to meet them.

"Cut off your fuel pumps, Buddy. Then flip your main cutoff switch. The big red one, remember?"

There was still a chance they were going to make it. Then suddenly Bill felt a powerful gust of wind jerk his plane to the left, shoving him toward the other plane. Wrestling his own plane straight, he keyed his mike to warn the boy to hold tight.

"Buddy," he called, and that was all.

The rest would play over and over in his mind for years—a horrible slow-motion loop: the tail of the other plane twisting left and snapping back in a counterclockwise circle, tilting the plane till the left wing found the ground. Tipping on this fulcrum, the little Piper cartwheeled on the wingtip, then collapsed in a heap, showering its deadly fuel in all directions.

Thirty yards away, Bill's harness was off and he was coming out his door. With the fire trucks still a quarter mile away and flames already spreading around the fuselage, Bill jumped on the crumpled wing of the burning plane, and began yanking at the door.

Peering inside, he saw that the boy had unfastened his safety harness and was lying on top of his father. Backing up, Bill slammed the full weight of his body against the door, inadvertently smashing the window glass. Jamming his bare hand through the opening, he yanked the door completely off its frame.

When the door came off there was a loud roar like a jet. A whoosh of dense black smoke rushed from somewhere under the plane and filled the cockpit as Bill laid two strong hands on the boy—so much smaller than he'd expected—and hefted him from the floor.

"My dad!" the boy cried. "We have to get my dad!"

Even if the boy's father had survived his heart attack and the plane crash, he was the responsibility of ground personnel. Bill had decided his job was to get the plane on the ground and get the boy out. But as he glanced over his shoulder at the cockpit, the flames leapt up from beneath the plane. In that instant the rush of fire sucked the smoke out of the cabin, giving Bill a view of the boy's father as he raised his arm to protect his face from the fire.

Hopping off the wing, Bill ran with Buddy in his arms, ten yards, fifteen, then twenty. Falling to his knees, he deposited the boy in the green, green grass and turned back to look at the burning plane. The rescue crews were racing up, and even with the wild adrenaline that coursed through his body, Bill was hesitant to dare fate a second time.

Then he saw the angel—hovering over the plane with her enormous wings wrapped around the fuselage, barring the flames from the cockpit and looking to Bill with large, dark eyes and an expression that seemed to say, "What are you waiting for?"

For the second time, Bill began to run toward the burning plane, his terrified mind trying to understand why he was running down a path marked by small puddles of fire. Only then did he look down and see that his right shoe was on fire and realize that these were his own burning footprints from carrying the boy away from the plane.

The heat at the wreck only drew him closer. With the angel still hovering above the wreckage and tall flames dancing at the door, Bill dove across the wing. Sliding through the doorway, he landed heavily against the other man's body. The heat tore at his lungs as he gasped for air, and it was only when he tried to heft the man onto his shoulders that he realized the father was too heavy to lift.

Dragging him to the door, Bill wrapped his own arms around the man's chest, then face-to-face they leapt out of the smoke and into the fire. As they sailed into the light, Bill saw that a yellow fire truck had stopped near the boy in the grass and that firemen were running toward the burning plane with foam hoses. Then both men landed heavily on the burning ground. When they stopped rolling, Bill was on his back with the other man on top of him, pinning him down.

With all his might, Bill pushed up but could not rise. And then he saw the stream of white foam rushing toward them, slamming into

*their bodies and drowning out the flames but not the terrible heat
that continued to consume his body.*

And that was all.

"Hey, Spaceman. You still with me?"

Bill raised his eyes from the empty blue ocean where the endless
wave patterns looked like a tapestry of liquid light. Mesmerized by
the motion of the waves and the intensity of his memories, he was
uncertain whether he'd actually told her the story or only relived
it in his mind.

Leaning closer, Kate placed a tender hand on the scars at the
back of his neck. A quick glance at his gauges showed that in his
reflections of long ago, he'd flown fifty miles across the ocean,
searching all the while for some sign of the boat below but almost
unaware that he was even in the plane, much less flying it.

Seeing how tired he was, she began to rub the taut, scarred
muscles on his neck.

"You believe in angels?" he asked.

Her strength suddenly gone, Kate's hands went slack on his neck
as she remembered that Michael had been her first angel, the man
who had rescued her with his love. Then there was Hope, a blessing
on a blessing, and finally—just two years before—another angel
had come into her life, a baby boy who for no reason had been
taken back to heaven. Believe in angels? Only enough to curse
them in long and sleepless nights.

"What's wrong with God?" she said to Bill in a sudden fit of
anger. "He takes my baby and I have to live with that! I have to live
with well-meaning people saying things like, 'You'll have another
child' or 'your baby's in a better place now.' Better for who? Not
me. Not for him, either—a tiny baby who never even knew one day
on this earth! That's so wrong," she sobbed. "And even that doesn't
make God happy, so he has to take the rest of my family too!"

"Kate," Bill said.

"Don't try to calm me!" she warned. "'Cause I don't deserve this!

If I do, then I didn't deserve Michael and Hope in the first place. Is this God's way of saying I took my husband for granted? I'd already figured that out! What did I do to God, anyway? Is he so bored he has to snatch away people's loved ones just to watch the show? If that's the case, screw him! I'll go it on my own!"

In the long silence that followed, Kate's entire body was trembling, but whether from rage or fear, Bill Frazier could not tell.

"So I guess that's a 'no' on the angels," he finally said.

Turning her head to him, Kate almost managed a laugh through her anger.

"Sorry," she told him. "I guess I'm a little wound up."

"Don't apologize to me. You think I'm not mad, that I don't curse God? We all ask that question 'why?' *Why do we suffer? Why does fate deal us a bum hand?* We live our lives hoping to find answers, but the only way to learn is to keep living, to fight harder, and somehow make it till tomorrow. That's what Mike and Hope are doing in that boat. And that's what we're gonna do, too. Right?"

Wiping her eyes, she nodded her head and said, "Yeah, that's right."

Turning her gaze back to the ocean below, she again lifted the binoculars and began to search the water. After a minute she said, "Thanks."

THIRTEEN

With the sun almost unbearable, Hope was huddled in the shadow of her sunburned father. For a couple of hours they'd been talking softly with hoarse, dry voices—first trying to remember all the places they'd ever been together, then doing the same with books they'd read—anything to keep their minds off the heat and the rolling of the boat.

Throughout the morning, the waves that had rocked them gently for two days had grown progressively larger. There were no storms visible on the horizon, not even a cloud in the sky, but as the boat rose and fell with each passing swell, it felt as if the sea was limbering her muscles for a display of her fearsome strength.

The hardest part was to keep up the watch, which was now possible only from the tops of the waves. As one particularly large swell held them high for a moment before dropping them, Hope pointed excitedly to the north.

"What's that?" she asked.

Michael jerked his head around quickly, but they were already falling into the next trough. Grabbing the makeshift mirror from Hope's hands, he leapt to his feet and was ready when they reached the next crest.

"I see it!" he shouted. "Looks like some tuna fishermen with their nets out—but they're way off."

Trying to catch the rays of the sun in the dull mirror, he tipped and tilted it in hopes of flashing the boat. And then they were falling again. As they came up the face of the next wave, Hope stood on the bow and waved the yellow emergency bag.

"Over here!" she yelled.

They were a mile beyond the range of a shout, but Michael waited until several waves had passed to tell her to save her voice. A hundred times they rose up the face of the swells, a hundred times they waved the yellow bag and tried to signal with the mirror, but the tuna boat continued unheeding on its way to the west. Within half an hour, the boat could no longer be seen, even from the tops of the tallest swells.

Exhausted, Hope sank down to the bottom of the boat.

"The mirror's not bright enough," Michael said as he sagged down at her side. Picking up the cloth, he again began rubbing the endless circular patterns on the aluminum box. The wounds in his arm had reopened again and again, and the throbbing ache was as constant as the beating of his heart. He was tempted to fling the mirror aside, but somehow he felt these absurd acts of desperation might help to keep them sane.

After a few minutes he slipped both mirror and cloth into his pocket, then rose carefully and moved aft to where the big plastic fuel tanks were tied. The second tank was nearly half full, but the first sat empty and useless. Crouching beside it, he untied the tank from its cleat on the rail.

"Time to send a signal," he said.

Taking out the pencil and a scrap of paper, Michael wrote a brief note in Spanish and English—requesting help, listing Campo Buenavista's phone number and his updated estimate of their position and course. Slipping the note into his empty medicine bottle, he sealed the pill bottle tight and dropped it into the open mouth of the fuel tank.

"Are we going to throw the tank out on the water?" Hope asked.

"You got it."

Screwing the cap back onto the gas can, Michael locked it down tight.

"But won't it just drift along with us?"

"No, it'll go its own way. It's lighter, so the current will push it faster than us, plus the can sits up high, so the wind will blow it faster, too. You want to do the honors?"

Taking the can in both hands, Hope tossed it out into the swells, where it landed with a loud splash, then rose up on the face of a wave and began to push away from the boat.

"In a few hours that gas can and our note will be miles away," he said. "Then they'll have twice the odds of finding us."

He tried to sound upbeat, but one glance at Hope told him that she knew his scheme was a million-to-one shot. The farther they drifted, the worse their chances of a rescue. And the longer it took to find them, the worse his own chances.

"It won't be long now," Michael said to no one.

In his cell in Bastrop Federal Prison, Michael lay motionless in his bunk for hours on end. All that had happened echoed endlessly in his mind, and he knew if he continued to lie there as he had for the two weeks since handing off his letter to Kate, there would come a time when he would simply go mad.

Three times a day his cellmate would rouse him from his stupor. With tattoos covering his string-bean frame, Sticks listened to head-banging music through Walkman headphones while reading and rereading the same dozen comic books.

"Time to eat," Sticks would say. "Hope it's sump'n good."

Generally surprised to see the cell door standing open, Michael would rise and walk out after Sticks, the two of them joining the single-file line to the commissary, where Michael ate without tasting, washed dishes without caring, then returned to his cell and lay again as he had before.

There was nothing else he wished to get up for. Considering his possibilities, he felt that all hope was lost: grandparents dead and gone, the River Ranch with them; his solemn promise to Wild Bill broken beyond repair. Find a reason to get up? Not without his friend and mentor, not without his license to soar above the clouds, and not without this amazing woman that, even on the day they first met, he'd known he would always love.

Hours into another endless afternoon, a guard wheeled a basket down the corridor and paused to toss a cardboard tube that sailed between the bars and hit him squarely on the head.

"Mail, you jerk-off!" yelled the guard.

Michael sat up sharply, then retrieved the tube from the floor. Just reading Kate's name on the return address was enough to send his heart racing.

"What ya got?" Sticks asked.

With trembling hands, Michael opened the tube and pulled out a rolled parchment, which he held in his hands, almost afraid to discover the treasures within its coil.

"Ain't ya gonna look?"

He did not have to open it to know that she had finally drawn the self-portrait that had cost her a college degree. Unrolling it slowly, he savored every detail as she was revealed to him from head to toe: her hair, even more beautiful than he remembered, a light in her eyes as she looked directly into his, her lips curved into a serene smile. Shoulders bare, her arms were wrapped around her legs, which were drawn up under her chin.

Breathless, Michael was seized with both joy and sadness.

"'Zat your girl?" Sticks asked.

Michael nodded.

"Lucky," Sticks told him.

Taking a deep breath, Michael felt the air rush into his lungs. It felt almost as if she were actually with him, and he knew all would be okay. He knew now that she would wait.

With her arms near collapse from holding the binoculars for two straight days, Kate wondered how seventy-year-old Bill Frazier found the strength to keep up his end of the search. In addition to scanning the ocean's surface as Kate was doing, Bill had to fly more than twelve hours straight, with the only break being one landing for fuel. Through much of that, he was on the radio—coordinating with Cooper at base and raising every craft they saw to check for information or enlist them in the search.

"How do you do it?" Kate asked. "The world's thrown so much crap at you, and you always come out stronger."

Bill let out a laugh. "You want to know if I've got some secret, is that it?"

"Do you?"

"Yeah, I do," he confessed. "My secret is to not ask too many questions. Then you never have to wonder why all the answers are so unsatisfying."

"That's a bunch of bull! I know you, and if you don't ask questions, it's so you won't have to take 'no' for an answer."

The longer she knew Bill Frazier, the more she wondered if anything could kill him. Having lived through more than he'd ever really wanted to, Bill had begun to think the same thing.

Transported by helicopter to the burn unit of Fort Sam Houston Hospital, the pilot who saved little Buddy Marucci and his father was already being seen on televisions all over the country. An Austin news crew, shooting with a long lens from outside the runway fences, had captured footage of the emergency landing, the crash and the rescue.

Kate saw none of this because the day of the crash she was seated in front of a large mirror, studying her body and staring into her own eyes, trying to find a way to put herself in that cell with Michael. By the end of one day, her drawing was finished. She'd taken just hours to complete a task she'd been unable to even begin for years.

"Have I changed that much?" she wondered.

The answer was yes, for now she realized that some piece of her had always been missing. In Michael, she'd found that piece. Now she was whole.

The next morning she rose early and set about her life, knowing the key to this time alone would be to appreciate all the moments of the day—sunrise to sunset, her swims at Barton Springs, her painting, and even the simple tasks of cooking and cleaning.

Opening the paper in search of information about Michael's case, she found instead the story of another pilot—a hero who had run twice into a burning plane. Recognizing Bill name from Michael's stories, she turned on the television and saw him running from the plane with the boy in his arms, then turning back to the fiery inferno for the father. His condition, the newscaster reported, was listed as critical.

Two hours later, she walked through the front doors of San Antonio's Brook Army Medical Hospital. Slipping past the reporters and television crews who were being briefed by a hospital administrator, she found the nurses' desk at the burn unit.

"Excuse me," she said. "I'm here to check on Bill Frazier."

"Are you a relative?"

"Not really, but I am a..."

The nurse cut her off abruptly.

"If you're not a relative, you'll have to leave. No press allowed on the floor; and no visitors except immediate family. Those are the rules."

With that the nurse spun around in her chair and resumed her work. Knowing she did not belong, Kate turned slowly and walked away. But as she pushed the button to summon the elevator, a doctor in a lab coat stepped up beside her.

"Miss, I heard you asking for Mr. Frazier," he said, "and you don't look like a reporter. Are you sure you're not family? We haven't been able to find any relatives."

Kate looked the doctor in the eye. He had a kind face, but tired eyes, and it was apparent that he wanted her to be a relative of their dying hero.

"We're not close," she said. Is he going to be okay?"

The elevator arrived and the doctor pulled her to one side as others got on.

"We don't know that yet," the doc told her. "He looks plenty tough, but I don't see much will to live. We can get his body through this, but only if that's what he wants. I don't know how close you are to your father—you did say he's your father, right? I don't mean to be personal, but the fact is, if he sees you it's bound to help."

To Kate, the look in the doctor's eyes would have excused any lie she cared to join.

"Okay," she said. "Let's go."

On the way back to the burn unit, the doctor gave her an overly honest summation of Bill's condition.

"There's lung damage from smoke and heat, so shock has set in from oxygen deprivation to his vital organs. He's receiving intravenous glucose, saline solution, whole blood, and antibodies. His face was burned too badly for an oxygen mask, so the first doctor at the site performed an emergency tracheotomy. You know what that is?"

In shock herself, Kate didn't answer.

"It means they cut a hole in his windpipe. There's a collar in the hole, and a tube to his lungs so we can give him oxygen. Dr. Becker's burn team worked on him for several hours, picked away the charred clothing and skin while fighting pulmonary edema with antibiotics and... well, you probably don't want to hear the rest."

Kate shook her head slowly.

"What have I got myself into?" she muttered.

Just outside the room, the doctor took her by the hand.

"I should warn you," he said as they put on masks to contain their germs, "the tracheotomy makes it impossible for him to talk."

Well, Kate though, at least he can't say, "Who the hell are you?"

When the doctor opened the door, she just stood there, her vision sweeping across the array of monitors, respirators, and IV pumps connected to skeleton stands holding bottles of liquid life. Finally her eyes settled on something or someone who looked more like a mummy than a man, a man of blackened fire transformed into a man of dazzling snow.

"Mr. Frazier." The doctor spoke softly but firmly. The mummy gave no indication of having heard. "Mr. Frazier, your daughter is here to see you."

Kate stepped forward tentatively and stood close to the bed. Finally she managed to utter a small "Hi."

Just enough of his face and eyes were visible through the bandages for Kate to see his surprise at having an unknown daughter visiting his deathbed. But whatever his doubts, she had to look a damn sight finer than the constant parade of nurses and doctors who caused him agonizing pain every time they touched him, when all he really wanted was to be left alone to die.

With their eyes locked on each other, neither noticed when the doctor retreated to the door.

"I'll leave you two alone," he said.

Both visitor and patient attempted to stop him, but neither could speak, one because the tube protruding from his neck had short-circuited the airflow over his blistered vocal cords, the other simply unable to find her voice. The heavy hermetic door swung shut like the entrance to a crypt, and sealed tight with a resounding echo.

For a long while, the two strangers simply stared, each wondering what the other was thinking. Finally Bill picked up the pen lying on his bed. In large block letters he wrote on a pad: "WHO <u>ARE</u> YOU?"

At that moment, Kate knew exactly who she was.

"A friend," she told him softly. "I'm a friend."

Dropping the pen, Bill moved his hand slowly across the bed until it came to rest in hers. Then, from beneath his thick bandages, Kate heard a muffled sob.

"I'm burning up!" Hope moaned to her father. "Please can I get in the water?"

"There might be another shark," Michael told her.

"It's like my head is on fire," she told him, "and the boat spinning is making me dizzy."

Glancing out to the horizon, Michael confirmed what he already knew—that despite the constant bobbing on the swells and their relentless drift, the boat wasn't spinning at all. Her face was red and her forehead hot to his touch, and he realized she was in severe heatstroke.

This could be bad. She needed to be out of the sun; her body needed to be cooled by ice or cold water, and she needed lots of fluids. Michael dipped his hand over the side to feel the temperature of the water. It was cool enough to lower her temperature, but even if there were no sharks, would he be able to get her back into the boat?

Her eyes were slipping shut now. Is it sleep or a coma, he wondered. Taking off his shirt, Michael dipped it in the ocean, and pressed the wet fabric against Hope's forehead. Only partially conscious, she cringed as she felt the salt water on her burned skin, but the relative cool of the water seemed to soothe her, and soon her eyes fell completely shut.

For twenty minutes, he dipped the shirt again and again, pressing it gently against her face and neck, shoulders, arms and legs. She was half-cradled in his arms now, her upper body in the shade created by his hat and his bare shoulders, which he felt turning red under the relentless attack of the sun. Looking down on her, his mind flew back to those late-night feedings in Hope's first year. Warming the mother's milk that Kate had pumped and refrigerated, he fed his perfect little girl, who drank with great satisfaction while looking deeply into her father's sleepy eyes.

Reaching now for their water bottle, Michael opened it and carefully filled the cap, which he tipped to Hope's cracked lips and let the water trickle in. Without waking, she swallowed reflexively, then he filled the lid and did it again and again, watching the furrows in her forehead relax as he dripped the elixir of life into her mouth.

With her skin cooled and the fresh water reaching her system, the alarming red in her face began to pale slightly, and Michael breathed a sigh of relief.

"You'll be okay," he said softly, even though she couldn't hear him. "The sun'll be down before long, Sweetie, and you'll be okay."

Despite the widespread insult to his flesh, Bill Frazier began to show a marked improvement only days after Kate's first visit. What she'd thought would be a one-time stop to check on the condition of Michael's mentor, quickly turned into a full-time job of sitting by the bed of a man who was beginning to remember his reasons for being alive. She had not yet told him that she was in love with or even knew Michael, so Bill had no idea why she'd dropped into his life. As far as he was concerned, she was the good angel, sent to make amends for the one who'd led him straight to hell.

Every morning she'd arrive carrying a newspaper, a book or a deck of cards with which to interrupt the parade of doctors and nurses who came and went speaking in terms like "damage maintenance" and "acceptable levels of pain." For long hours, she passed tiny pieces of crushed ice into his mouth to chill his scorched tongue and throat. When she stopped, the pain and thirst would return, and his burned lips would press together and silently form the word "more."

To help them both pass the time, she read to him. Bill never seemed to tire of the easy lilt of her voice. After she finished <u>Love Story</u>, he wrote, "kinda dopey," on his pad, but she saw it had affected him nevertheless. When she finished Mario Puzo's <u>The Godfather</u>, he simply wrote, "Wow!" One day she came in with Tom Wolfe's new book, <u>The Right Stuff</u>. It turned out that Bill knew many of the early test-pilots-turned-astronauts, so as she came to their stories, he would sometimes scratch a comment on his pad. About Gus Grissom, he wrote, "railroaded;" about Chuck Yeager, "a good man."

She gave him his meals by slipping a rubber tube into his mouth, encouraging him to sip the clear liquids that the doctors said would provide the protein, vitamins, and calories to keep him going. When he resisted, she described the way her mother had taught her to make biscuits—kneading the flour, baking powder, and butter together with her bare hands, adding buttermilk, then rolling the sticky dough on a floured board.

"When I take them out of the oven," she told him, "I crack one open to make sure it's steaming and wonderful just the way my mother did when I was little."

At some point in her descriptions, Bill would inevitably take the tube into his mouth and begin to drink.

"When you get better," she told him, "I'm going to bake some chocolate chip cookies. We'll hide them in your drawer and you can eat them whenever you want."

Even through his bandages, she could see his smile.

"You hang tough, pal. We'll beat these doctors yet."

She knew by his reaction to every opening of the door that the doctors had become his enemy. Twice a day she took a long break from his bedside while the medical team came into the room to change his bloody suit of lights, peeling away the crusted bandages, and laying bare the burned flesh and bone.

An essential part of burn therapy is the continuous job of debriding dead tissue and infectious fluids, then sterilizing the body with antiseptic ointments and replacing bandages which themselves must be pulled painfully away just a few hours later. Though Bill prided himself on never crying out, deep inside him a silent scream would gather and rage from every nerve in his body before finally rushing out of his mouth in a tidal wave of mute agony.

There are some things in life for which the only help comes from within. And so it was with Bill, who learned to live with these horrors by taking his mind to a better place. Among the curling cirrus commas, he soared in the open cockpit of his old biplane.

The cold air blew upon his face and turned his nose and ears bright red, while the oxygen, thin as a contortionist at the circus, rushed in and out of his lungs in a high-altitude high. Through the golden hours of late afternoon he would soar, sailing through the tops of thunderstorms, bursting in and out of darkness and light. With a Mexican pig as his passenger, Wild Bill Frazier kicked the angels out of bed and dared them to come along. And when the blue sky had gone to black and the gold and the horizon to a blood-red band, he'd search for a place to put himself back on the ground, the battle won again, with Kate waiting for him.

"Daughter," he called her when he was again able to talk. "Daughter..." just as they'd been introduced.

Surprised now to hear him call her this after so many years, Kate turned from her search of the water below to the man on whom everything now depended. It took only a moment to see that Bill didn't know he'd spoken. The long hours in the plane had sent both their minds wandering, wondering how all this had come to pass.

When his jet was hit over Korea, Bill Frazier left a trail of smoke as he barely topped the mountain ridges and—unable to make a carrier landing—he'd ejected into the sky and parachuted into the icy waters below.

In an army hospital in Japan, a nurse from Kansas had cared for him by day, and come to him in the night to care for him in different ways. Thirty years later, he had not forgotten the coolness of her body or her alabaster skin. After the war, his nurse had returned to her husband in Kansas, but in the burn unit he sometimes dreamed that the nurse had borne his daughter. And in his dreams, that daughter was Kate. Sometimes in his dreams, though, it was hard to tell nurse from daughter, or the life he had lived from another he might have lived.

People always wanted to make a hero of him. When he was a strapping lad of thirteen, he was roundly hailed in the Kerrville Daily Sun for diving into the flooded Guadalupe River and rescuing a curly-headed girl named Oida Dawson, who was being swept rapidly downstream. Only Bill knew that the driving motivation to risk his life had been neither noble nor honorable. What drew him into the maelstrom was not bravery, but the chance to hold sweet Oida in his arms as he pulled her to shore. What he had risked had been in hope of a kiss of thanks from a girl he worshiped from afar.

In fact, when he received that kiss of gratitude, so sweet were Oida's lips upon his cheek that he briefly considered pushing her back into the river for another go at the whole affair. Instead he was declared a boy hero and his picture plastered in the newspaper for all to see, neither of which prevented the Dawson family from moving back East with their curly-headed girl in tow. Leaving town in the backseat of her father's old Ford, she had given Bill a final tiny wave—farewell, I'll never see you again, though I might have loved you forever, my hero.

Returning from Korea, he'd been hailed a hero once more, though he knew better and was not afraid to admit it.

"Marvin was the hero," he told Josh Parker. "I'm just the one who came home."

Heartbroken at the loss of his only son, Josh Parker took Bill at his word. There would be no forgiveness from Marvin's heartbroken parents for the sin of living, and Bill Frazier knew he was no longer welcome at the Parker ranch.

"Hero." The very sound of the word sent a shudder through his soul, while the medals on his uniform burned so hot he could feel them brand the scarlet letter "H" through his shirt and onto his skin.

He had helped Buddy Marucci land that plane because that was part of being a pilot and a teacher, and because the boy needed both, but not because he was a hero. He had run into that burning plane to rescue Buddy because a boy has a full life ahead of him, while a sleepless old man has only the growing awareness that the darkness of night seems so much longer than the light of day.

And finally he went back into the conflagration a second time because an angel waited there, beckoning him to someplace away from all his sadness and guilt. An angel, by God! Either she would protect him, or she would show him the way to heaven. Instead, she led him straight to hell—a place of eternal fire and a never-ending barbecue of human flesh and soul. "God in heaven," his mute voice cried out, "will it never end?"

To Bill, the world no longer seemed bright before him.

All morning long, the skies over the Cortez had grown more and more cloudy. Bill and Kate were still flying well under the deck and, if anything, the lack of glare in the shadows of the clouds reduced the strain on their eyes. With Bill having to periodically add saline drops to his eyes, as he had done for thirteen years since the fire, the clouds were welcome relief. But the lack of sun combined with the motion of the waves made it increasingly difficult to pick out objects on the surface of the water. After returning to Buenavista for fuel, food and coffee, Bill decided to finish the day at a lower altitude.

"Lower is good, right?" Kate asked, not wanting to consider what the clouds portended.

"Good for clarity, but bad for the size of our search area," Bill told her. "The lower we go, the more passes we'll have to make to cover our grid."

"So we'll make more passes."

"We can only search till dark, so a lower altitude means covering less area. I'm sorry, Kate. But I still think it's better than taking a chance on missing them."

"There!" she suddenly shouted. "A boat!"

"How far?"

"Half a mile."

Now they both saw it, bobbing above the big swells, disappearing, then rising up again. Coming closer, they made out the shape of the panga, the hull painted white with a blue rim like the description of Nacho's boat. Neither Bill nor Kate said a word, but Kate's heart was beating so fast she thought she was going to faint. At an altitude of two hundred feet, they passed directly over the panga, with the plane in a steep bank to give Kate a better view.

Below them, two young Mexican men waved enthusiastically, big grins on their faces to see anyone but a couple of crazy hand-liners this far from shore.

Crestfallen, Kate looked to Bill, her sad eyes slowly welling with tears.

"Let's get back on our track. There's a couple more hours before dark," he told her. "We found one boat; we can find another."

For the time being at least, Michael felt that Hope was out of the danger from heatstroke, but he knew it had been a close call. An hour earlier, he'd moved her to the stern and tied the emergency bag between the rail and the top of the motor to give her more shade. With the sun approaching the horizon, Michael stowed the bag and the nearly empty water bottle. Their rationing plan was shot now, but she'd needed the fluids. Somehow, they'd get by.

His dead reckoning told him they were now close to a shipping lane used by the ferry from La Paz to Las Mochis on the mainland. If only he could spot one before dark, the low angle of the sun might reflect off his makeshift mirror.

As he continued to polish the cover of the lure box, his fingers were slowly burning from the friction of cloth on aluminum. He could have dipped his hand over the side to cool it, but then his wet hand would've cooled the cloth and box as well. Heat was what he needed to resurface the box's brushed-aluminum finish. Pausing for a moment, he gazed at the box, trying to see his own reflection, but all he could make out was the hazy outline of a man.

"Is that all I am?" he wondered. "Just a blur? A man that's disappearing?"

Lost in a reflected shadow of himself, his insulin depleted and reserves exhausted, Michael's mind slipped away to the sounds of the wind and the waves as they whispered their hidden message.

When Bill Frazier's bandages were removed from his face and arms, the doctors set about changing the mummy back into a presentable hero. As letters and telegrams of encouragement came in, Kate read through them haphazardly. Somehow they all seemed the same, but then one stopped her cold.

"What is it?" Bill rasped. "Am I being sued?"

"No, it's a letter. A letter from a friend."

"Well, read it, by Gar! I'm tired of listening to a bunch of weepy-eyed strangers."

With a trembling hand, she opened the envelope.

"Dear Bill," she began, thrilled just to see the handwriting again, and not noticing Bill's reaction to the emotion in her voice.

You old buzzard! I hear it's not enough to talk 'em down out of the sky; you've got to get 'em out of the planes, too! Let me tell you—you're such a damned fool of a hero that I got promoted from washing dishes just because I know you.

I'm writing to tell you how sorry I am for having betrayed the trust you put in me. Should I get another chance, I am determined to do better.

Do you remember how you always told me to slow down? I was rushing so fast to get to the next part of my life that I forgot about the one I was in. All that changed when I met someone who finally made me see the beauty of every moment.

Her voice failing her, Kate paused to reach for a glass of water. By this time, both Bill and Kate were so caught up in Michael's words that neither of them had noticed the effect it was having on the other.

"Keep going," Bill told her.

Kate cleared her throat and carried on.

I hadn't realized that I'd never been in love before. And now that I am, the days and nights fly faster than a jet. Grandpa Josh once told me that time is just an old magician's trick that separates good times from the bad. You're in the bad times now, and I wish I could be there with you. But since I can't, know that the old magician will bring you back to the good times again. When both of us get free of our bonds, I hope your forgiveness will allow us to see some of those times together.

If I am truly lucky, someday I'll introduce you to the woman I love even as much as I love you, you old goat.

Michael

Folding the letter slowly, Kate let it drop into her lap.

"You're a lucky girl," Bill told her.

"What?" she sniffed.

"I'd have given anything to be loved by someone the way he loves you."

Kate had so often pondered when and how to tell Bill about herself and Michael that even when confronted by the truth, she found it difficult to admit.

"What do you mean?"

"Hell, Daughter. Why else would you fall out of heaven and land in my lap right when I needed you most? It sure wasn't because of my god-damn good looks!"

"Or your language," she laughed, fighting back her tears.

"How long have you known him?"

"Truthfully?" she answered. "One day."

Bill looked her up and down and realized she wasn't kidding.

"One day!" he laughed. "Well, I guess that's understandable. He made quite an impression on me the first day, too."

Once their mutual connection to Michael was revealed to Bill and Kate, the illusion of time returned to its normal pace. One day the doctors came in with big smiles on their faces and said those magic word that every displaced person dreams of hearing: "You can go home."

At Bill's insistence, he left via the same route he'd entered—through the emergency room. He had no desire to be paraded in front of news cameras like a freak. He also knew he'd have to return for more reconstructive surgery, but this was the symbolic moment—the going home of a man who most people had thought would never go home again. To wish him well, a gentle gauntlet of medical personnel lined the hallway.

His physical therapist was there, a patient man who'd helped him to stretch his taut-as-piano-string tendons and taught him to walk upright again. So was Dr. Becker, who'd suggested that Bill buy a toupee to cover his scarred head. And here was Bill walking past him with only a soft blue Yankees cap on his scarred dome. Here, too, was the accountant who had come to Bill's room and shuffled papers and double-talk into piles of illogic so that Bill finally said, "Lay it out straight, Bean Counter. How much is it gonna cost?"

And the pencil pusher snapped his briefcase shut and said, "Nothing. Not one damn cent. With insurance and donations from well-wishers, your debt is paid."

"Well it's damn lucky people are so charitable," Bill said as he fingered the scars on his arms. " 'Cause you sure couldn't take it out of my hide!"

In a group were the three plastic surgeons who'd grafted his skin and given back his smile. Unfortunately, his ears did not line up, a cause of great consternation to the doctors until Bill explained with a laugh that they'd always been that way.

And finally, at the end of the line of well-wishers, Kate stopped pushing Bill's wheelchair as they came to two people who did not work at the hospital, but who had also spent time within its white walls.

The first was a large man in his late forties, a business executive who had one day discovered just how much he had to lose, and who, because of Bill, had lost none of it. The second was a boy, twelve years and three days old, holding the slingshot that Bill had given him on his birthday and wearing a blue Yankees baseball cap just like the one on Bill's head. The bond between these three was eternal. Hadn't they sat in Bill's room and watched the Yankees win the World Series, with Reggie Jackson hitting three home runs on three pitches in the triumphant sixth game? Hadn't this boy come again and again to bring Blue Bell ice cream for Bill's scorched throat? Hadn't he read all of <u>Treasure Island</u> to Bill during the week when Kate was barred from the burn unit because of her flu?

Now Bill looked from son to father, and saw that Charles Marucci was crying. Shamelessly and helplessly, the tears were pouring from his eyes and rolling down his face. Through his tears he said, "Thank you."

"Yes, thank you," echoed little Buddy—who was an almost perfect miniature reproduction of his father.

Somewhere behind his eyes, Bill, too, felt a welling of emotion and the push of tears that wished to fall. The doctors had told him his tear ducts were blocked and that he would never cry again. For a moment, Bill thought he might prove them wrong, but only the ghosts of tears emerged from his eyes.

Rising from his wheelchair, Bill held Buddy's hand—only partially to steady himself—then he stepped to the boy's father. Since the accident, Bill had discovered that Charles Marucci was a kind and thoughtful man, as big of heart as he was of frame. And Bill was fully aware that the poor soul felt a terrible guilt for having been the cause of so much pain.

"Charlie, I want you to know something. I've thought it all through a hundred times, and if I was back up there in my plane, and I heard this boy on the radio, even if I knew then exactly where it would take us, I'd do it all again—not one thing different. Now you got a boy here who says he wants to be a doctor. You make sure he gets what he wants, cause I think he'll be a good one. You two come see me up in Austin next summer like we agreed, and we'll all go flying."

Now as he and Kate flew endless patterns above the empty Sea of Cortez, one thought stood out in Bill's mind.

"Why can't I be the hero now?" he wondered. "Why can't I save the family that I love?"

Too soon, they were running out of light. Above them the sky was gray and threatening; below, the troubled water was growing rougher by the hour.

Two days of searching and not one sign, Kate thought. This is not good. Her eyes and her arms were exhausted from scanning the sea for ten straight hours. "How long can we keep this up?" she wondered.

"Would you look at that?"

Hearing the tone of his voice, Kate lowered the binoculars and the water fell from her view, replaced by a flame-red sky wearing a sunset like a coat of many colors.

"You know what they say, "Red sky at night, sailor's delight."

"Is it a wives' tale or is it true?" she asked.

"Hell, I don't know. But tell me, truthfully, ain't it a sight to see?"

Bill had obviously decided it was time to cheer his partner in this damned depressing business.

"Well," Kate said, "I guess it all depends on the beholder. If Michael and Hope were in this plane with us, then I'd have to say it was the most beautiful sunset in the history of time."

"But they're not up here," he said. "Not yet—so what do you think about it now?"

"An illusion, a masterful trompe l'oeil."

Raising his vision from the water again, Bill studied the sky of whirling fire and said, "They're watching this sunset too, you know."

Both of them knew that on this last leg as they headed back to Buenavista, they were flying over close-in areas that they'd been over five times before. And Kate knew that Bill was simply trying to make the best of it. She cursed herself for giving in, even briefly, to the nagging depression that welled up from the pit of her stomach.

"I know they are," she told him.

"And they know you're watching it, too."

Kate glanced at him. "What do you mean?"

"Think about it. They know I'm up here searching for them. And they know you're here, too. You know how Mike has the uncanny ability to see things through others eyes. So when Michael looks at that sky, he sees it through your eyes, the eyes of a painter. And he sees it through mine, the eyes of a flyer. And that's why I think it's a beautiful sky—because Michael knows I'm an old fool who loves that sort of thing."

The binoculars forgotten, Kate was now staring at Bill. Already he was lining up the nose of the plane with a visual on the runway at Buenavista.

"Even with the troubles you two have had lately, he knows you love him, and that I love him, too. And however much Michael means to us, Hope means that much more. He'd lay down his life for that girl, and he knows that we would, too."

"They're still out there," Kate told him.

"Yes, they are," Bill told her. "Now I know why I lived through that fire. We will never give up our Hope."

FOURTEEN

"Dad, wake up!"

Dusk had come and nearly gone, and the sky's last touches of red were fading into a haze-shrouded darkness. Despite Bill's certainty, Michael had not been watching that dazzling sky. Instead he'd fallen asleep at his daughter's side, their careful watch forgotten as the boat rose and fell on the growing swells of the Cortez.

Awaking without any memory of her heatstroke, Hope sat up to look at the horizon, but saw only the ocean, rising above them, then lifting, peaking, and dropping—motion without end.

"Dad, wake up!" she said again, jostling his shoulders. "I feel sick."

From far away, Michael heard her calling. Coming toward the sound of her voice, he opened his eyes and found the dim outline of not one, but two Hopes.

"Can you hear me?" they asked in unison.

Unable to form words in the desert of his throat, Michael nodded his answer and tried to focus.

"I feel sick," she said. "Like I'm gonna throw up."

As the boat rose high on the face of a swell, then plunged abruptly to the trough below, Michael also felt a surge of nausea.

"We shouldn't throw up," he told her. "Not if we can help it. It'll dehydrate us even more."

With some effort he stood into a low crouch and stumbled forward. In the bow, he untied a piece of line that held more than a dozen pieces of fish that had dried in the sun.

Breaking off a piece, he held it out to her.

"Eat this; it'll make you feel better."

Hope took the little filet and looked at it suspiciously.

"I can't. It's too gross!"

Tearing off a second piece of fish, Michael began to chew on it slowly.

"Well, I gotta admit," he said. "It's not quite as good as McDonald's."

For years they'd had a running battle over where to go for burgers, and Hope knew all too well her father's low opinion of chain restaurants.

"Wanna hear something funny?" he asked. "Even now, a Big Mac doesn't sound that good to me."

"Yeah, right!"

"Hey, if you'd ever had one of Gramma Parker's burgers, you'd never eat one of those cardboard things again."

This time she wasn't buying it.

"Dad, I'll make a deal with you. I'll eat the fish if you don't tell me a bunch of stories about your Gramma's cooking and how this is supposed to taste like fried catfish, and how Uncle Leon always patted his big belly at the end of dinner and said, 'I'm full as a tick!' Deal?"

"Deal," he said, then they each took a bite.

"How is it?" he asked.

"Tastes like raw, dried fish."

"Don't talk with your mouth full."

Hope laughed, then took another bite.

As easy as that, the two of them were filling their stomachs with the smelly, dried fish, both pleased that they'd convinced the other to eat.

"I wish I'd known them," Hope told her dad.

"Who?"

"Your family."

"You're my family now."

A dark look came across Hope's eyes.

"What?"

"Mom and me, *we're* your family! Not just me. It has to be Mom, too. It has to be the three of us. She needs you and you need her, and I need both of you. I don't want you to be mad at each other, can't you see that?"

They were into it now.

"So why are you mad at me?" he asked.

"Because when something goes wrong, you always run away! How would *you* like it if *I* ran away?"

Michael thought back to when he was Hope's age and younger, to a thousand times when he, too, had felt completely alone. Among all his stories, he'd never told her about the bad times: growing up with a picture of a soldier instead of a father, with a mother who wasted away in grief. He'd never realized it, but he'd felt alone for much of his life. His fierce independence had been an act of self-defense—proof that he could get by without his grandfather, without Bill, without the baby boy he'd never even seen, and finally without Kate and Hope. Cut loose by Kate when she was lost in her own pain, he'd drifted away on an ocean of sadness, losing his bearing in the same way that he and Hope were drifting away on this indifferent sea.

"Okay," he promised. "No more running away. I need both of you, too. Without you, I'm nothing but memories and stories."

"I like your stories," she said, leaning her head on his shoulder.

He knew he didn't have much time, and saw that the stories spinning round his brain were the fundamental atoms that connected his body and soul. Sometimes he tried to improve their order, but always they fell back to their own quantum levels, some receding from him, and others carrying him along, toward some higher altitude, perhaps, from which he could survey all the triumphs and mistakes, joys and sorrows of his life and the lives of everyone he'd loved and lost; toward some higher orbit where a better perspective might finally help him understand the meaning of it all.

Now he was starting to grasp that, hidden among the spinning images and nearly forgotten voices, among tastes of foods long since eaten and music no longer heard, dancing from behind first kisses and awkward groping for love in the front seat of his old pickup, and more than anything else, peeking out from behind a glorious array of Kates—there among the phenomenal electrical essence of a man waited one whirling idea that had outlasted all the dimensions of time and space in order to make itself clear to him. He wished to call that spirit forward, but did not know its name. Still, he knew that it was burning brighter inside him all the while, racing through his body in search of someplace from which it could speak.

"Dad," said Hope. "Dad!"

Michael's head gave a little jerk.

"You didn't finish your fish yet."

Michael saw that Hope had eaten both the pieces of fish he had given her.

"Okay," he told her. "You want some more?"

She grinned at him, patting her stomach.

"No thanks. I'm full as a tick!"

There was a long pause, then both burst out laughing, a defiant duet that rippled out across the darkening ocean in an attempt to fight back the coming storm.

"I've been down before," thought Michael. "Down to the bottom of the well with only a glimmer of light to see me through. I made it then, and we can make it now."

As Bill endured the hell of his burn therapy, Michael endured life in a small cell in Bastrop Federal Prison. Twice his lawyer came to visit him, full of remorse at having allowed his first client to receive a harsh sentence for a crime he may not have even committed.

"I'm p-p-putting together an appeal," he told Michael. "Turns out people don't normally p-plead guilty at an arraignment."

With Bill in the hospital and in need of help himself, Michael now grasped at every straw of hope. What kept him going were the letters from Kate that described Bill's improving condition. Then miracle of miracles, one of the letters also contained a note in Bill's scratchy handwriting.

Hang in there, kid. I'm working on something. We'll beat this thing yet.

Within a week, a prison official came in with a stack of papers and said, "Sign here, here, and here."

"Maybe I should let my lawyer look 'em over," Michael replied.

"You don't want out?" the man asked. "You're conviction's been overturned. But you have to sign or you aren't going anywhere."

Michael grabbed the documents, and raced through them, pausing on certain words and phrases: mistrial, the sworn affidavit of a previously unavailable expert, eyewitness testimony from a reliable source in Mexico. What all that meant, he suspected, was that Bill had convinced the feds that Michael had been framed, and probably persuaded Victorio DelaRosa to do the same in Mexico, most likely trading Sada's freedom for Michael's.

As if to confirm all that, as Michael's personal belongings were returned to him in the warden's office, he picked up the morning paper and found a photo of Wild Bill with his doctors and nurses. And there on the front page of the paper was the explanation for everything, a headline that read, HERO GOES HOME!

Yeah, after he went to the courthouse, Michael thought.

Looking closer at the photo, he saw something even sweeter than freedom—standing at Bill's side was the woman Michael loved.

When he stepped out of the darkness of the prison with Kate's self-portrait tucked beneath his arm, his pupils tightened against the bright Texas sun. But when his blue irises allowed him to focus, he saw her standing across the way, more beautiful than in any drawing or memory, a serene smile upon her face and a white cotton dress blowing back against the curves of her body.

Resisting the urge to run, he strode across the last thing in the world that separated them, a ribbon of black asphalt, the Texas heat shimmering off the pavement so that each appeared to the other as some kind of desert mirage. Then the illusion became reality and she was in his arms.

"One rule," she said, pulling back so she could look in his eyes. "Love me."

For the first time in all those weeks, he smiled, and with a nod of his head, the deal was done. There on a lonely road, two people united their lives into a whole that was infinitely larger than the sum of their individual souls.

After steak and cheap champagne on the shores of Lake Austin, they found each other in the little bedroom of Kate's Airstream trailer where Michael's fingertips traced brushstrokes across her back. Through the open windows, a breath of wind lifted the curtains to them, a wedding veil raised to a trembling kiss that rocked the foundations of time so these two hearts could beat as one.

As they kissed beneath the billowing curtains, far across the hills thunder began to echo through the valley where a teenage Michael Parker had first dreamed of sharing such love. Gathering strength through the night as it rolled through the Texas Hill Country, the storm began to rain down on dry summer ground that opened itself and drank eagerly of this marriage of land and sky. And in that night, the fallen water swelled long-dormant seeds, and new life began its tentative journey from out of the earth, fighting gravity and struggling toward the sky.

Sheltered in a trailer beside the water, two lovers listened as the rumbling storm drew near, and the pent-up passion of their own long drought flashed between them like fire in the sky. Reaching upward, their voices danced with the thunder while the rain poured down and washed away the dams that all people build in caution and fear around their carefully guarded hearts, so that finally—entwined as one—they were unable to tell where one's touch ended and the other's began.

Before the storm had moved down to the sea, a second blessing had been given. Life would spring from them, and so long as they honored the bond they made that night, nothing would go so wrong again.

"Dad, are you awake?"

Though the stars were bright, the moon had not yet risen, and it was impossible to see each other.

"What is it?"

"I'm scared."

Michael pulled her closer.

"Listen, champ. There's nothing wrong with being scared. Fear is a sign of great intelligence. So anytime you're scared, I want you to tell me about it. Maybe I can be scared with you. Is it the dark?"

"No, it's the stars. There's too many of them. They make me feel so small."

Michael looked up at the Milky Way stretching from northeast to southwest, bisecting the sky with a billion stars. And the stars cast across the rest of the night canopy seemed somehow even brighter, for they were set against the infinite backdrop of the universe that was blacker than the deepest well.

"Fear comes from uncertainty," he told her, "from not knowing what you face. Remember telling me you were afraid of changing schools in the fall?"

"Yeah, but middle school's gonna be a breeze after this."

"Almost everything will seem easy compared to this. But the thing that scared you about middle school was the unknown. As soon as you learn about something, it's not really scary anymore. See any stars you know?"

"The Big Dipper," she said. "And Polaris is where you showed me, but it's a little higher, right?"

"Yeah, we're still drifting north. But I've got another star for you now—higher up, and over to the right. It's the brightest star in the sky."

"I see it. What's it called?"

"That's Vega. It has a solar system like ours, but the planets are hiding in clouds of dust. There may even be life on those planets."

Staring upward, Hope tried to picture it all.

"Who knows? Maybe someday, some brilliant kid like you will look up there and, bam, the mysteries of the universe will suddenly unfold in his mind."

"Or *her* mind."

"Exactly. Someday it'll all come clear."

Her fear forgotten, Hope stared at the sky in wonder. "Dad, when we used to wish on the stars, did your wishes ever come true?"

"I don't know, Hope. I think it's more about making the wishes than whether they really come true."

"Do you remember all the stories you used to tell me?"

"Some of them."

"Well I remember them all. I always thought you should be a writer."

"Oh, I don't know, Kiddo. I didn't really *write* those stories. I just told them."

"You wanted to be a rancher, right?"

"When I was young. But then I wanted to be a pilot. And the older I got, the more I realized that what I really wanted were other kinds of things."

"Like what?"

"A family; I wanted to love and be loved. I also wanted to be curious about what I didn't know, and certain about the things I did. I wanted to feel as if Grandpa Josh would be proud of the way I spent my life."

His voice was weak, but to Hope his words were strong. Filled with the need to hear him talk; she pushed away the thought that it might be his last story.

"Do you think Josh watches over you?" she asked.

"Sometimes I do. And that helps me to do things right. When I was about your age, Josh told me one summer morning that we were taking the day off. It was a Wednesday, and he never took a weekday off from working the ranch. But this time he said there was something he wanted to tell me, something important. So I saddled up Blue and he saddled Stupid."

"He called his horse Stupid?"

"Yeah, cause when Josh bought the horse, Gramma Parker said he'd have to be stupid to buy a horse at his age, so he said she must be talking about the horse. Anyway, Josh and I spent all that day riding up into the high canyons in the back pastures of the ranch. We talked about the kind of stuff we always talked about: whether the rain was coming, how the deer and cattle were doing, about the trees, the birds, anything we saw, but not anything that seemed real important. And when we got up to the high country, we turned around and rode back home."

"What was it he wanted to say?"

"That's what I asked him when we were taking the saddles off the horses at the barn.

"And?"

"He said, 'Weren't you listening?' And then he went into the house for supper."

"I don't get it."

"I didn't either, not for a long time. But when I finally figured it out, I knew I'd never forget it. I think what he wanted was for me to remember who I was and where I came from, and for me to realize that he'd been talking to me my whole life. Maybe it was all worth remembering."

There was a long silence as the two pondered the vastness of the night. It was Hope who spoke first.

"You and I've been talking my whole life, haven't we?"

"I guess we have. And it makes me feel better to know that you'll always have my stories."

"Me, too," she said.

"Hey, guess what?" he asked, his tone suddenly upbeat.

"What?"

"I just realized something: when we're rescued, we won't be the same people as when we started."

"Yeah, we'll be all sunburned and skinny."

"You're right; we'll look different. But we'll act and think different, too. We'll be changed."

"How?"

"Well, we won't take each other for granted, will we?"

"No, I guess not. And I'm gonna enjoy every bite I eat."

"Even your veggies?"

"Especially my veggies. And I'm gonna drink a thousand glasses of ice water and sleep for a month."

"You'll have to pee for a month first."

"Ha-ha," she said, nudging him in the ribs.

"We'll also be different because we won't be afraid of the thing people fear the most."

"You mean dying?"

"No. I mean living. Think of the pleasure we'll feel when we're safe on dry land with the knowledge of having been tested by the sea and all its power. You'll carry that feeling with you your whole life, a confidence in who you are and what you can achieve, and a satisfaction in knowing the value of life and love and... I don't know, all the ice cream you can eat."

"Yeah, Dad. I'm never gonna be afraid of a math test again."

"Good for you."

He was about to lean over and give her a hug when her gaze fixed on something in the distance.

"Wow! Look at that!"

Looking to the east, Michael saw the gold upper rim of the moon as it rose above the horizon.

"It's beautiful," Michael told her. "I hope your mom's watching it, too."

In the moon's yellow light, he saw a serious look come to Hope's face.

"What?" he asked.

"When we get home, you have to do something for Mom."

"Anything. Just name it."

"You have to dance with her."

"You're kidding, right?"

"You never danced with her, not even once. She told me."

"I don't know how."

"Then you have to learn. Are you chicken of something as easy as dancing?"

"Okay. When we get home, you can give me dance lessons."

"Not then," she told him. "Now."

Holding the rail to steady herself in the swells, Hope rose to standing.

"That's sweet, Kiddo, but the water's too rough."

"Come on, Dad. It's a new kind of rock 'n roll."

Looking him in the eye, with the moon climbing over her shoulder, she held out her hand to her father.

"May I have this dance?"

In a flash, Michael thought back to the dance invitations that he'd declined—the lost opportunity to dance with Jackie at the senior prom, with other pretty girls in the years he'd been single, with Kate from the night he met her till the last time he flew away.

Then he reached out and put his hand in his daughter's and rose slowly to his feet. Hope took his left hand and placed it formally on her hip.

"It's easy," she said. "You just have to listen to the music."

"There isn't any music."

"Sure there is. Can't you hear it?"

Listening closely, Michael heard the sound of the wind and the waves, which were making a music of their own fashion. Then with the ocean as her rhythm, Hope began to hum a tune. After a moment, Michael softly sang the words of their favorite song.

Pack up all your cares and woes
Here I go singing low,
Bye bye blackbird.

Following his daughter's lead, Michael took one step, and then another. Rocking to and fro, shuffling their feet and circling gently in the center of the boat, father and daughter danced and sang, the outlines of their bodies silhouetted against the golden moon at the horizon. Together they sang.

Make my bed and light the light
I'll arrive late tonight,
Bye bye blackbird.

As they danced, in his mind Michael took a fifty-centavo piece from his pocket and tossed it into the luminescent sea. The coin drifted down, sinking into the deep where giant creatures glide silently through phosphorescent trails never seen by man. As it fell deeper still, with the white boat hull far above it just another speck in the star-studded canopy of night, he made a wish.

In the dining room of Campo Buenavista, Kate stared out the windows as the moon climbed higher and reflected off the waves as they rolled high up the beach. She'd expected the dining hall to be full of boat captains and fresh pilots. The food was set out on the table, but she was the only one there. When Coop came in, he walked over to her, but said nothing.

"How many planes did we get?" Kate asked, already knowing that there had been no other planes at the airstrip when she and Bill landed at dusk.

Looking out at the moon, Coop knew there was no good way to tell her.

"They're not coming," he said. "I'm sorry, Kate. We've got a tropical storm warning and these guys are recreational pilots. Their insurance companies don't let them fly into the eye of a storm."

"The skies are clear," she protested.

"The skies change quickly here. Even if they made it down, there's a chance they wouldn't be able to fly tomorrow. Put the two together and there's not enough justification to risk it."

"A twelve-year-old girl isn't justification enough?"

Through this exchange, Wild Bill had been listening at the door. Now he crossed to her and led her from the window.

"Bill, what are we going to do?" she asked.

"I'm gonna eat." Bill said, grabbing two plates and handing one to Kate. "And I think you should do the same."

"Absolutely not. I'm not eating—not until I know Hope can, too. And I don't see how you can put one bite in your mouth when you know she's out there without food or water!"

Bill dropped a thin steak on his platter and began squeezing fresh lemon juice on it.

"Hell! Knowing Mike, they're probably having an evening snack of dorado and seaweed sandwiches at this very moment. Besides, you don't eat, you're no help."

Next to his steak, Bill added a piece of fish and a scoop of Mexican rice.

"Okay," she relented. "Maybe a little fruit."

"That's the way," he told her. "There's nothing to be done tonight. We'll eat and sleep and hope the weather lets us start early tomorrow. We've covered two-thirds of our search grids and we're bound to be getting close."

A few other boatmen were coming in now, all of them avoiding eye contact with Kate. Determined to show them she was strong and the situation was not hopeless, Kate managed to eat most of a decent meal. It was not until Juana brought out a platter of desserts that Kate slid back her chair and stood quickly to leave.

"What is it?" Bill asked.

"Flan," she told him flatly. "Hope's favorite."

With that, she was gone. It served no purpose for the others to see her at her worst.

Opening her door, Kate switched on the light and was crestfallen to see that the room had been cleaned and the beds made. Turning back the covers, she stretched out on the bed that had been Michael's, but hot water and bleach had banished his smell.

The fatigue that plagued her body was also allowing doubt to creep into her mind. What if the search failed? What if the boat had already sunk? So far she'd refused to even consider the possibility of failure, but once she allowed that doubt into her mind, she knew it would be almost impossible to banish.

Looking to Hope's bed, she noticed something leaning against the pillows. Sitting up to look closer, she realized it was Hope's diary. The maid must have found it when she changed the linens, then left it where Kate would see it.

Picking it up, Kate clasped it to her chest. Michael had found the handmade book at a street vendor's stall in Oaxaca and given it to Hope on her birthday as a way to find her heart. But even as Kate opened the front cover, she was remembering her solemn promise that she would never ever read Hope's diary.

About to put it down, Kate realized there was more at stake here than her word. What if Hope had written where they were going? In that case, Kate held in her hands the secret to finding them both. Trying to stay true to her daughter's wishes, Kate resolved to read the last entry only.

Glancing at the pages as she searched for the final entry, she was almost dumbstruck at the similarities of Hope's diary to her own journals. The book was filled with sketches and poems, and with long sections of dense writing, and it took all of Kate's resolve to keep turning the pages to the last entry, marked, *June 14, 1991. Baja, Mexico.*

The next words were almost more than Kate could bear. *Dear Jamie,*—God in heaven, her daughter, who was lost on a stormy sea, had written her diary to a baby brother she had never known.

Kate had been so sure that no one else could know that loss the way she had. Now she knew how wrong she had been.

The reading did not get easier. *Why can't they see how much they love each other?*

It was almost more than Kate could bear. Once upon a time, it had been unthinkable that her marriage to Michael could fail, but she'd allowed herself that doubt, and look what it had led to. For so many years, the words "I love you" had practically been her mantra. Now she was unable to even remember when she'd last said them to him; now she realized Michael might die thinking she didn't love him.

"I took everything for granted," Kate sobbed. "I had everything, and then I let it go! God, please let them come home!"

When she lost her baby, Kate felt that a part of her had died as well. Now she had come alive only to learn how incomplete she was without Hope and Michael. The three of them shared their hopes and their dreams; they shared their pain. There would be no healing if this went wrong, no going back to what she had been when she was alone. That person had been Kate, but now she was Kate and Michael and Hope. Without them, she was wounded. She was dying.

What had Bill told her, something about people allowing the bad times to wash over the good? Kate realized that she needed to do the opposite; she needed the good times to bring her to some temporary peace that would help her rest for tomorrow. Those wonderful years with Michael and Hope were still there, calling out to her like a lighthouse in the dark night of her despair. She thought of Hope, a four-year-old girl attending college classes with her mother, listening as the professor spouted nonsense about capturing the essence of life on paper. So small on the tall stool, Hope sat beside Kate with her own easel and colored pencils, drawing pictures of the places and things that her father had told her about—giant blue whales in the Sea of Cortez or a pair of scarlet macaws in the jungles of Belize.

"No. No. No!" the professor said as he circled past his students' best efforts. Suddenly he stopped behind Kate and let out a triumphant yell. "Yes, yes, yes!"

Feeling a rush of satisfaction, Kate turned to see that he was looking not at her drawing of birds in flight, but at Hope's sketch of a chameleon, barely visible as it concealed itself on a brown twig.

"You see," he concluded. "You must paint with the eyes of a child!"

At the time, Kate was miffed, shown up after twenty years of art classes by the untrained eye of her daughter. But now she knew that day was a treasure. All their days had been treasures. Above the bed in the dimly lit hotel room, the fan blades spun round and round, a whirling propeller that pulled her into the sky on summer vacations with Michael and Hope. The places they visited and the adventures they found were grand in her mind, but what she treasured most was simply the memory of the three of them flying to a horizon that held nothing but promise.

Kate was smiling now, remembering Hope's first day at school, her parents each holding one of her hands as they wished her luck. "Don't cry," Hope said to her mother. "You'll be okay."

Back in the car, Kate sobbed and sobbed. Her little girl was growing up.

In the second grade, Hope came home from school one day with a card she'd written for her mother, a little poem surrounded by wildflowers she'd pressed in the pages of a book.

Butterflies hover near my mother, it read. *Whispering that I dearly love her.*

That night, Kate and Michael decided to try to have another baby. It had taken some time for Kate to overcome the scare of her first delivery. Growing inside a mother with a slender frame, Hope had been a big and impatient baby, eager to escape the womb and see the world. It wasn't the amount of blood Kate lost during Hope's birth that scared her so, but the look on Dr. Ward's face as he tried to stop her bleeding.

But as Hope grew, the memory of that trauma began to fade. A second child would double their blessing, and Michael wanted a boy to carry his family's name. Kate smiled now, remembering the whole experience, the home pregnancy kits she used time and again, Michael sitting on the edge of the bed, nervous with excitement as she came out of the bathroom shaking her head slowly. He would hide his disappointment and offer his encouragement, working up to a sly look on his face. All they had to do was try again. But at some point they began to tire of their own urgency. Making love became a task instead of a joy.

Sitting again in the doctor's office, Kate looked at the walls covered in countless photos, kids of all ages with big smiles and shining eyes, all of whom had been delivered by Dr. Ward. In a few minutes, he came in with a folder containing the results of her examinations and tests.

"Kate," he said, "your tubes are blocked—adhesions we call them. There may have been an infection from the bleeding after Hope's birth. When we don't catch that, it can leave scars."

Kate and Michael exchanged an uneasy look.

"There's no danger," he told her. "But you won't be able to conceive unless we intervene... surgery... in vitro. The options are all involved procedures, and you should take some time to think it over."

As much as they wanted to get pregnant, there was little to think about. They'd been blessed by Hope, and that was more than enough.

The years flew by, marked by summer vacations for the three of them in Mexico: fishing in Buenavista, horseback riding in the Sierra Madre mountains, and fending off gulls to rescue baby sea turtles as they emerged from the golden sands of Careyes. In all these places, Kate had assumed that her days with Hope were days without end.

And just as she'd done many years before on the shores of Half Moon Caye, in all of these places Kate had rested her head upon her lover's chest and fallen into peaceful sleep. Now with the waves sweeping up the beach outside her window, she closed her eyes and imagined herself lying once again with her head on Michael's chest, and let the rhythmic beating of his heart carry her to sleep.

FIFTEEN

As the moon moved across the sky, the waves continued to roll beneath the open boat, lifting and dropping Michael and Hope as if some distant phantom was toying with its dolls.

The stars had wheeled further around Polaris when Michael began to see flashes of lightning on the southern horizon. Soon he knew that the source of the lightning was either growing stronger or coming closer, for its intensity and frequency increased to the point that there seemed to be one continuous electrical display, flashing so bright that the water around them was fully illuminated. Having seen countless storms from his plane, Michael knew this one could be fifty or two hundred miles away, just as he knew that it could dissipate with the dawn, or roar upon them with all of nature's fury.

But he also knew that he would not last much longer without insulin or water. Though her body was stronger and not ravaged by diabetic ketosis, Hope also needed water. With their fate woven into the progress of the storm, he found himself unable to avert his gaze. The waves, in their constant progression, grew ever larger, and the boat rose and fell in a hypnotic rhythm, while the flashbulbs of distant lightning played tricks on his tired mind.

I've seen lightning like this before, he thought, seen it rolling down the riverbed, the clouds like sheets of fire in the night, the thunder growing louder till I thought I'd never sleep. But I always did. I loved to sleep in that old rock house with the rain pelting down on the tin roof.

In the morning after the storm, the air smelled so sweet. At first light he slipped out of the barn, crossed the shearing pens, and walked his horse through the gate into the River Pasture, which stretched for two miles along both banks of the South Llano.

After the rain, with the river running full, Michael rode Blue along the muddy banks, keeping an eye out for snakes and burrows, and for arrowheads that might have been uncovered by the storm. Though he had ridden this way countless times, Michael never seemed to tire of it, for there were always new things to discover. Love of the natural world had a hold on him and was showing no indication of ever letting go.

Then he saw something that raised the hair on the back of his neck—something many said would never again be seen in these parts. In the muddy riverbank were tracks of a mountain lion—fresh tracks, made in the hour or two since the river had receded at dawn. The smell of the animal still hung in the air, for Blue, who was disciplined enough to control her equine fear even when she once stepped on a rattlesnake, was now skittish as a young colt.

Following the tracks upriver, Michael lost the trail more than once at places where the big cat had crossed rock outcroppings. But cutting back and forth across the line of where he thought the tracks would reappear, he eventually relocated the sign, knowing he was again on the trail by Blue's reaction even before he saw the shallow depressions in the mud.

Not carrying a gun and certainly not wishing to kill a lion, Michael was drawn on by the chance of just seeing the animal. After an hour on the trail, he also began to sense the cat's presence. With the passing of the storm, the wind had swung around from the west, the same direction his quarry was tending, which swept his human scent behind him. The potential danger of the situation was something he kept penned in one corner of his mind, for he felt that there are quests that lie above and beyond peril, achievements beyond fear, and destinations that defy the very nature of logic.

His heart leapt when a flock of quail burst into the air around him, their wings beating the air. Blue—more skittish than he'd ever seen her—reared back at the sound and nearly dumped him in a thorny agarita. But Michael calmed her and they pressed on.

As the trail led further upstream, his biggest fear was that his prey would reach the upper boundary of the ranch before his search was done. Then he'd be faced with the decision of whether to climb the fence and continue on foot through land that was not his to cross. Sanctity of ownership and respect for fence lines had been instilled in him since his earliest days, and in all his thirteen years, there was no time when he had stepped beyond the outer fences of the River Ranch.

The fence at the far end of the Parker ranch bisected the uppermost hole of water on the South Llano, an isolated cove of deep blue sheltered by a spring-dotted cliff that occasionally dropped massive boulders into the water below. This accumulated pile of rock harbored a grove of tall trees—pecans, sycamores, and oaks—all of them playing host to one of the largest turkey roosts in Texas.

He was in the shade of both bluff and trees when he eased his nervous horse around a pile of driftwood and saw the big cat just twenty yards in front of him—a full-grown mountain lion, casually sunning on a log as if it were Sunday afternoon at the zoo. Golden in the morning light, the lion's fur was thick and soft, giving her lean body the look of some pampered animal in the court of kings. Her face was turned away, but her long, fat tail swooped and dove through the air about her, flicking for a moment at some flying insect that dared enter her presence. To Michael's surprise, there were two beautiful lion cubs rolling and tumbling over each other just below her. Evidently they weighed too little to make tracks in the mud, but their presence explained the slow speed with which the lioness was moving.

He wondered if she would stay here till evening when the turkeys returned to their roost, then make a meal for her brood on two or three plump hens. But Blue, catching a whiff of the lion's scent, whinnied in protest, and the lion whipped around to evaluate her danger. For long moments, boy and lion stared at each other, cool on the outside and seized by indecision within.

With the intensity of her gaze burning on his eyes, Michael glanced away for one second. When he looked back, by some hidden signal she had already moved her cubs. Then in the wink of an eye, she was gone too, like a mirage that you try to approach, only to wonder if it was ever truly there. He didn't even know which way she'd gone.

On the ride back to the house, Michael told the story over and over in his mind, rehearsing just the way he'd brag to Josh and to his friends at school how he'd stared down a wild mountain lion, the likes of which had not been seen in these parts for thirty years. He wondered if people would believe him, then decided that they would.

The prints along the riverbank would prove his claim. Word of the lion and her cubs would soon circulate through the Hill Country, then hunters and trackers and everyday fools with dogs, ropes, and guns would come in search of this prey. Though they might not find her, they would certainly drive her farther away. In the end, he told no one. Not Josh, who would likely have ridden out to check for newly killed sheep or calves, and not his friends, who would never have understood.

The one time he took Kate to see the ranch, the foreman loaned them a pair of crummy horses and they rode out into the river pasture so Michael could show his wife the land from which he had sprung. The rain had been plentiful that year, the springs were running and wildflowers blanketed the old county road where Wild Bill had once landed his plane.

As they came to the final pool, Michael was about to tell Kate about the mountain lion, but stopped when he discovered that the pool of water was even larger than he remembered. The pecan trees had grown, and there was a loud gush of spring water coming from high up the bluffs. It was too much: too beautiful, too heartbreaking. The color drained from Michael's face and he found himself rendered unable to breathe by the sheer perfection of it all. Gasping for air, he looked around with all of it swirling through his brain, and there on a log above Kate, the mountain lion called out, teeth bared and growling loudly as if to leap to attack. Michael tried to utter a warning, but instead he woke with a start and found himself lying in the dark—he knew not where.

And then he felt the hardness beneath his back and shoulders, and the boat rolling in the swells. It was not Kate who was in danger; it was Hope. Over and over, his mind played back through the images of his dream, trying to separate what was real from what he had conjured. Realizing that he could no longer tell, he propped himself higher so that he could watch for some light.

Unseen by Michael, clouds had blown in, and the moon was now shrouded in a glowing halo, its light reflecting eerily off the white tops of the windblown waves. This time he was determined to stay awake. Half an hour later, his vigilance paid off as the darkened outline of a small boat grew larger and larger before him. Coming almost straight toward them, cutting up and down through the swells, was a panga with red and green running lights.

"Gilberto!" he shouted as he hopped to his feet. "We're over here!"

Waking to the sound of her father's shouts, Hope also leapt to her feet and began to yell.

"Here we are! Help! We're over here!"

"Flare!" Michael called to Hope. "Hand me a flare!"

Tearing open the waterproof package, Hope pulled out one of the two flares and placed it in Michael's hand like a relay runner passing a baton.

Michael was about to crack the flare when Hope grabbed his arm with both hands.

"Wait!" she yelled. "Where is it? Where's the boat?"

Michael pointed to one side but saw nothing. Spinning his head around, he looked to the other side to see if the boat had somehow passed. But all he could see were the faces of the swells. The boat had vanished.

"It was right there," Michael told her as he sank down on the seat. "Right there, coming toward us. Did you see it?"

Hope took his hand. His skin was hot to her touch.

"No, Dad. I didn't see it."

Around them the waves themselves glowed with an eerie phosphorescence, a glow that revealed the look she gave him, the look that said, "You got me into this and now you're going crazy."

In that same glow, Hope also saw that he had recognized her scowl, and immediately she regretted it. Her father was sick, and she knew it. Perhaps he was dying, and she could not bear the idea of his feeling guilty.

"Maybe it was the ghost panga," she offered.

"Maybe so, sweetheart; or maybe I was dreaming."

Reaching forward, Hope found the bottle that held the last few drops of their water.

"Drink this," she told her father.

After a bit, he said, "Okay," then opened the bottle, tipped it carefully to his lips, and drank the last two swallows of their precious water.

"Better?"

"Yeah, I'm okay now, so you lie back down. It's not your turn yet to stand watch."

As much as he hated to face the facts, it was impossible for Michael to ignore that forty-eight hours of wind and sun and very little water had left every inch of his being so severely dehydrated that he could almost feel the cells themselves calling out for water. Somewhere beneath his thirst, the acids building inside him were robbing his muscles and mind of the one thing they most needed—oxygen.

Like a computer with a faulty power supply, his mind was starting to blink on and off, First he was pulling fish at midnight from the Blue Hole with Josh, then he was on the ocean with Hope. The swirling canvas of stars above him, golden orbs against a background of midnight blue, became Kate's re-creation of Van Gogh's <u>Starry Night</u>, rendered in Crayola during her morning sickness before Hope's birth when Kate could not stomach the smell of her paints. So fine was her work that it now hung in the sky over the oceans of Mexico. What artist could say more? It was good to be within her sky, to be looking down from Kate's stars to the rocking boat where Hope lay sleeping.

On the surface of the ocean, he saw yet another boat, but his waking self reminded him that it was only the ghost ship, coming back to trick him again. Only this was like no ship he'd ever seen—huge and black and leaking steam from every vent and seam. He knew it could not be real, even as it came closer still. Even when the pounding drone of its engine grew loud upon his ears, he was certain he was dreaming.

When the ghostly giant was nearly upon them, Hope stirred beside him and opened her eyes. With her piercing scream, both of them came fully awake. Bursting out of his trance, Michael realized they were about to be crushed to the bottom of the sea.

The bow wake of the big ship was already lifting them as Hope screamed again, her hands flying up to protect her face and head. As the little panga was shoved up and out, pitched toward the night sky, Hope was tossed into the air. But as she flew out of the boat, she saw her father's long arms reach up and felt him grab her the way a leaping cat snatches a bird from flight. Father, daughter, and panga all landed as one, slapping hard on the ocean and scraping along the barnacle-encrusted ship hull.

Holding Hope in the bottom of the panga, Michael wedged his legs and back against the rails and seats until the little boat was sucked around the stern of the ship and tossed like driftwood into the churning prop wash. Caught between the wake and the ocean's own rolling waves, the panga bounced to and fro—a refraction trapped in a house of mirrors.

When he was certain they would not capsize, Michael leapt to his feet and popped one of the flares. Bright as day it burned, arcing back and forth above his head, but doing no good, for the freighter continued south, with the helmsman intent on rounding Cabo for the Pacific before the storm reached the Cortez.

"Turn around!" Hope yelled. "Please turn around!"

As the flare sputtered to an end, Michael was already untying the remaining gas tank from its cleat. Unscrewing the cap, he took the can in both hands and swung it around his body like an Olympic hammer. With all his strength, he heaved the half-filled can as far from the boat as possible.

"The other flare!" he yelled to Hope.

Stumbling to her father, she quickly handed him their last flare, only to have him stare after the ship, doing nothing.

"Hurry, Dad! They're getting away!"

"Not yet! The gas is too close."

Finally he popped the flare, blinding them again in the sudden red light, then he heaved the burning torch toward the can on the water. A red arc cut through the air, spinning as it flew, illuminating the iridescent trail of floating gas. As he pulled Hope below the rails, the flare found home and flames shot across the surface toward the can. After the slightest pause, the can and fifty square yards of the ocean ignited all at once, the explosion shaking the panga as the darkness turned to day.

But even in that burning light, with the flames dancing just away from the rising and falling panga, somehow the ship continued on its way. With all hands looking south toward the storm, not one soul looked back to the fire. After a few minutes, the heat and light around Michael and Hope faded, the ocean flickered, and then it was dark again.

"Dad!" Hope sobbed. "It was so bright! How could they not see us?"

"I don't know, honey. Maybe they're on autopilot; maybe they just weren't paying attention."

The days and nights on the ocean had been too much for a twelve-year-old girl, and this felt like the final blow. Lost in her tears, Hope did not see her father sag to the bottom of the boat, pain stabbing at his stomach, his legs so numb he could barely feel them.

When she saw him there, Hope let out a small scream and fell to her knees beside him.

"Daddy!" she called out.

Her voice sounded as if it was coming from across the ocean, but he could hear her asking if he was okay. He wanted to say "yes," but that would have been another lie. He'd lied to keep her from losing hope. He'd lied to contain her fear. But the lies were over now.

"Only the truth," he promised himself.

"What?" Hope asked. "I couldn't hear you."

He looked up at her beautiful face, so much like her mother, but already so much her own woman.

"Hope, I'm sick. I wish I wasn't. I wish I was strong, but I'm not."

"Dad," she asked, helping him to sit up against the side of the boat so he could steady himself against the swells. "Are we gonna die out here?"

"I don't know, Hope. If we don't get something to drink, we could be in trouble. But if it rains, we should be okay."

"Should I pray for rain?"

Even in jail, in the depths of his troubles, Michael had not put his faith in prayer. As a boy, he sometimes said grace at meals, but in his heart he refused to seek assistance from the same God that had taken his parents, who had enjoyed this earth only long enough to have a son who would always miss them. He'd seen prayer as the constant companion of Gramma Parker, who felt it her role to pray for the wicked and the righteous alike, to ask forgiveness for sins Michael knew she had not committed, to pray for those who had cheated or stolen from the ranch, to pray for the everlasting soul of her beloved son and daughter-in-law. As far as Michael knew, none of it had done any good. But in the drought of the fifties, when the green hills had withered to desert and the river dried to hard-cracked mud, Josh Parker had joined his wife to pray for relief, to beg for the angels to look down upon their plight and cry copious tears of sorrow that would heal the land. And when the rain came that night, it was in giant drops that soon gave way to sheets, then waves, then torrents of falling water.

Just five years old, Michael knew he would never see such rain again.

"Thank the Lord!" Gramma Parker said. "Our prayers are answered. The angels are crying!"

"Yes, sweetheart," Michael told his daughter as he peered out across the Cortez. "I think you should pray for rain."

SIXTEEN

For two years Kate had been plagued by this nightmare, the recollection of the terrible night that she would never erase from her mind. Leaping down upon her like a wildcat, this monster had nearly consumed her until she finally learned to lock it away where it would not be easily roused. But sooner or later, she knew the beast would break free to haunt her again.

"Go away," she moaned in the dark room at Buenavista. "I can't do this now!"

But it was too late. The beast was loose again, leaping down to devour her heart and soul, leaving behind only an empty shell, a body without spirit, breasts without purpose, arms without a beloved baby to hold.

From deep in sleep, covered in sweat, she'd wake with the sheets wet, knowing her water had broken. But when the light came on, the bed was wet with blood, not water, and Michael was springing to his feet. Then they were driving, sliding around corners—horn honking and lights flashing, all of it echoing the driving pain within her.

They'd been so excited when they learned she was pregnant—"a miraculous conception," Bill Frazier had called it.

Looking back now, Kate thought of the last day she'd lived without fear. Thirty weeks into her pregnancy, during a routine sonogram, with Michael standing beside her, the two of them were looking at the first image of their baby boy.

"Good news," Dr. Ward told them. "It's a boy."

There was a long moment of pure happiness, then Kate saw that Dr. Ward was not smiling.

"What's wrong?" she asked.

Adjusting the display to make the image clear, he took a breath. "The baby looks fine," he said. "Strong heartbeat—you can see it right there—everything normal. But he's flipped around feet first."

"Breech?" she asked.

"Instead of curling up with head down, he's basically standing in the womb."

"What does that mean?" Michael asked.

"Nothing to worry about," Dr. Ward assured them. "He's just eager to arrive and start walking around. Breech babies often flip around on their own. In five or six weeks, we'll do another sonogram. If he hasn't reversed by then, we'll try an external version, do a little pushing here and there on your belly, and see if we can coax him around the other way. I'm sorry, it can be painful; but it's worth it if it works."

"If it doesn't?" she asked.

"Well, if you try for natural childbirth with a breech baby, when your cervix opens, it can allow the umbilical cord to drift down and cause all kinds of problems. We can't take that chance, so we'd have to do a C-section. Considering your bleeding last time, it's probably best anyway."

That evening, she and Michael asked Hope to sit with them on the dock at dusk, with the tall bluff across the lake illuminated in a red reflection of the sunset. When they'd explained it all to Hope, she had only one thing to say.

"If I'm going to have a brother, he should have a name."

Kate had never loved her daughter more than at that moment.

It took so little time for the three of them to decide. Before the light had faded from the bluff, Michael and Hope laid their hands on Kate's belly, then Kate gently placed her own hands on theirs.

"I name thee Marvin James Parker," Kate proclaimed softly, honoring two fathers who had gone on too soon.

Leaning close, Hope spoke to her brother. "Hi, Jamie. I'm your sister. My name is Hope."

Despite Dr. Ward's assurances, Kate could not shake her fear that things had already gone wrong. For much of the previous year, Michael had been teaching her to fly. If something happened to him, she wanted to be able to land the plane. But there was more to it than that, for Michael knew her secret. Despite her brave front, she'd never lost her fear of flying.

"If you learn to fly," he told her, "I mean really learn—if you solo and land alone, if you put in the hours to get your license, your fear will melt away."

"Are you sure?"

Taking her hand, Michael had looked in her eyes and said, "I promise."

For months, she studied and practiced, logged the required hours with Michael as her copilot; did touch-and-gos and landings. He was a good teacher. With Michael at her side, she became stronger than her fear.

All that remained was her first solo.

Two years later, she still didn't know why she froze as the runway came up to meet her. And even though she'd walked away from the plane, she knew that fear had won.

A week later, she learned she was pregnant. Michael couldn't have known any more than she did, but he had promised that all would be well, and he'd encouraged her to do something that endangered their baby.

A few weeks after learning the baby was breech, the new sonogram showed Jamie to be growing at a normal pace, his heart beating strongly, and both feet still firmly planted at the bottom of his mother's uterus. Printing a photo of the image on the screen, Dr. Ward handed it to Kate who stared at it a long while. Then she slowly spun the photo around till the baby was in the proper position—feet up, head down. It seemed so simple.

The actual attempt to rotate her baby was somewhat more horrific—two doctors literally crawling atop Kate on the hospital bed as they shoved at various angles on her swollen belly while Kate gritted her teeth, trying not to scream as they pushed and prodded at the baby inside her, watching all the while on the sonogram scope to see if they were having any success.

Biting her lip, Kate held her mind to the rhythmic music of Jamie's beating heart, amplified into the room through a fetal monitor to ensure that the procedure didn't cause him too much stress.

After ten minutes with no progress in the manipulation, Kate thought she heard the steady heartbeat begin to slacken.

"Stop it!" she ordered. "You're hurting him!"

The C-section was scheduled to take place in two weeks.

In the hotel room at Buenavista, with the wind whipping the tops of the palms outside, Kate took out that first black-and-white sonogram photo of her dear baby Jamie. For two years she'd carried it with her everywhere she went. Kissing the photo, she held it to her heart, then placed it on the table beside the bed and tried to find some rest.

But in her uneasy sleep, Jamie gave her no rest as he pushed at the confines of her womb, as Michael raced to the hospital, lights flashing, the horn echoing as they skidded to the emergency room doors.

Wheeling her in on a stretcher, a nurse asked the space of her contractions.

"One minute," she told them through clenched teeth, thinking these people were acting far too calm. "But the baby's breech."

At the mention of the word, everyone froze for one long moment then the room sprang into a panic. Kate wanted Dr. Ward, but he was nowhere to be found. Pulled away from Michael by unfamiliar nurses, Kate was wheeled into a trauma room—the wrong place for newborns—and the door was shut in Michael's face.

"She's dilated eight centimeters," a nurse told the doctor when he rushed in, still putting on his gloves.

"I have to push!" Kate told him. "He wants out!"

"Not yet," the doctor told her sternly as another contraction came on. Gritting her teeth, Kate fought against everything her body told her.

"I want fetal tones!" the doctor ordered.

"We're trying," a nurse said in a panic.

"Call a surgeon to assist," the doctor said calmly.

Through her pain, Kate realized for the first time how young the doctor was. He looked like he should be making coffee. At that moment the doppler on her belly picked up the baby's heartbeat.

"I got it!" the nurse said. "Pulse is one hundred; no, it's ninety."

"Too low," the doctor said.

"Now it's eighty."

"Fetal distress," the doctor said. "I need scalpels. We're going to open."

"Michael!" Kate called out. "Michael, I need you!"

She could hear him outside the room calling back to her, but she didn't know that two orderlies and a cop were holding him tightly, saying, "Calm down, pal. The doctor knows what he's doing."

But what the doctor knew was that a footling breech is one of the most dangerous births. Hope's baby was stuck, half in this world, half in his mother. Frozen for a moment, Kate heard the panicked nurse say, "Can we push him back up?"

"Seventy," the other nurse called out.

The scalpel was in the doctor's hand when the nurse said, "Wait! The baby's descending. The hips are clear."

When they told her to push, Kate did her best, but it all unraveled in a blur of panic and pain—pulse at sixty, then fifty, Jamie's shoulder hung in her pelvis, the cord pulling tighter and tighter by contractions she could not stop.

She screamed in pain when they twisted Jamie to clear the

shoulder, but then he was free and the pain was gone for one moment until she saw her baby, his body blue, his eyes closed as in a gentle sleep. Kate was crying now, "No, no, no," as they put him in the incubator and did all that they could, using words no mother should ever hear—aspirate, intubate, endotracheal... CPR.

"It's my fault!" Kate cried. "It's all my fault!"

She'd never imagined anything so sad. Her tiny baby, already gone as the doctor wrapped both hands around his body and began rhythmically squeezing Jamie's chest with his thumbs, counting out a pulse he could not restore.

Outside the room, the men could hold Michael no longer. Dashing in, his mind crazy with fear, Michael froze at the sight of his son's tiny body, the blue color already turning pale as the nurse put her hand on the doctor's shoulder and said, "He's gone. You did all you could."

"No!" Kate wailed.

As Michael came to her, through her sobs she kept saying, "I did something wrong. Michael, what did I do wrong?"

"Nothing," he reassured her.

But Kate didn't hear him. After a moment, she looked up to her husband and said, "Where were you?"

With the storm raging outside, Kate knew she would never sleep. Opening Hope's little diary, she read the final words their daughter had written to the lost spirit of her baby brother.

Dad and I are going fishing tomorrow. I'm going to catch the biggest fish in the ocean, and I'm gonna give it your name—Jamie—then I'm gonna let it go. Then the fish will be you, and you'll be the fish—the master of the seas—swimming wherever you want to go. You'll be free. Forever.

The rest of the page—and all the pages that followed—were blank. Closing the diary, Kate wondered how she could be so foolish, and her daughter so wise.

Outside, the first light of dawn was beginning to show as she kissed the sonogram photo of the baby they had all loved but none of them had known, and placed it back on the dresser. Then taking Hope's diary with her, she went out the door to find her family.

SEVENTEEN

One hundred miles to the north, Hope shook her father's shoulders.

"Dad!" she told him loudly. "You have to wake up! I see something."

Opening his eyes, Michael peered up at the blue sky and knew that the storm had not come. His throat was swollen and his tongue thick as if he had slept with his mouth full of sand and salt. If there had been anything in his stomach, he was sure he would have thrown up.

Lifting his head against the pitching of the boat, he looked across the ocean in the direction that Hope was pointing. At first he saw nothing. Then his eyes began to focus, and he realized there was definitely something on the horizon. The shape bobbed up and down with the waves like a boat in the distance, rising into sight, then disappearing below the jagged line of swells that separated Michael and Hope from what might be their salvation.

For half an hour they watched it coming slowly closer, tantalizing them with the possibility of rescue. And then it came to the top of a wave that was bigger than the rest and revealed itself, much closer than they had thought, and consequently, much smaller.

"Oh, shit," Michael said. "It's the gas tank."

"No, Dad. You blew it up. Don't you remember?"

"Not that one; the other one. The one with our message."

Hope looked closer and realized he was right.

"No!" she shouted at the tank. "Go back! Go find someone! We don't want you here!"

The tank floated closer, returning because the winds had shifted and were now blowing from the north, blowing the tank back to them but also keeping the storm away to the south. So specific was the tank's intent that within minutes Hope was able to lean over the side and bring their message back into the boat.

Dropping the fuel can into the bow, Hope sank down around her father's legs.

"I don't want to do this anymore," she sobbed. "I want to see Mom! I want to go home!"

Now that the dam had broken, Hope's emotions rushed out in heaving sobs that stabbed at Michael's heart. Stroking her hair to calm her, he tried desperately to think of something he could do. Their food and water were gone, the school of fish following the boat had abandoned them, and the storm appeared to be no closer.

Finally he had to admit that the only thing left to do was perhaps what he should have started with.

"Dear Lord." Though his lips formed the words, his burned vocal cords barely made a sound. No matter, he thought. If he can see me, then he can hear my words.

"Dear Lord!" he murmured. "Don't let this happen to my little girl. She's too good and too young to leave this earth, too fine for the world to lose her grace. I've had my chances, but she's only just beginning. Her life is promise, and it's wrong to make her suffer. Take me if it makes you happy, but save this girl, and send her back to her mother."

He tried to think of more to say, but then he thought that if his muffled words could be heard, then God could just as easily see into his heart. What need was there for words when all the angels had to do was look down upon this sad scene and let their tears come. As his dried, cracked lips parted for a final "Amen," the north wind slowly died, and they were left floating in a dead calm.

Within minutes, he saw the first bird coming toward them, a herring gull, its white body a bright spot against the gray sky. Then he saw another, and another. Behind the first wave of gulls came an immense flock of seabirds, thousands of them, strung out from horizon to horizon in a seemingly endless line of brown boobies and white albatrosses, black-winged shearwaters and night-black storm petrels—all of them flying to the north as fast as they could go.

"I've never seen so many," Hope said in wonder.

"They're fleeing the storm," Michael was able to say.

"No," she said, "The birds are bringing it to us."

For the next hour they sat silently and watched the rain coming closer. Though he tried to stay in the present, Michael's mind kept slipping back to the River Ranch where he and Josh would sit on the porch and watch the clouds and rain roll down the riverbed toward them, each hill obscured by the approaching downpour until they could see only the bluff across the way, and then not even that. When the first cool gusts of wind reached them, the carpet of leaves beneath the old oak trees would stir as if to make the ground ready for the blessed rain.

"Sometimes it seems like the rain is all that really matters," he told his grandfather.

"What's that?" Hope asked.

"I smell the rain," Michael told her.

A smile tugged at Hope's cracked lips. "The angels heard my prayer."

"Get the water bottles." He told her. "We have to be ready."

Sitting in the dining room at Buenavista, Kate stared numbly at the black coffee before her. The sound of the gale-force winds tore across the thatched roof above her head, and she knew they couldn't fly until the weather had passed. Hope and Michael were at the mercy of the storm.

Suddenly the door flew open and banged against the wall. The wind rushed in and the room flew into motion, with papers and maps taking flight as Bill Frazier and Ray Cooper pushed their way in.

"You check the tie-downs on the plane?" Coop asked Bill as he pushed the door closed with his shoulder.

"They'll hold. I just hope we don't get any runway damage. What's the weather report?"

"You don't want to know."

"Try me."

"Tropical storm warning for Cabo. Sunny and clear for here."

"Sunny and clear?"

Bill shook his head and looked out across the bay at the approaching storm, now a black wall obscuring Punta Colorada from sight. And then he saw something on the water—a panga coming toward them, cutting like a knife across the jagged waves, racing the storm for shore.

"Who the hell is that?"

Jumping up, Kate ran toward the door.

"It's them!" she called. But before she could get outside, Coop caught her hand and pulled her back.

"No, it's Gilberto. He's coming back with his scientists."

Crowding to the window, they watched as Coop's manager, Tomás, came out of the office with a rain parka and ran to the beach. The surging waves—windblown into ugly brown crests—were far too high for Gilberto to tie off to one of the buoys anchored in the bay. The only permanent dock on driven pilings ever built at the hotel had washed out with the first major storm. Colonel Cooper's response was to construct a massive wheeled dock that was rolled into the water every morning by a bulldozer and dragged out again in the evening. With the storm approaching, the dock had already been dragged back to high ground, which left Gilberto and his passengers at the mercy of a violent sea.

Circling once, Gilberto surveyed the situation, his bow slamming into each wave and raising a V-shaped geyser of spray that blew back upon them in the open boat. Fifty yards out, he turned and headed straight for shore, gunning his motor full out to push the skiff up onto the crest of a tall, rushing wave.

"He's crazy!" Kate said. "They're gonna crash!"

"He's gonna beach the boat," Coop told her. "It's the only way."

With his two passengers holding on for dear life, Gilberto raced the motor till he was nearly in the break of the waves at the beach. One second before certain doom, he cut the engine and dropped the panga just behind the crest of the wave. The water surged ahead of them and crashed violently onto the beach, obscuring the boat from sight with a giant splash of water and foam that bounced high into the air. In a curtain of windblown spray, this orphan sea hung in the air, frozen for one impossible moment, then the picture roared to life as the panga came crashing through the airborne wave. Landing hard in two feet of water where only sand had been a moment before, the fiberglass boat glided up the beach. In a split second, Gilberto and the wave had moved the panga from true peril on the ocean to the safety of the shore.

Coop and Tomás ran across the beach to lend a hand. Tying one end of a tow strap to the boat and the other to the back of Tomás' old Toyota pickup, Gilberto gave a shout and Coop raced the truck inland, dragging the panga farther from the waves.

Coop and Gilberto were soaked to the skin when they came into the bar. For a moment Gilberto's face was a filled with a big, happy-to-be-alive smile, but then he saw Kate and froze in his tracks.

"Por que?" he asked. "Why are you here?"

After three straight days and nights of this disaster, Kate felt her stoic reserve melt away. Huge round tears began to roll down her cheeks. Bill put his arm around her shoulders and turned her away from the windows and the storm.

"Michael and Hope," Coop explained. "They didn't come back."

Gilberto looked gravely stricken. "When?" he asked. "The day I left?"

As Coop nodded, a terrible realization swept across the boatman's face.

"Donde ván? Tell me where you've looked!"

"South," said Bill. "Beyond Pulmo in the Pacific current. God knows how far they've drifted by now."

"No! Not south!" stammered Gilberto. "North! They left toward Isla Cerralvo. In the outer current, they have gone far to the north!"

"Oh, Christ!" exclaimed Bill. "We've been looking in the wrong ocean."

"We have to start over?" asked Kate, panic in her voice. "There's not enough time!"

"No! This is good," Coop told her as he shoved his arms back into his slicker. "Now we know where to look. I'm going to the radio. If they're far enough north, someone might find them before the storm."

Within half an hour, he was back.

"Good news," he said. "A tuna boat radioed to say they saw a panga west of Mochis yesterday."

"Mochis!" said Bill. "Hell, that's over a hundred miles from here. Could they have drifted that far?"

"Certamente," said Gilberto. "It could be them."

"Oh God," said Kate.

Coop continued. "The harbormaster in Cabo says it's already clearing there. The storm's hauling ass to the north and we may be able to search before dark."

"What do we do till then?" asked Kate.

"Wait until the storm passes," said Coop.

In the boat Michael was beyond pain or thirst, had forgotten about the storm, and had even forgotten that Hope was there beside him. All that he knew was Kate—lying on their dock in the early evening, the waves of Lake Austin lapping at their desire. After so long apart, it seemed as if they were once again new lovers touching for the first time. But this time there was no urgency in their passion. That old magician time was weaving his spell to help them turn the minutes into hours, to show them that the hours could turn into days and weeks and years.

He could still feel the breeze that caressed them there that first night by the lake, could still taste the sweet salt of her skin and the sadness of her tears. Like a man dying of thirst, he drank her tears away, and when he had taken her sorrow inside himself, her need made him stronger, and made the two of them whole again.

Even in his depleted physical state, Michael was dimly aware of the growing sound of distant thunder. Smiling, he found himself inside his own life with one rain becoming all rains. In the same moment he was leaning against his grandfather, holding Kate in his arms on the shore of Lake Austin, crouching with his daughter in the boat, and holding hands with his grandmother in the nursing home.

It had been so long since that final day with Gramma Parker when the love in her heart briefly overcame the numbness in her brain brought on by Alzheimer's. Mistaking her sixteen-year-old grandson for a doctor, she was telling him about her aches and pains when she suddenly looked deeply into Michael's eyes.

"Do I know you?" she asked.

"You used to," Michael told her.

"Have you lost something?" she wanted to know.

"Some<u>one</u>," Michael corrected her. "I've lost someone, and I am looking for her."

"Someone you loved?" she asked coyly, smiling at him as if she were hearing the innermost secrets of a young man on the hunt for true romance.

"Yes," Michael told her. "Someone I love very much."

"Well, if you really love her, you'll see her again. There is no loss than cannot be redeemed by love."

After a moment, she looked out the window and sighed. "I wish it would rain."

Feeling someone shaking his shoulders, Michael looked up to his daughter.

"Dad! It's raining!" Hope sang out. "Open your mouth and taste it. Isn't it beautiful?"

The first drops fell upon them, splashing off the boat and their skin, taunting them with promise as they tilted back their heads and opened their parched mouths to catch large, sweet drops. Within minutes, the splattering had increased to a steady shower, reviving Michael's mind and body so he could help Hope stretch out the yellow emergency bag and begin funneling the rain into one of the empty water bottles, no easy task with the boat pitching on the swells.

"It's filling!" Hope said excitedly. "It's filling up!"

But then she looked closer and saw something was wrong.

"No!" she cried. "The water's yellow and gross!"

Michael glanced at the bottle, but kept his focus on holding the bag to catch as much rain as possible.

"Just fill it up, Kiddo. Then switch to another bottle. The gunk and salt are washing off the bag. Maybe the next one'll be cleaner."

Sure enough, the second and third bottles filled with clean, clear water. Sensing that the rain was likely to continue, Michael emptied the first bottle of its foul-smelling fluid and began to fill it again. Only after each of them had drunk to their satisfaction and all three bottles were full did they sit back in exhaustion and huddle together against the storm.

"We're gonna be okay!" Hope yelled above the pounding rain.

Michael was not so sure. The first burst of rain had knocked down the wind, helping to calm the ocean around them. But now the wind had picked up again and was driving the rain sideways against them in sheets. Hiding below the rails, Michael tried to shield Hope, both with the yellow bag and with his body, but as he glanced over the side, he did not like what he saw.

The swells rolling at them were twenty feet high, with the distance from crest to crest having grown to the length of a football field. Instead of a constant bobbing up and down, they were riding now in God's own theme park, climbing for fifteen or twenty seconds to the face of the wave, hanging there for one long moment, then racing down the back side, the force of their fall driving more water up into the air and into the open boat.

As the wind increased, the tops of the waves began to blow off, creating walls of water that slapped at the side of the panga in deafening cannon shots, jolting Michael and Hope with an unending succession of violent blows.

Michael could see how terrified Hope was, but there was little he could do except help to brace her against the next jarring shock. And with every wave the water gathering in the bottom of the boat grew deeper.

"We're gonna sink!" Hope yelled to her father. "We've got to bail!"

"No, it's okay," he told her. "The water in the boat pulls us down in the waves and keeps the wind from flipping us over."

"So what do we do?" she asked.

"We have to wait until it passes."

EIGHTEEN

Two hours after it began, the rain at Campo Buenavista slowed, then stopped. The cloud ceiling remained, however, at just two hundred feet, making it all but impossible to fly.

"Damn it!" Coop said as he ran into the dining room again, "I wish we could get a decent weather forecast!"

"What is it now?" Bill asked.

"Tropical storm warning—high winds and heavy rain."

Bill glanced out the window to a few brighter patches in the clouds. "Looks to me like it's moving on."

"That'd be my guess, too, but the boys in Mexico City say there's more coming."

"You believe 'em? I'd hate to go out in a lull and find out the real McCoy's not here yet."

"Who knows what to believe?" Coop said. "It's Mexico."

Kicking hard at a chair, he launched it across the room.

"Shit!" he yelled, limping on a hurt foot to the bar.

Agua mineral," he told Elvis, wanting a beer or a shot of tequila but knowing it was out of the question. Feeling a hand on his shoulder, he turned to find Kate standing close.

"Cooper," she asked, "what are we doing wrong?"

"Hell, I haven't done anything right," he answered. "Not yet, anyway."

"But we're going to find them, aren't we?"

Coop didn't know what to say. Like Michael, he didn't find it easy to lie, and he didn't know the truth.

"Yeah, I think we will."

"Not *think*," she corrected him. "We *will* find them. We have to."

Looking beneath the veneer of her controlled exterior, Coop could see that Kate needed all their strength to help her keep it together.

"We'll find them," he told her.

Elvis set another mineral water on the bar for her.

"You ever get homesick?" she asked Cooper.

"This *is* my home," he told her. "When I was growing up—the Colonel moved us all over the world. Every year or two he'd get transferred, then a month or two later my mom and I would pack up everything and get on an Air Force plane to someplace new."

"Did you hate it?"

"Shoot, no. I was Air Force, Air Force all the way. I loved the jets screaming over the base and climbing straight up into the stratosphere till their sonic boom was all they left behind. I wanted to be a jet jockey, and was counting the years till I could go to the Academy."

"And?"

"I think they called it the sixties. When the old man got home from 'Nam, I was sixteen and hearing bad things about the war. He told me to have a little faith in America and to get a haircut. And then he told me all those damn hippie protesters ought to be lined up and shot."

"Uh-oh!" Kate said.

"Yeah. That's when I told him he could go to hell."

"By the time he got back from his second tour in 'Nam, I'd moved out of the house and we didn't speak anymore. It was bad as it can get between a father and son. As far as he was concerned, I was dead."

"But you got back together anyway."

"We didn't talk for five years," Coop looked away at the agitated ocean. "Not even at Mom's funeral. Then one day the Colonel calls me up. Says, 'Hey, I'm retiring. Thinking of moving down to Baja and opening a fishing lodge.'"

"I thought he'd lost his mind."

"Then I heard the Colonel take a deep breath, like when he was mad or had to spit out some command. 'Don't think I can manage it on my own, though.' he said. 'You want to be my partner? It's a big step and you can think about it if you want.'

"I told him I didn't have to think about it. He was quiet for a bit, then he said, 'Yeah, sure, I understand.' And I said, 'No, you don't. I want to do it.'"

"And you've been here ever since?" Kate asked.

"Even with him gone, this is my home."

"He was a great man!" came a voice from behind them where Bill had listened to Coop's story. "War hero. Bullshitter! Best damn pilot I ever met!"

Holding his coffee cup aloft, Bill clinked it against Cooper's water glass.

"What do you think he'd say if he were here now?" Coop asked as looked out at the heavy weather

It didn't take Bill long to come up with an answer.

"Screw the storm. Let's go get 'em!"

"Yeah, I guess he would."

Bill stood up and reached for his raincoat. "No, I mean *screw the storm, let's go get 'em!*"

"What about the clouds?" Coop protested. "You won't be able to see."

Bill bent over to look up from the window to the solid gray cloud cover hanging so close over them that even the fisherman's steeple on the hill behind the hotel was obscured.

"We'll fly low."

As the wind and rain began to slacken, Michael peered over the side and saw the light starting to shine through the clouds to their south. Then he saw something else on the horizon, something coming toward them.

"Hope. Look over there. Do you see that?"

Hope raised her head and stared out across the misty water.

"I see it," she said. "It's another bird. Poor thing got caught in the storm."

Flying just above the waves, the bird came closer, a large pelican, brown and white with traces of yellow plumage on its head. Heading straight to the panga, the pelican pulled up fast and landed heavily on the bow.

"Hello, bird," Michael growled. "I wish we had some food for you to steal, but we don't."

For a moment he considered eating the pelican—an act thought by ancient mariners to be a bad omen and a summoner of ill fortune.

"The last thing we need," Michael laughed to himself, "is a run of bad luck."

Rocking back and forth with the movement of the boat, the pelican hardly seemed to notice the woeful castaways. Then, ever so slowly, Michael leaned forward and began to creep toward it.

"What are you doing?" Hope whispered.

Crossing over the center seat, Michael had already closed half the distance to the bird. Watching nervously, the pelican hopped forward onto the point of the bow. Still Michael edged closer.

"Dad..." said Hope. But before she could finish, Michael sprang forward. The pelican spread its huge wings to take flight, but Michael was already there, reaching wide to pin the bird's wings.

"No!!!" Hope screamed at her father. "Let him go! I don't want to eat him. I don't want to!"

Fighting for its life, the pelican opened its cavernous beak and snapped hard at Michael's hand. Michael jerked the hand back just in time, and the beak slammed shut with a loud and frightening whack. To complicate matters, Hope sprung forward and began pulling at her father's waist, trying to drag him off the bird. Michael turned back to her, and when he did the bird snapped at him again, biting hard this time on the tattered bandage of his forearm.

"Ow!" Michael cried, looking to the fresh blood shining on his arm.

Seeing her father bleeding again, Hope released her grasp on his waist and dove now for the pelican.

"I'll get you, bird!" she cried out. "Leave my dad alone!"

By now Michael had one arm wrapped around the pelican's body and one hand holding its head. With the battle over, Hope sat back, out of breath.

The big bird, nearly blinded with fear, was paralyzed by the arms of this monstrous man.

"Do we have to eat him?" Hope asked. "He's so beautiful!"

"We're not going to eat him. Get the water bottle—the one we've been drinking from."

"I got it. What do I do?"

"Open it and pour it out."

Hope looked at him like he'd lost his mind. "No," she said. "I can't do that."

"Drink it, then. Drink all of it."

Trusting that he had a plan, Hope opened the bottle and drank all of the rainwater inside it.

"Now open up the empty fuel tank and take out the medicine bottle with the message."

She did as he said, but still didn't understand.

"Reach into my pocket," he told her, unable to let go of the bird with even one hand "Get the pencil and change the position on our note. I want it to say '50 miles east of Loreto.'"

Hope wrote on the note and Michael told her to read it back.

"SOS!" she read. "50 miles east of Loreto. Contact Campo Buenavista."

"Now put it back in the medicine bottle and seal it up tight."

All this time he'd kept the pelican locked in his grip. Now he could feel the bird surrendering to its fate.

"Dad, we already sent out a message in the fuel tank. It didn't work."

"Yeah, 'cause someone had to find the tank and the ocean's too big to count on that. But a bird can find someone else the same way it found us. Now, get me the last piece of fishing line."

Hope turned back around with the piece of scrap line, then held the pelican's head with both hands while her father half-filled the empty water bottle with the brine water from the bottom of the boat. Hefting the bottle to test its weight, he poured a little of the water out, then dropped the medicine bottle with the message inside. Finally, he sealed the water bottle and tied it to the pelican's leg.

"How can he fly like that?" she asked.

"Not very well, I hope."

"You think he'll get to shore?"

"Maybe not."

"So he'll just land in the water?"

"I don't think so. The bottle's too heavy. If he lands in these waves, he won't be able to take off again, so maybe he'll find another boat and land on it to rest."

Summoning what little strength remained in his aching body, Michael lifted the bird into the air and the pelican extended his wings to their full six-foot span. Releasing his hold, Michael watched as the pelican soared away from the boat. Not expecting the weight of the bottle, the bird suddenly plunged almost to the surface before flapping its wings harder and finding some lift.

"Fly!" shouted Michael. "Fly, you beautiful bird!"

"Fly bird!" called Hope. "Fly away home!"

Together they watched the bird fly east, barely staying above the surface of the water until it disappeared beyond the horizon.

Sitting on the runway at Buenavista, Bill leaned forward to study the gusting winds as Kate surveyed the wet sand and crushed seashells on which they'd have to hit seventy miles per hour in order to take off.

"You ready?" Bill asked as he raced the motor.

As soon as she nodded, Bill released the brakes and the plane struggled to climb out of a wet patch and start to roll. With trips back to refuel, they'd already landed and taken off half a dozen times from this strip, but every time Kate had managed to distract herself by thinking of Hope. But now the wet runway conquered her remaining bit of calm. Even when she'd flown here in years past with Michael, she'd hated this runway. For starters, it was not flat. From just above the hotel, the runway ran for two thousand feet at an alarming climb alongside a dry river wash. Only now that wash was surging with floodwaters coming down from the mountains. Ordinarily you took off and landed facing up the slope of the hill. But this time Bill had decided to take off into the winds that were blowing strong off the beach. Now as they came tearing down the muddy runway, splashing in puddles that filled the low places, Kate looked to the rushing flood in the wash that ran beside them. Even as they gained speed, they didn't seem to be going faster than the flood, which created the sensation that everything was standing still. Ahead of them, the ocean grew larger and larger. With her grip tightening on the armrests, Kate's knuckles turn white. Then Bill pulled back hard on the wheel, and the plane bounced into the air, dropped precipitously for one sickening moment, then began to climb.

At the beach, Bill banked to the north and jostled through rough air into the wispy trails at the bottom of the clouds. Below them, the little town of Buenavista passed in and out of view.

"The storm's turning off to the east," Bill said as he studied the wind patterns on the waves. "I figure we'll trail up the lee side of the weather and move farther out over the water as it clears."

Just then the plane hit an air pocket and bounced roughly as it dropped. Bill pulled it back up and looked to Kate, who seemed to have stopped breathing.

"Take the wheel," he told her. "I want to double-check the instruments."

Tentatively, Kate put her feet on the pedals and her hands on the copilot's yoke, all of which she'd done her best to ignore for three straight days.

"You got it?" he asked, his voice nonchalant as if she were steadying the steering wheel of a car while he glanced at a map.

"I got it," she told him. "It's not the kind of thing you forget."

"Yeah, I bet you thought you were all through with flying?"

"That was my intention."

"Well, it's funny the cards life deals you sometimes."

For two years, he'd been waiting to ask her something, something he now needed to know.

"Kate, you flew with Michael for years, no problem, you landed a dozen times with him sitting beside you. So why did you freeze that day?"

As she considered the answer, Kate checked her instruments, scanning the panel to reassure herself that all was well. The feel of the airplane was coming back to her.

"One day, Michael had me land the plane. Then he got out and said, 'You're ready.'"

"Just like I did with him," Bill said, remembering how he'd sent Michael up on the flight no pilot ever forgets—his first solo.

"But I wasn't ready. I took off and it all looked the same—the airport, the runway, the tower. But one thing was different."

"You were scared?"

"Terrified. I needed Michael, but he wasn't there."

A strong gust of wind sent the tail skidding to one side. Bill was ready to grab his yoke, but Kate muscled the plane back on track.

"But you knew you had to land anyway," Bill said. "Even without him."

"I came in too fast and Michael yelled on the radio for me to go around, but it was all a blur. I ballooned the landing, and when the wheels hit the second time, I started braking, but couldn't remember how to steer and went off the runway into a ditch. The next thing I knew, Michael was pulling me out of the water."

"I'm not surprised you didn't want to fly again. Nothing like an accident to remind us we're not immortal."

"Yeah. And it wasn't just me. A week later I found out I was pregnant."

"So, Daughter," he said, his voice so soft that she took her eyes off the water to look at him. "Do you blame that accident?"

"What do you mean, do I blame flying for losing my baby?"

"No. Do you blame Michael?"

It was a question she'd kept buried for two years. She'd been bounced violently during that botched landing, and her unborn baby had been as well.

"After we lost Jamie, Michael kept saying it wasn't my fault. So whose fault was it?"

"No one's," Bill said. "It just *was*."

"Take the wheel," she said. "I hate flying."

As she relaxed her arms, Kate's gaze turned to the water below, where a pod of pilot whales were also moving north in the lee of the storm.

"Listen," Bill told her. "What do you hear?"

"The plane," she said automatically.

"No, listen!" he told her, holding up his hand to grab her attention. "What do you hear?"

Now she began to concentrate.

"I hear the engine," she tells him, "and the propeller."

"What else?"

They flew on, the whales receding in the distance behind them as Kate relaxed into the sounds around them.

"I hear the wind on the wings. And some noise from the tail that's been there all along. What do you hear?"

"I hear Michael," Bill told her. "No, I'm not crazy. I don't hear him calling to us or anything like that. But I still hear him. Listen to your heart Kate; his voice is still there. You thought he got over losing your baby too soon, but the truth is he'll never get over it. But he tried to put his loss aside because he was afraid of losing you, too."

"Mike and I went flying last year, a few months after you lost the baby. I got the idea he wanted to talk, and up here is where we've done our best thinking. But all he said was, 'Why? Why did it have to happen?'"

"What did you tell him?"

"I told him I didn't know. I still don't. Some things can never be known. Otherwise, there's no point to life."

After a moment, Kate reached into her bag and pulled out something to show Bill.

"You know what this is? It's Hope's diary. We're not supposed to read it, but I found something in here that I want you to see."

Opening to the first page, Kate held out the book for him.

"It's a map of the places she's been with Michael: Hill Country rivers, the Monarch butterfly reserves in Michoacán, the Sea of Cortez. It's all there."

"Does it say where they are now?"

"They're on here somewhere. They have to be."

The clouds were continuing to move off to the east, and just ahead was the eastern tip of a desolate island of rock. As they crossed over the barren shore, Bill and Kate looked down at the barren scrub that covered the little mountain in the sea, and at the tiny strip of sandy beach that separated the harsh land from the rich sea.

"Isla del Espiritu Santo," Bill told her. "The Island of the Holy Saint."

"You'd have to be a holy saint to want to live down there."

"And yet," said Bill, "some man came to that place, running away from something, or searching for something else. Either way, he was on a quest to understand the same things we want to know. *Who am I? Why am I here? Where am I going?* We all search for that hidden secret that can flood our souls with light."

"You're talking about miracles," she said as Bill banked into a right-hand turn and set the first track of their new search pattern.

"Life is a miracle, Kate. Look at me. Who'd have thought I'd still be around? I don't know why you lost your baby, and I'm not sure the *why* matters anymore. It just *is.*"

This time she nodded her head in agreement.

"When things that don't matter fall away, we're left with essentials. Maybe the point of Mike's life is just to get Hope through this thing. Maybe all three of us were put on this earth to help Hope along her way. That wouldn't be so bad. If you lived your whole life just so you'd be there that one moment when you were needed, wouldn't that be worth it?"

Kate suddenly knew again what she had known all along, the one undeniable fact that could never be unwritten.

"I love them both so much," she blurted out, her voice choking with emotion. The most important thing in the world is for me to tell them both that I love them."

"You'll tell them," he said. "I swear it on the Holy Saint."

Unfastening her belt, Kate leaned over and kissed him on the cheek.

"Bill Frazier, you beautiful old man. It'd be worth it to live your whole life just to hear you think."

"Thinking's about all I got left," he told her. "I got to make the most of it."

NINETEEN

What little strength Michael had hung on to through three days at sea now seemed to have been exhausted during a battle with a bird. Slumping down after the pelican disappeared over the horizon, Michael moved his chest in and out in shallow breaths as Hope braced against the swells and tipped tiny sips of water into his mouth, the same care he'd given to her the day before.

Was this how Josh had felt in the hospital in Kerrville? Michael wondered. *I did the best I could, but Hope is too young for this. Twelve years... I wish I had them all over again, all my years with Hope... and Kate, too.*

And then he was standing on the dock at Lake Austin with the Reverend Wild Bill Frazier, a five-dollar minister ordained by a mail-order church. Walking toward them, Kate was nine months pregnant and proudly dressed in white.

"You look..." Michael said, pausing to find the right words to describe her radiant beauty.

"Like a great white whale," Kate concluded.

After their vows, Michael's songwriter pal Fromholz sang for them.

I'd have to be crazy
plum out of my mind
To fall out of love with you.

Two days later, Kate gave birth to a beautiful baby girl, and through her joy and pain, curses and prayers, tears and laughter, she'd come to some new understanding.

"We're connected," Michael told his wife that night. "To those who came before and to those who will follow."

Hearing him mumbling beside her, Hope brushed the hair from his forehead. "Try to rest," she told him.

I hear her voice, almost grown, he thought. How can that be when she's just a baby, her eyes falling closed for the first time as she sleeps in my arms? When she's just starting to walk, when she still listens to my stories.

"The King of Cats," he'd told her, "saw that there wasn't enough food for so many cats in such a small kingdom, so he sent them all across the world, where they found new homes in the houses of people." She loved that story, hearing how the scraggly cat they'd adopted from the wild had come to live with them. And 'The Rattlesnake with No Rattle,' who stole the rattle from a baby's crib to make rattlesnake sounds to keep people from stepping on him. Kate wrote those stories down, drew the cats in their kingdom and the guileless snake in the crib, and sold them as a children's book to a publisher in New York. Who told those stories to me, he wondered. Where do any stories come from?

And then Hope was four. "At night," she whispered, "horses spread their hidden wings and fly off to the stars. It's a secret; don't tell anyone!"

In the boat he smiled. He'd never told a soul.

"I am Nature Girl!" she declared one day.

"What are you going to do with it all?" he asked his little collector of leaves, bugs, reptiles, and fossils. "Look," she said, bending to pick up a perfect arrowhead from the ground where it had lain undetected for a thousand years. "She's right," he thought. "The world Hope lives in is full of magic."

Drifting across the Sea of Cortez, the little girl is replaced by a bigger one: a girl who loves to shoot hoops with her father and to paint with her mom; a girl who swims long laps at Barton Springs as if she were born to the water; a girl who breaks her arm falling out of a tree, then climbs the same tree with the arm in a cast. A girl who loves to read and write, and who listens to a good story the way a starving man tastes food. Sometimes Michael could not quit talking about her.

"You do not suffer from a lack of pride," Bill had told him.

Beside her father, Hope had ceased trying to understand the whisperings of his heart. He'd moved on to another place, and fear was on her face. Seeing her dad shivering in the cool breeze, Hope pulled the waterproof bag up over him. Despite the rainwater they'd both drunk, she didn't think her father had much time.

"Dad," she said softly. "Can you hear me?"

"Hope, you're so far away," he tried to say.

"Don't go away, Dad," she told him. "I can't grow up without you."

Her voice brought him back to her, but his was hard to find.

"Don't grow up, " he mumbled. "It's a trap."

Hearing his joke brought a smile to her cracked lips. "You and Mom were the best adults ever," she told him.

"We did pretty good. And then we lost Jamie and we got lost, too."

"I should have been a boy," Hope told him. "If I'd been a boy, everything would have been different."

Finding his hands, he reached up to touch her face.

"Don't think that. I wouldn't have one thing about you different."

Even as he denied it, it all came clear to him. He'd told Hope how great it was going to be to have a baby brother, and she'd ended up feeling she wasn't good enough for him. It was only after Hope was born that he'd really begun to want a son. One good kid inspires another. And there was the name, of course, the lineage of Parkers and knowing that Josh would have wanted the name to carry on.

The goodness and strength that had been passed from one

generation to the next would carry through to Hope, of course. Michael had always reacted in the worst way to bad times. After Josh died, he'd gone to the bullfights on a fool's errand. He'd pled guilty to a crime he hadn't committed. He and Kate had lost a baby and he'd locked that pain inside of him. What did he want, for the world to feel sorry for him?

Turning his face away, Michael stared at the whitecaps slipping off the tops of the waves. Then he looked back to his daughter.

"Do you know how much I love you?" he asked.

A smile came to her face. "This much?" she asked, stretching her arms as wide as they could reach according to the rules of childhood.

"More than that."

"As big as this boat?" she asked.

"Bigger."

"Big as the ocean?"

He shook his head slowly.

"As big as all creation?" she asked without getting a reply. "I don't get it, Dad. What else is there?"

"I love you, Hope, as big as I love your mom."

A radiant smile spread across her sunburned face.

"Both of us?"

"More than you can ever know."

"We love you, too, Dad," she told him softly, but Michael gave no indication of having heard. Dropping his head on his daughter's shoulder, he closed his eyes and drifted back into sleep with Gramma Parker and Josh taking their turns in giving him comfort.

And then Kate was with him, stroking his forehead as gently as Hope had done only moments before.

"Be strong, Kate. Be strong for Hope," he tried to say. And then he sank further into Kate's arms, trusting she would keep him afloat a while longer, knowing their story was not yet done.

"Just think," Bill told Kate. "This time tomorrow we'll all be finishing a big lunch at Coop's place—you, me, Hope, and Michael."

They were cutting their third track across the new search grid, and it was dawning on Kate that once again they had a lot of ocean to cover.

"What makes you so sure?" she asked.

Opening a storage compartment next to his seat, Bill took out an old leather flying cap and tossed it to Kate.

"Take a look at that."

Kate ran her hands over the dried, crinkled leather.

"How old is it?"

"Forty years. It belonged to Michael's father, Lieutenant Marvin Parker. It was his good-luck charm. He wore it every flight—from training school all the way to Korea. Right from the beginning, Josh blamed me for his son learning to fly, for joining the Air Force, for going to Korea. But old Marv was the gutsiest sumbitch I ever saw. He never followed nobody nowhere, and I thought it was an honor just to be in his shadow."

"So what happened to him?"

"We were flying off the Essex, the 'Fightin'est Ship in the Fleet.' Four or five missions a week, taking off in rough seas with your stomach already in your throat, anti-aircraft fire over the targets, Russian MiG fighters trying to pick you off on the way back. I was scared every minute of every day. But Parker kept me going. Then one day I woke up sick as a dog, fever all over me. I couldn't fly, so he took my slot."

"And he didn't come back?"

"Yeah, but it's worse than that. He had a premonition. Before he left, he asked me to hold onto that helmet for him. If anything went wrong, I was supposed to take it back to Texas, give it to his kid, and tell Michael how much his father loved him. Hell, that was all he could talk about the whole damn time we were in Korea—how much he loved that kid."

"You never told Michael?"

"That's what I was doing when I flew to the ranch to meet him.

I gave Michael the helmet, but I was afraid to tell him the truth, afraid that he'd blame me as his grandfather had. I chickened out, just like I have a thousand times since."

"Wait a minute. You came back with every decoration for bravery, but you call yourself a coward?"

"Yeah, I got a whole box of medals. Every one of 'em was because of something that happened after Parker died. I wasn't being heroic; I was suicidal. I had to bail out twice into freezing waters. Both times I thought I'd just sink right down to the bottom of the ocean, maybe have a peek around for Parker while I was there. But when I went under, my fear was greater than my death wish and I always fought my way back to safety. And I had that helmet with me every time. Maybe that's what kept me going. Knowing I had an unfinished job to do. "

"After his grandfather died, Michael walked into my hangar in Kerrville. He was the last living descendant of the finest family I ever knew. He marched over, tossed that helmet in my lap, and said, 'you owe me a flying lesson, not a thrill ride and a worn-out hat.' "

"So you taught him how to fly."

"And he taught me how to live again. For the last twenty-five years, I've carried this damn helmet on every flight I've made. Every flight... except for the fire."

Looking to him, Kate saw that his face was averted to the water below his window.

"I was so mad at him for breaking his word that I didn't take it with me. So listen and listen good. I'm gonna give him that damn helmet and tell him that his father loved him. And then I'm gonna tell him how much he's meant to me, how he's kept me going all these years. Do you think an old man like me can do that?"

Kate looked at Bill and somehow knew that it was true, knew that they would find Michael and Hope.

"Yes," she said. "I know you will."

"Me, too," said Bill. "Me, too."

They flew on awhile in silence, both searching the water below until the radio grabbed their attention.

"Hope Two, this is Hope One. You read me?"

Bill reached for his microphone. "Cooper, you got Hope Two here. What's up?"

"You're not gonna believe it."

"Try me: I'm gullible."

"A fishing trawler named *Anna Maria* just called on the ship-to-shore."

"They see something?" Bill asked.

"Right at the tail end of the storm, a pelican landed on her."

"A pelican landed on a fishing boat," said Bill. "Why am I not surprised?"

"There's more. The pelican was so tired he could barely move, and there was a bottle tied to his leg."

"Say again, Coop. Sounded like you said a bottle."

"Roger that. A bottle, half filled with seawater."

Perhaps for the first time since the fire, Bill felt goose bumps rush across his scarred skin.

"That's our Mike!" he said. "Always thinking! Lemme guess—was there a note inside this bottle?"

"Bingo!"

"God-damn yes!!" Bill shouted. "We got 'em!!"

He looked to Kate, whose hands over her face could not hold back the tears.

"Now shut up and listen!" Coop ordered. "The note says: 'SOS—50 miles east of Loreto.' Repeat: 50 miles east of Loreto."

Bill keyed the mike. "Roger that: fifty miles east. But he's just guessing, right?"

"It's gotta be dead reckoning."

With Kate showing him their position on the map, Bill banked the plane.

"Coop, that's not gonna narrow it down much. What's the position of the trawler?"

Coop gave him the coordinates.

"We're on our way. In the meantime, find out how far a pelican can fly with a weight on its leg."

"How do I do that?"

"Ask Gilberto's marine scientists. They ought to be able to figure it out. Tell them it's not every day they get to save a little girl's life."

"Okay. Keep your ears on."

Signing off, Bill turned to Kate, who'd said not a word during the only good news they'd had in days.

"Did you hear that, Daughter? They're okay."

Already she had the binoculars up and was intently studying the sea to their north.

"How much fuel do we have?" she asked.

"Couple of hours."

"How long till dark?"

Bill checked his watch, then glanced at the sun shining through the clouds to his left. "About the same."

"Is it enough?"

"Yeah," he told her. "It has to be."

TWENTY

"If you look long enough, the pieces all fit."

Josh had told him that all those years ago. For three days they'd been building a stone wall from a big pile of rock they'd gathered. But the closer the wall came to completion, the more Josh sorted through the remaining pile of loose rocks in search of that one perfect rock for the next spot.

"Why don't we just chip one down to size the way the Mexicans do it?" Michael asked the old man.

"'Cause we don't need to," Josh told him. "If you look long enough, the pieces all fit."

For the first time, Michael now understood what his grandfather had meant.

Still trying to support her father, Hope studied his face. Despite his sunburn, his skin seemed to have lost all its color and he was white as a ghost.

Feeling her gentle touch, he reached down deep inside and found some hidden reserve of strength.

"You'd make a good doctor," he managed to say.

Relieved to hear his voice, Hope wanted to keep him alert.

"No way, Dad. Too much school to be a doctor."

"Okay, he told her. "All I want is for you to be happy. What you want in life is up to you."

"But how do I know what I want?"

With so many stories from Michael's past, they'd never really talked much about the future. Now Hope was no longer tending to her father. Instead she dropped the cloth and bowed her head slightly as if to listen more closely, to hold onto and never forget her father's words. Michael saw this change in her and he knew this was too much, too fast, but he also knew that time was shorter than she realized and there was much to say.

"I don't know, Hope. Life is a little like our time on this boat, not hard like this, but it's still a journey without maps. There's no chart that tells you where to go—just the compass of your heart."

Michael paused to let his thoughts catch up with his words. When he started to speak again, his voice was failing and Hope held the water bottle to his lips. After he took a sip, he spoke again

"There's one task that stands above all others."

"What is it?" she asked.

"To find love. To search it out; to give it and earn it with all your heart."

"But I love you, Daddy! And I love Mom."

"There'll come a time when you'll find another love. To see it, you have to love who you are, too. Then you can give yourself to it—heart and soul."

Hope was staring at her father's lips now as if that would help her gain more meaning from his words.

"But Dad, how will I know? At school they teach us everything about sex and nothing about love."

"That's why they call it sex education. You want to know what they taught us about sex in Junction?"

"Not really."

"That sex is the dirtiest, most dangerous and disgusting thing on the face of the earth, so we should save it for someone we love."

"Dad!"

"Yeah, they got us a little confused. I kept trying to lose my virginity, but it just kept following me around."

"It's not funny," she told him. "It's scary!"

"Hope," he said more seriously, "there's one person on earth for whom your choices mean the most. Not me. Not Mom."

"Who?"

"You."

Now Michael lay his head over to one side and looked out at the afternoon sky, the trailing edge of the clouds moving away, the sun behind them, a shrouded ember falling toward the horizon.

"Love is a mystery, Hope. It can never be anticipated. You can't know. You can only listen to your heart and trust what it says to you. Only one thing went wrong between your mom and me—we stopped listening. So I want you to tell her for me that the trust came back. Okay?"

"Daddy," she pleaded. "Don't talk that way. I hate it when you talk like you're going to die."

Lying silent for a time, Michael felt he had crossed a bridge that could not be re-crossed. His legs were a million miles away, his feet dragging the bottom of the ocean, his head lost in the stars. The only way was to press on.

"Sweetheart, your pop doesn't feel so great, so you just have to let me speak my mind. If I feel better when they find us, I'll take it all back and we can laugh at how silly I was."

The word wasn't easy to say, but Hope managed a small, "Okay." Then softly but surely, tears began to run down her cheeks and splash onto the crook of her father's arm.

Michael looked back to the sky, streaked in blue and red, the kind of sight he would have thought so beautiful just a few days before.

"You won't be alone," he told her. "You and Mom will find a way to carry on together. She's going to need you. In many ways, you're stronger than she is, so it'll be up to you to look her in the eye and tell her that everything is going to be all right. Think you can say that? Everything's gonna be all right."

Michael held her away a bit so that he could see her, so he would know that she could say it.

Hope wiped away her tears, attempted a little laugh, and then she said it: "Everything's gonna be all right."

"That wasn't bad. If you need something to pass the time, you practice that for when you see her."

As his eyes fell closed, Michael managed one last thought. "I love you, Hope."

Suddenly Hope was seized with regret. How many times had she withheld those words?

"I love you too, Dad."

She wasn't sure if he'd heard her, but as he slept in her arms, she thought she felt him respond with a gentle squeeze of his hand.

"Come in Hope Two, this is Hope One," squawked the radio.

Bill keyed the mike that was still in his hand.

"Coop, whadaya got for me?"

"I talked to the scientists. They say with a weight around its leg, he could fly maybe twenty miles."

"Twenty miles! Hell, that's a thousand square miles of ocean. What good is that?"

"Twenty miles," answered Coop. "Unless the bird was tired already."

"Like after a storm."

"Exactly. Then maybe five miles or less."

"Now you're talking."

"Bill," Kate interrupted. "I see it. Dead ahead."

Bill squinted out at the horizon and zeroed in on the squat outline of the fishing trawler, plowing through heavy seas.

"Anna Maria," Bill called into his mike as he swooped over the boat. "This is Beech 1201, searching for a lost panga. Do you read us?"

There was a long pause, then the radio squawked back with a crackle of feedback, and a voice from out of the blue.

"Hola, Gringo! You lose someone?"

"Looking for a panga, Capitán. Have you seen them?"

"No, Señor. Just the bird."

"Did you see which way the bird came from?"

"Wait. I ask my crew."

Bill made a big loop and circled back toward the trawler. After a minute the captain came back on the air.

"Amigo. My mate is on a very steady watch for twelve hours now. And he says he sees the bird. Sees it coming from a long ways off."

"Which way?"

"From the west: 275 degrees."

"Can you come about and help us with a rescue?"

"*Lo siento, no.* We have damage from the storm and bilge pumps running."

Bill took a moment to consider the importance of not just finding them but having a rescue boat on scene.

"Señor, there is a little girl on the panga—twelve years old."

"You can do it!" Kate whispered softly, trying to convince him by the unknowable mystery of a mother desperate to protect her loved ones. "You can do it!"

When he spoke, the captain sounded tired and resigned.

"I am only the captain," he said. "The owner in Mazatlán orders me to port. *I am sorry.*"

"I understand," Bill told him. "Keep your radio on."

"Of course. Happy hunting, Señor."

Bill turned to Kate. "Just a few miles," he told her. "We're almost there."

For half an hour, Michael had been shivering in his sleep, at first with little tremors that ran up and down his body, and then with increasingly violent shakes. Hope had tried to hold her father still, first his legs and then his arms. Finally she stretched all four feet eleven inches of her body atop him and hugged him tightly. Whether it was from the strength of her muscles or the warmth of her body, she did not know, but at last his tremors diminished and then stopped completely.

For a time Michael knew that she was there with him, but he

was tired and somehow couldn't remember how to open his eyes or find the right muscles to speak. And still his mind played tricks on him: taking him to the ranch, to the shores of Half Moon Caye, or to Kate's loving arms. There had been the ghost ship, the real ship, and now he heard something else, a distant droning like a bee. No, something louder, a sound he knew. It was Wild Bill, flying his old biplane down the valley of the South Llano. Beneath Michael, Blue skittered as they searched for some escape. "Easy," he whispered. "Easy."

"That's good," Hope told him. "Easy."

And then she heard it, too. "It's them!" Hope shouted, jumping to her feet and grabbing the aluminum case they'd been polishing for three days. Holding it above her head, she tried to catch some ray of the low-lying sun, but saw that it was partially obscured by the clouds. The plane was visible now, just beneath the clouds way off to the south, and passing by without turning toward them.

If they don't see us, Hope realized, they won't get back before dark.

"What do I do?" she cried. "What do I do?" But her father could not hear her.

She was about to drop the mirror and begin waving the yellow bag when the sun dropped below the broken clouds. Resplendent in golden light, she tilted the mirror left and right, unable to see where the reflection was flashing.

"Please!!" she cried. "Please look!"

In the plane, Bill and Kate were growing glum. Their fuel was already too low to make it back to Buenavista, and they were pushing their luck on La Paz.

"I've plotted a course for Loreto," Bill told Kate. "Hope and Mike have water now, so they should be okay till morning."

"Just one more pass," Kate pleaded. And then she saw it.

"There!"

Her hand shot up and pointed to the north.

"There on the water—I saw something! I saw a light!"

Bill turned to look and the light flashed again.

"There!" Kate yelled again. "Did you see it?"

After the fire, the doctors told him he would never cry again. Now he proved them wrong.

"I saw it," he said, his voice choking with emotion. "Bright before me!"

Hope had almost given up when the plane started to bank toward the panga. She could see them coming now, growing larger as they approached—the buzz of the engine growing louder as the plane dove, rushing toward them with all good speed. Two hundred feet above the surface, the plane roared over the panga and Bill rolled his wings from side to side in greeting. As the plane tipped right, mother and daughter saw each other—their eyes meeting for one exhilarating and desperate moment—and then they were moving apart.

"Mom! Mom!" shouted Hope, jumping and waving with abandon. "We're down here! You found us!"

As the plane moved away and began to circle back, Hope knelt by her father.

"Daddy, wake up! It's Mom!"

Just as they came over the second time, Michael opened his eyes and saw Bill's plane.

"Hope is going to be okay," he thought. And then his eyes fell shut.

When they'd made the second pass, Kate looked to Bill with a look of panic. "Hope's waving," she said, "but Michael's not getting up!"

"Open your window," Bill said as he climbed for more altitude. "When I say 'now,' throw out the emergency kit."

From the backseat, Kate grabbed the waterproof bag and the float attached to it. Opening the bag, she began to inspect its contents.

"It's all there," Bill assured her. "I've checked it a dozen times:

insulin, syringes, glucogen, juice, water, food, first aid, flares. Here it comes. Get ready!"

Kate closed the bag again and opened the little window. The wet salt air blasted in on her at 170 miles per hour.

"Ready," said Bill. "One. Two. Now!"

In the boat, Hope saw the package drop, a small chute unfurling behind it. It was falling straight toward the boat, but then she watched in horror as the wind snatched the package and stole it away.

"No!" she shouted. "Come back! Over here!"

The kit landed with a splash about two hundred yards from the boat. Hoped looked from her father—still asleep —to the rough water that trailed after the storm.

"I'm too tired," she cried to no one. "I can't make it."

"Christ! We missed!" said Kate. "It's not close enough."

Bill moved back into a steep climb, snatching at the radio mike as they were pushed back into their seats.

"Hope One! Hope One! Come in, Buenavista. We need you."

"I got you, Bill," Coop barked back over the radio. "Tell me something good."

"We found 'em."

"Yeah! Yeah!! Come on, give me a position."

Bill took the map from Kate and read the coordinates twice to Coop, who repeated them, then repeated them again.

"Listen up, Coop. Michael's down and it's getting dark. The chute missed, so I need you to contact the Mexican Coast Guard in La Paz and Loreto. We need a boat out here, and I mean <u>now</u>!"

"Bill," replied Coop, "That's gonna take some time. The crews don't live on board."

"Then radio the captain of that fishing boat, *Anna Maria.* Tell him I want to know who the captain is, him or some *pinche* owner in a big mansion?"

"What else?"

"Tell him there's a beacon on the boat."

There was a pause on the other end.

"A transponder? How you gonna do that?"

Bill set the mike down and looked to Kate.

"Take the wheel."

Not giving her any choice but to obey, Bill unfastened his belts and moved to the rear seats. Opening a duffel on the seat, he took out a second emergency kit, then cut the line to its float.

Flying the plane in buffeting winds, Kate couldn't turn to look at him.

"What are you doing?" she called over her shoulder.

From the duffel, Bill removed an emergency transponder and turned on the power switch.

"Bill, we don't need heroics here. We need a plan!"

Looking back at him, she inadvertently tipped the plane and sent Bill tumbling against the sidewall.

"Hold it level," he told her. "And contact Loreto. The frequency is on the com card. See it?"

"Yeah, but..."

"Give 'em our position and ask if they see us on radar."

Kate did nothing.

"Right now," he told her. "They'll speak English."

While Kate flipped the radio to the frequency and made contact with Loreto, Bill reached to the back storage compartment and pulled out a parachute. Slipping into the harness, he opened up the belly pack that held the backup chute and spilled the yards of silk onto the floor of the plane. Taking out his knife, he slashed at the tangle of shroud lines and cut the second chute free. Then he began to load the empty belly pack with the contents of the emergency kit: water, food, insulin, the transponder, and a flare gun.

"Did you get them?" he yelled to Kate.

"Yeah. Bearing 285," she replied. Then she saw him wearing the chute.

"No!" she yelled. "Absolutely not! Not you. Me! It's my family and I jump!"

"It's my family, too," he told her. "And you never jumped out of a plane in your life."

"Bill, you're seventy years old!"

"Seventy-two," he corrected as he knelt at her side. "Kate, it's windy. Even if your chute didn't get fouled in the air, you'd land a half a mile from the boat."

"Bill..."

"You'd be in rough seas with two hundred shroud lines trying to wrap you up. You won't get to them. There's only one way and that's to land close. That means an experienced jumper. Hell, I can probably land *in* the boat."

She turned her head to look him in the eye.

"I can't land the plane," she said. "I can't do it."

"Hell's bells, Kate! Of course you can. It's the same as before, but this time you'll be alone, no one else to worry about, no tiny baby inside you; nothing to do but set her down easy the way Michael taught you."

Reaching to the storage compartment, Bill took out the leather flying helmet and put it on.

"You really think I can do it?"

"I know you can. But first you've got to get rid of me. Climb to three thousand feet, east to west, then throttle back to 4,000 rpm's. I'll be in the door. After I'm clear, set a course for Loreto. Declare an emergency. Tell 'em to clear the runway. It's a big airport with lights. You can't miss it."

He turned to go, but she grabbed his arm, pulled him down and kissed him on the lips.

"You just can't help it, can you?" she told him. "You always have to be the hero."

The boat was just ahead as Bill opened the door.

"Bright before me," he said. "Bright before me."

"Bill, wait!" she called. "Tell Michael..."

But he was already gone. At the door, his shoes marked the spot from which he'd jumped.

He was free—free of everything. The air rushed past him as he plummeted, his hands fumbling for the handle of the ripcord tangled in his jury-rigged belly pack. At the same time he was trying to judge the wind and his altitude, wanting to drop straight on the boat as long as possible before pulling the chute and opening himself to the wind.

When was the last time he'd jumped? Thirteen years ago, to celebrate after his final reconstructive surgery. He had been baptized by fire. And now would come the water.

At a thousand feet he wrapped both of his heavy scarred hands around the handle and yanked away from his body. The chute fluttered out above him, marking his descent with a white ribbon against the fading sky. Then the canopy popped open and jerked at his body like a puppeteer.

He was only disoriented for an instant, then he found the boat below him. Pulling on the riser toggles, he did his best to turn toward Hope and Michael. With fifty pounds of emergency gear, he saw the ocean rushing to him, and the fear crawled out from his stomach to every inch of his body till he thought he would throw up.

At fifty feet the surface winds slammed against him, tipping his chute and shoving him further from the boat. He could see Hope there, just thirty yards away, standing in the boat, waving at him. And then the fear was gone as his mind flashed back to his plunge into the freezing waters off Korea.

If I had sunk to the bottom like I intended, he thought, everything would have been different. But now he was finally sure that he wanted everything to be as it had been.

The shock of hitting the water rattled every muscle and bone. Plunging through the glass ceiling, he continued to fall into the darkness below. He had filled his lungs with air to bring him up sooner, but the chute and packs still dragged him down.

Up, not down, he thought. Must be lighter. Lose the chute and hold the belly pack. Everything depends on that.

He tore at the releases on the main chute, opening one and then the other, and then he began to claw at the ocean above him. Instead of water, he found cords, a giant octopus of parachute lines that wrapped around his arms and neck, an endless web of sunken sail enveloping him in a terrifying shroud of the deep. He kicked his feet and the movement only tightened the lines around his throat. It was not possible to scream, only to kick harder and hold the remaining air in his scarred lungs.

Clawing now at his face, he pulled the silken shroud away and saw light above him. Two more kicks of his legs and he came into that light, breaking the surface and rising up into the sweet salt air, gasping for breath. A heavy swell passed over his head. He choked on the seawater and coughed it out. Then he saw the boat and began to kick free of the lines.

Hope called to him. "Uncle Bill! We're over here! Swim!" Her voice sounded thin and far away.

Bill kicked for the boat but the weight of his clothes and the belly pack seemed to anchor him to the bottom of the ocean. Thirteen years since he'd jumped, but how long since he had swum? He had no idea, but Hope was there in front of him, twelve years old, the same age as little Oida Dawson who rewarded him with a kiss after he pulled her from the river. But now he swam for more than a kiss. Now he swam for Hope's life, for Michael's, and for his own. Slowly he began to close the distance.

"You can do it!" Hope shouted. "Come on!"

He kicked harder, but a swell crested over him and pushed him back. He'd come so far and gotten so close, but God, he'd never been so tired. With his arms flailing against the water, he realized he wouldn't make it.

Then he felt something against his arm, and his hand closed around the rope that Hope had thrown to him. She tied the other end to a cleat at the back of the boat, and then she began to pull, using all her weight and the power of her legs and arms the way she had with the marlin to drag her rescuer toward her, and toward her father, who lay motionless in the bow.

When Bill came alongside, Hope grasped his wrist and raised his arm till he was clinging to the gunwale of boat.

"You have to climb in," she said. "I can't pull you up."

For a long moment he hung there, clinging to the safety of the boat, saying nothing, happy only to bring the air in and out of his lungs. With an effort he flung the other hand upward. The heavy pack came out of the water, tumbled over the rail and fell into the boat.

"Help your father," he told her. "Then you can help me."

TURK PIPKIN

TWENTY-ONE

Alone in the plane, Kate knew it was important to hold her course, conserve her fuel and make all haste for Loreto. She was an unqualified pilot and any unnecessary maneuvers might lose both her life and Bill's plane. But somewhere behind her, Bill was falling out of the sky, falling toward Hope and Michael, and there was only one way to know if he made it to the boat.

Banking left in a wide circle, she pushed the throttle forward and began to dive toward the water. The panga was barely visible on the surface but Bill was nowhere in sight in the air above the boat. God, she thought, had his chute failed to open? Coming over the boat, she saw Bill struggling in the water. Hope was throwing something to him, and then Kate was past, climbing and banking to turn.

On the second pass, Bill was at the side of the boat. Hope was holding tightly to him, but Kate thought she saw Bill raise one arm to her, waving her to the west.

Even together, with all their strength, Hope and Bill could not drag his body out of the water into the boat.

"Take the rope," he told her, "and tie a loop in the end."

When the loop was done, just big enough for a foot, she tied another loop above it, and another above that. The other end of the rope she made fast to the cleat on the opposite side of the boat.

Then she hung her improvised ladder over the side.

"Hurry," she told him. "I can't wake Dad."

Putting his bare feet into the loops of the rope, Bill climbed one loop at a time to the rail, then heaved himself into the boat. Moving to Michael, Bill placed a hand on his cold forehead.

"Mike," he called, patting his cheek. "Mike! Wake up! They're coming for us, but you have to wake up!"

Feeling a faint pulse at Michael's wrist, Bill lifted his eyelid and looked into the blank whites below.

"Daddy, wake up!" Hope called to him.

Bill tore open the seal on a syringe and plunged it into a bottle of fast-acting insulin. When the needle went into Michael's arm, Hope thought she saw a sign of life.

"He moved!" she cried. "I saw his eyes move."

She shook him gently.

"Daddy, wake up!" she said with a sob. "Please, Daddy, wake up!"

Closing the distance between herself and Loreto, Kate watched in despair as the sun sank behind the distant mountains of Baja and the world fell into shadow. In constant contact with her, the controller at Loreto had given her a course and then a slight correction, and the plane was humming along. She kept thinking back to what Bill had said, that he knew she could land the plane. She wanted desperately to believe that he was right.

Her mind flew back to the lessons Michael had given her. They'd been intense, a thousand emotions but never a wasted word.

"Methodical and alert," he'd told her. "A good pilot is methodical and alert."

And now she was neither. Passing over a small island, she saw the lights of Loreto up ahead, the mountains behind the city only dark silhouettes. The coastline was coming up in front of her and the controller was telling her about the approach and wind speeds, and she'd heard none of it.

"Say again," she spoke into the mike. "How is the wind?"

"Calm," he said softly. "We are in luck. All is calm."

As she descended through a thousand feet, she saw the beach at Loreto and a hundred pangas tied in the little harbor. Then she was over the old city, the road along the seawall lit with cheerful lights. As she banked toward the airport lights, she looked down and saw people walking by the sea, people whose lives had not gone so terribly astray.

"Methodical and alert," she said to herself. "Landing checklist."

Looking to the placard mounted next to the controls, she already knew she'd waited too long to go through the fifteen steps listed there.

But Michael had taught her well—GUMP—Gas, Undercarriage, Mixture, Prop, the landing checklist of all good pilots. She went through them in order—checked the fuel tank, flipped the lever to lower the gear, moved her fuel mixture to rich, and checked her throttle.

Then she saw it. Ahead of her was the airport, not an empty strip like the one at Buenavista, which she'd approached half a dozen times with Bill, but a real airport—a paved runway with lights, a control tower, all the images locked in her mind from the day she'd frozen in flight.

Mesmerized, she looked at the lights, uncertain what to do, and doing nothing. Then she heard Michael's voice, speaking to her just as he had during their long hours of lessons.

"It's like putting a baby to bed."

"Just pick a spot on the runway," he told her.

"Pick a spot," she thought, "then check my glideslope."

Focusing on a group of tire marks on the runway, she calculated her descent to intercept that spot. But holding the plane steady, she saw that the spot was moving lower on her windshield. She was going to overshoot!

Suddenly the controller was shrieking at her over the radio.

"Too high! Too high! Too fast!"

Quickly and nervously, the controller yelled to her. Do this, do that, chattering nonstop in his accented English, making it impossible for her to think. Now the dials and instruments all looked the same. Where was her speed indicator? The RPMs? What do you do when you're going too fast? The controller's voice grew louder and her mind fixed upon one thing and one thing only.

"I'm going to crash."

"Pull up! Pull up!" the controller shrieked. "Pull up and go around!"

Kate looked at the fuel gauge and saw the needle resting on empty.

"I don't know what to do!" she said in a panic made even worse by the shrieks of the controller.

Breaking all the rules, she reached up and switched off radio, silencing the controller's irritating noise. Now the only sound was the smooth hum of the engines, carrying her to where she had to go.

Steady on the wheel, she increased her pitch and reduced power until she was back on track. But when she chose a new touchdown point, her target was still moving lower on the window.

Something was wrong! Power, pitch, gear... it was all too much. Again panic seized at her throat, and her hand tightened on the wheel. And then she heard Michael as clearly as if he was in the plane with her.

"Flaps," Michael told her. "Extend your flaps."

Fumbling with the lever, Kate extended the flaps. Immediately the drag pushed against the plane. Descending quickly now, she saw the runway coming up at her, coming up too fast. She wanted desperately to pull back on the yoke but was afraid she'd stall. The runway lights shone bright in her eyes as she glanced to one side to check her altitude. Just as the front wheel was about to slam into the runway, she pulled back on the yoke to flare the nose up. Then exactly as the stall warning sounded, she felt the back wheels go down and stay down.

"Ease off the throttle," Michael told her

She did it, and the nose wheel went down, too. She was rolling at sixty miles an hour now, veering from the centerline toward the edge of the runway where water from the storm stood in long pools that reflected the airport lights in her eyes. But trusting that Michael was with her, she knew what to do.

Pushing the rudder with her left leg, she brought the plane onto the tarmac. Then she powered back, and felt the shudder as the weight transferred from the wings to the wheels. Holding it steady, she stepped easy on the brakes, slowing as she rolled. And then she was stopped. Reaching forward, she switched off the fuel pumps and the main power.

Behind her, a fire truck was racing up the runway. For a time she waited to see if Michael would speak to her again. When he did not, she unfastened her harness, climbed out, and walked away.

In the boat, Bill was leaning over Michael, knowing there was nothing else he could do, but listening to his labored breath and slowly counting his weak pulse.

Without warning, Michael's eyes sprang open and he called out loudly, "Kate!"

"Kee-rist!!" Bill hollered, jumping back in alarm. "You scared the be-Jesus out of me!"

"I saw Kate," Michael said hoarsely. "In the plane."

"Hope saw her, too," Bill told him. "When we flew over the boat. And God am I glad to see you awake!"

Slipping a hand around Michael's shoulders, Bill gently pulled him up to a position where he could eat and drink. Beside her father, Hope gave him a sip of juice then slipped a piece of a cracker into his mouth.

"Daddy, we're going to be okay," she told him.

But Michael did not look okay.

"I was flying," he managed to tell her.

"Where did you go?"

"I don't know. You were older and there was a little boy with you. He had blue eyes like you, and he was crying big tears that ran down his face to the corners of his mouth."

"Why was he crying?"

"I don't know. But you wrapped your arms around him and said everything was going to be okay."

"Did he stop crying?"

"Yeah. Because he knew you were right."

"That's a funny dream."

"I know. Can you remember it for me?"

"Sure, Dad. I'd never forget that."

Hope was tired, tired beyond belief. Now that her father was awake, she laid her head upon his shoulder and closed her eyes.

"Mike, I want you to drink a little more juice," Bill told him. "And then I want you to eat some glucogen."

Bill poured a sip of juice into his mouth and a thin smile came over Michael's face and eyes.

"Bill, guess what?" Michael said softly, his voice barely audible. "It took my whole life, but I finally figured it out."

Bill didn't want him to talk, but he wanted even more to keep him awake. Perhaps this was the best way.

"What, Mike? What did you figure out?"

"All for love," Michael told him. "We do it all for love."

As if these words were the only reason he'd awakened, Michael allowed the fatigue to sweep over his body. He felt himself slipping away from the brooding ocean to times long left behind, to times unchanging.

I love the banks of the river, he reminded himself—the blazing days of summer and the last wildflowers standing tall against the coming sun. The legs of the spotted fawns grow so quickly from spindly to strong, the better to escape the mountain lions we thought would never return. The bass have finished their spawn in the shallows, and the mayflies have given over to the fireflies that dance like stars in woods. I never thought I'd see them again, but now I know they're waiting for me. Look at them: the fireflies, the fawns, the fish, and the lions, dancing about me on the Sea of Cortez, waiting for me to come home.

And so he learned that on the river nothing has changed except the leaving of a boy who loved a place too well to understand why he could never go there again. On the Cortez, that boy gathers the sea of stars like a sky of fireflies, and in that vision he sees that all places on this vast blue planet are one place, and all its people one person, and all his thoughts the same thought that all who come this way must know.

For Michael Parker has tried and seen, has loved and wanted, and finally he has found satisfaction. And all that remains of his dreams, he knows, lies with her dazzling head asleep on his shoulder. And his grace rests in knowing that he has given her what he could in the short time any of us are allowed.

"Farewell, Princess," he managed to say. "I love you."

Either from the touch of his lips or the sound of his voice, Hope stirred for a moment, and murmured, "I love you, too, Daddy. I really do."

In his torn and dehydrated body, no tears remained, but Michael felt what Bill had known all these years—the ghosts of tears as they gathered in his eyes, but could not fall. Beyond tears, he thought, recalling his feelings after they lost the baby. Perhaps his grandmother was wrong, for theirs was a loss that had not been redeemed by love.

"All we needed," he thought, "was a little more time."

"Take care of your mother," he whispered into Hope's sleep. At the mention of her mother, the corners of Hope's mouth turned involuntarily upwards in a knowing smile from the other side of consciousness.

Certain she was asleep, Michael laid his head back again so that he could stare at the stars.

"Mike," Bill said. "Can you hear me?"

Michael nodded.

"Mike, I want to tell you about your dad."

Clutching the old leather flyer's helmet that Bill handed him, Michael listened to Bill's story, and for the first time in his life, he saw that his father had watched over him, and had found a way to love him after all.

Perhaps that was all that he'd been waiting for.

Then he was in the water, swimming through the night. His breath came in and out at a slow cadence—inhaling with each rising wave, exhaling with the fall—a perfect syncopation to the endless rhythm of the sea. The stars were shrouded from his sight by the blackness of the night, but he knew that Kate was out there, knew that she was coming for him. As the night stretched on, his body grew tired. He'd been swimming for so long, his entire life fighting tides he felt but could not see, driving toward and pulling away from the things he loved. Now he wondered why he'd fought so hard.

How did the song go? He could barely remember.

Pack up all your cares and woe,
There you go, sinking low.
Bye Bye Blackbird.

Letting out his breath, he felt himself sinking down, plunging to mysterious depths where giant creatures glide silently through phosphorescent trails never seen by man. And still he sank further, passing even the silver coin he had tossed into the ocean, heading toward the light until his feet found ground.

Opening his eyes, he found himself in a land of cold springs and blue skies, of work to be done among green pastures of plenty. On the breeze that stirred the trees, he heard the laughter of his lost baby Jamie. Painted high over his head were the symbols of ancient man, at his feet the bubbling waters of Contrary Creek.

Now all was clear, the meaning of the glyphs and the word spoken by the spring and by the whale passing in the night were one and the same, repeated for all who listened. And the word was... *"remember."*

"Michael," his grandfather said softly, leading him to a grassy place where a picnic had been set out. "Rest here a while. You must be tired."

"No," said Michael, "I can't leave yet. What about Hope?"

"Mike, she's right here," Bill told him. "We're right beside you."

He tried to answer, but Bill was too far away.

It's so much easier here, he thought. And I am so tired.

Far above him, he saw Kate gliding in the wake of the storm, her swimmer's body cutting through the waves like a seal. Even in this place he yearned for her, for the warmth of her body. He wondered if they could be drawn together by shared dreams.

Then, like a miracle, he felt her arm slide past his head and wrap tightly around his chest. Her shoulder pressed against his parted lips, her body tasting of salt and Kate and of all things that men dream. Just above them, he could see the surface and imagined the water sliding off their bodies in sheets.

As his arms wrapped around her, she tried to pull him higher, but instead he slipped away, and plunged into the deep.

TWENTY-TWO

As the lights dotting the shore began to switch off at midnight, a group of people were drawn to the dock that jutted out into the Puerto Escondido, the safe harbor just south of Loreto. Parked at water's edge were two ambulances and a police car. The people who had arrived in them waited at the end of the pier.

Not far away, a woman stood tall and alone. Looking out beyond the entrance to the harbor, she watched the rusty trawler *Anna Maria,* its running lights blazing as it came between the outer jetties. Cutting through the smooth water, the trawler's wake spread behind it in an ever-widening V, two small rolling waves that opened out to the world like a window on its past.

Inside the V, trailing by a long, thick rope, was a small fishing boat, an empty orphan skating to and fro on the foam. As both boats drew closer to the dock, Kate saw Bill Frazier's figure standing alone at the rail of the trawler, and a tiny sound of fear escaped her throat. But then she saw her daughter, sitting atop a heavy coil of rope in the bow of the trawler. Stretched out beside Hope was Michael, his head cradled in her lap. Kate's hand came up to cover her mouth, but whether to keep in her voice or her breath, she did not know.

Lines were thrown and the trawler made fast to the dock. As the gangplank was passed across, Kate elbowed past two men carrying stretchers and ran first onto the deck. Flying to Hope, but looking to Michael, she threw her arms tightly around her daughter.

"Mom," Hope told her, "it's going to be okay. Dad told me to tell you that. He told me to tell you that it's going to be okay."

Kate's arms fell slack.

"Mom! Listen to me!" Hope insisted. "He made me promise. Do you hear me? Dad said it was going to be okay."

Holding her daughter at arm's length, Kate looked in her eyes and saw how much she needed this.

"I hear you, honey, I do."

Bill came over and put his arm around Hope's shoulder.

"Come on, Tiger," he told her. "I see a doctor. Let's show him how tough you are."

Kate turned to Michael, lying motionless on the coil of thick rope, then sank down beside him. Gently, she touched his face, so burned by the sun; his eyes dark and swollen, but closed as in a peaceful dream. Leaning down, she kissed his rough and swollen lips, then spoke the words that had haunted her for months.

"Wait for me."

Still far beneath the surface, he felt her hand behind his neck; then her mouth found his, and he felt the power of her breath. Knowing now that she needed him, he saw the light growing closer. Then, together, they burst through the surface into the light, and he drank in the sweet air around her.

Seeing his eyes open and the smile come to his lips, she laid her head upon his chest and listened to the most glorious sound she had ever heard—the rhythmic music of his beating heart.

CPSIA information can be obtained
at www.ICGtesting.com
Printed in the USA
FFOW02n1615100518
46537921-48510FF